The Kona Shuffle

by

Tom Bradley Jr.

This is a work of fiction. Any resemblance of characters to actual persons, living or dead or otherwise, is purely coincidental, and possibly even regrettable. Most of the places and settings depicted are real, but the events described as taking place in them—to the best of my knowledge—did not really happen.

The Kona Shuffle
Copyright © 2013 by Tom Bradley Jr.
All rights reserved. This book or any portion thereof may not be reproduced or used in any manner whatsoever without the express written permission of the author/publisher except for the use of brief quotations in a book review. I mean it.

Warning: This story contains criminal activity, dirty words, a smattering of smut, immoral thoughts expressed by characters heretofore disclaimed as fictional, and the insertion of at least one syringe into male buttocks. Otherwise, it's loaded with such uplifting delights as a baseball game, a kitty cat, and lots of food. Still, no matter your predilections, some of you are bound to be offended.

Cover design © Tugboat Design

For DB,
who I hope reads
all the chapters in order

Chapter One:
The Tension Settings

She didn't know it at the time, but late one evening as she waited tables in Las Vegas, Noelani B. Lee found her true calling.

* * *

On a slow Wednesday night at an overpriced seafood place in a second-rate casino on the Strip, Noelani Lee stifled a yawn and allowed her mind to wander.

In the restaurant's subdued lighting, she watched a young couple at one of her booths, who spent more time making out than eating. Every few minutes, they surfaced for air and admired the rings each wore on their left hand before they continued their public display of groping.

Newlyweds. Congratulations on your fifty-fifty chance of making it to seven years.

She shifted her attention to her other table, where three guys talked, a lot. Well, two of them spoke plenty. The third one said next to nothing; he just chewed his salmon and pilaf and listened to the other two men call each other names. Noelani noticed he'd sometimes offer a half-smile or a raised eyebrow but said little because he couldn't sneak a word in edgewise.

For entertainment purposes, Noelani eavesdropped on them, but she caught little of their conversation. Except, she heard words like "CPA" and "Phoenix" sprinkled with profanities, which the talkative ones directed toward their quiet partner. She decided to keep her distance until they signaled for their check.

About eleven o'clock, two men in navy blue suits, red ties, and American flag lapel pins, with a pair of buxom, tipsy working girls on their arms, entered the restaurant. Noelani figured one of the men was in his late forties; he had neat, trimmed hair, and a warm complexion. The other was silver-maned, with flushed, blotchy skin.

The maître d' parked the quartet in a booth and then pulled Noelani aside. He instructed her to "take special care of the governor and his guests." Not the least bit impressed, she painted on a smile and cranked up the fake charm. She kept it up even as the quartet got bombed on vodka tonics.

At one point, when the bimbos jiggled their way to the restroom, the older man—the governor—copped a feel of Noelani's thigh. He said, "You know, it's been a while since I've eaten Chinese."

This type of inappropriate behavior was nothing new; this was Vegas, after all. But Noelani was too tired to laugh it away this time, as she sometimes did with intoxicated patrons. She wanted to tell him off, but with the maître d' watching her every move, she instead played nice. "Well, sir, next time you should try our Asian Sea Bass."

"How about instead I have some of your sweet Asian ass?"

Noelani waited a beat, leaned in close and dropped her voice an octave, phony smile still in place. "Keep it up and you'll see my fist in your veiny old nose."

The governor leered. "Speaking of 'veiny'…"

The younger man said, "Can it, Joe, the girls are coming back."

A few minutes later, Noelani checked on the three guys at her other table. One of them—the quiet man, older than his dinner companions—said, "Any trouble?" He nodded toward the governor.

Noelani watched as the state's highest elected official buried his face in the brunette's generous cleavage and said something like, "Joey like big mushy muffins."

One of the quiet man's friends—younger, rounder, and dressed like a low-rent rapper—said, "Jesus Christ, Tommy, who cares?"

The third man, in nice clothes and with frosted brown hair and snow-white teeth, thanked Noelani and asked for the check. As she walked away, Noelani heard him tell his friends, "It's on me, dipshits."

At shift's end, as she walked to her car in the parking garage, Noelani felt someone pinch her butt. Hard. She jumped and turned and looked straight into the eyes of the governor.

"Hiya, my tight China doll," he said. "How about you and me have us a little egg roll in the hay with creamy Joe sauce?"

"Sir, you've had too much to drink," she said, as she backed away from him. "I think you should call someone to give you a ride home."

Before she could take the pepper spray from her purse, the governor grabbed both of her wrists and pushed her against her car. "Maybe," he said, "but that's when I'm at my best. You know what they say about 'having a stiff one.'"

He thrust his crotch against hers. She resisted as best she could, kicking and squirming, and was about to scream when the younger man who'd been with him at dinner stepped around Noelani's car and pulled him away. "Joe, come on, knock it off."

The governor raised his eyebrows and looked at Noelani. He winked and blew her a kiss. "Maybe next time, China doll."

She leaned against the car, near tears, trying to breathe, her heart pounding.

As the two men walked away, the younger one turned and stared at Noelani. He gave her a look she knew too well after three years living in Vegas.

The look said, *What happened here never happened.*

The next afternoon, at the two-bedroom apartment Noelani shared with her cousin, the younger man visited, unannounced. He carried a silver attaché case and introduced himself as James, first name only.

How he found where she lived, he didn't say and she didn't ask.

They sat in the living room, him in a recliner and Noelani on a sofa. "First, I want to apologize for my friend's, uh, inappropriate behavior last night," he said. "Nice guy—he just gets carried away sometimes when he's had a few too many."

Noelani, woozy from a sleepless night following her encounter with the governor, curled her five-foot-eight-inch frame into a corner of the sofa. She said, "I almost called the cops, you know. I planned on telling them about the security cameras in the garage."

James said nothing, just nodded.

She thought he looked familiar, like maybe she'd seen him somewhere before the incident, in the papers or something. "But I get the feeling they wouldn't believe me."

"No reason why they should," said James. "Now, I'm prepared to make sure no one else does, either." He placed the attaché case on the table and opened it. "This is fifty grand for you to keep your trap shut."

The last time Noelani saw so much money in one place at one time was on the news when she was a kid, when prosecutors presented gym bags overflowing with currency as evidence in her father's racketeering trial.

She uncurled her legs and sat upright, placing her bare feet flat on the dirty beige carpet. "What's he running for?"

"United States Senate."

"Is he going to win?"

"What, you don't watch TV?"

Noelani scanned the bank-wrapped bundles of cash. She heard herself say, "I think you're short another fifty thousand."

James sat on the edge of the recliner. He rubbed his palms together and said, "Where'd you move here from?"

"Hawaii."

"Thought so."

"How come?"

"Your whole mixed-up exotic melting pot look. Cross between Asian of some sort and who knows what else."

"I suppose I should be flattered."

James patted the cash. "Ever think of moving back?"

"Until now, no."

"Ten."

Noelani rose, crossed the room, and picked up the Yellow Pages. She started leafing through the listings. "Um, should I look under 'A' or 'L'?"

"'A' or 'L'?"

"'Attorneys' or 'lawyers.'"

James grinned. "Amusing. But it won't get you anywhere. Fifteen."

Noelani sat down and took a moment to study him. He was heavier than she remembered from the restaurant and had grayer hair. "Well, you're off to a good start. How about thirty?"

James stared at her. After a few moments, he said, "All right, this is what you do and there's no more negotiating, okay?"

She sniffed. "Fine."

"Take this money, move your tush back to the Aloha State,

and keep your mouth shut. Follow those simple instructions and in a year, you get another twenty thousand. Final offer."

"Sold."

James lifted the attaché and dumped the cash on the coffee table, and then he left the apartment without another word.

The next day, Noelani quit her job at the restaurant and her other gig as a keno runner at an off-Strip locals casino. She gave her cousin, Wanda Tess Fong, a song-and-dance about homesickness, without mentioning the incident in the parking garage or the money.

Within a week, she was back in Hawaii.

* * *

A year later, DHL brought her a package—a rectangular white box containing jewelry—with a note: "This settles it. Your friend in Las Vegas, James Vartoogian."

Jewelry. Not her thing.

Noelani never saw the other twenty grand.

One day she caught them in passing on C-SPAN.

A reporter interviewed the governor, now Senator Joe Whatever, a moral, upright family man who championed legislation for abused women.

Then the reporter spoke with a man named James Vartoogian. C-SPAN called him the foremost political operative in the West and a rising star on the national stage. He ran a profitable advertising and PR agency and knew the president on a first-name basis.

* * *

Seven years later…

On a Tuesday evening, Noelani Lee stood in the bedroom of her little house in Hilo, on the Big Island of Hawai'i, packing an overnight bag. Her cousin, Wanda, was set to arrive from Vegas the next day. She'd talked Noelani into spending a week "playing tourist" in Kona. Noelani instead wanted Wanda to stay with her in Hilo and "play local," but Wanda said she'd already made hotel reservations. *Take some time off, cousin,* Wanda said. *We're gonna have us a staycation.*

Noelani gave in. She hadn't seen Wanda since she fled Vegas. *No use arguing and besides, what the heck.*

She was about to zip her bag closed when she remembered one last item. She opened her closet.

Hanging to her left were pressed jeans, Capri pants, and blouses in solid colors. Several pairs of espadrilles and leather flip-flops in bright, feminine colors sat on the floor below. To her right, long-sleeve tees and threadbare jeans hung above brown rubber flip-flops and a pair of black Chuck Taylors. Trucker caps and straw fedoras rested on the shelf above. Camera cases piled atop a three-drawer file cabinet in the middle of the closet separated the dissimilar wardrobes.

A small safe sat on the floor next to the file cabinet. She opened it and took out a rectangular white box, which she carried to the bed.

Master Po, her overweight flame-point Himalayan, lounged on her pillow. Noelani said to the cat, "Want one last peek?"

Master Po looked at her. Then he licked his balls.

On the TV in the corner of her bedroom, a sports reporter raved about a baseball team on the Kona side called the Diamond Kings and its star player, a muscular Dean Something. From what Noelani gathered, he had the talent and potential to be a big star. Best player on all the islands. There was talk of him one day playing in the Major Leagues.

Noelani sat next to Master Po, opened the box, and examined its contents—a pair of earrings, solitaire diamonds set in white-and-yellow gold plumeria flowers, and a matching necklace.

She considered the irony of James's "gift." She hated jewelry. She never wore it and thought it was just a bunch of useless, overpriced rocks and minerals. Shiny and pretty but lacking a true purpose.

She read the lettering printed inside the box lid: *Another Island Creation—from the Beautiful Kona Coast of Hawai'i— Handcrafted by Jules.*

Noelani closed the box and slipped it inside her overnight bag. Then she shut and locked the safe, leaving in it her Ruger SR9.

* * *

In his shop in Kailua-Kona, on the other side of the island, Jules Matsumoto dumped the contents of a white plastic shopping bag on his desk: watches, a bracelet, rings, and a locket.

"This is the best he could do?" Jules said.

A huge woman, five-ten and three bills, stood motionless in front of his desk, arms folded across her enormous chest. Jules avoided direct eye contact as he looked up at her.

She said, "What you mean by that shit?"

To Jules, the woman—Esther Halekealoha—resembled a mountain. And, like Hawaii's volcanoes, she sometimes blew her top and laid waste to everything in her path if things didn't go as she thought they should. Jules knew this, having once witnessed her son on the receiving end of her considerable wrath. Since then, he exercised caution whenever he dared criticize the materials she delivered.

"Esther, I appreciate the effort but there's not much here," Jules said. "I think he's losing his touch. Are you sure you don't have him chasing after too *much* crap?"

"Cameras ain't crap. Them i-thingies, they ain't crap."

He opened the locket. Even with his naked eye, he could tell it was made from nickel with thin gold plating. Inside was a tiny color photo of an attractive woman and a smiling baby. "Maybe not to you."

"Hey, taking jewelry ain't easy to do," Esther said. "People getting more careful. It makes it tough being da kine wholesaler."

Jules closed the locket and set it aside. He picked up a watch, a digital Timex. "This I can't use. It's cheap stainless steel."

"C'mon, thing's waterproof to like fifteen feet."

"What I mean is, I can't do anything with it. As far as what I'd need it for."

"You lose then." Esther snapped up the watch and stuffed it in her bra. "'Kay den, what about that?"

Jules picked up a handsome gold-and-diamond tennis bracelet. He figured it set the buyer back at least a grand. "Now I definitely can do something with this."

"Boy had to be extra quick to get it, he told me." With a finger as round and as dark as a sausage, Esther pointed at the rings. "And them? They gotta be made from real gold."

"They're okay. Not great but okay."

"What does 'okay' come out to?"

Jules took a deep breath as he studied the jewelry. "The bracelet alone, maybe a hundred. The rest combined, fifty."

No response. In his peripheral visions, Jules glanced at a baseball bat leaning against the wall, beside his desk. He kept it there in case of emergencies.

Esther said, "You're getting cheap, Jules. Used to be you buy all this for twice as much. What, you got yourself a cash flow problem?"

"It's what the market will bear, Esther. Besides, I'm expecting a delivery this week and this guy, he's wants serious cash."

"How serious?"

"Almost all I have in reserve."

"Must be one big damn delivery." Esther grunted. "All right, whatevahs. My fat ass is getting too tired to argue with you. Make it an even two hundred, we call it good."

Jules stood, took two hundred-dollar bills from his wallet, and handed them to Esther. "I still say he's losing his touch."

Esther crumpled the money inside a meaty fist. "Boy sometimes gets his priorities all outta whack—what're you gonna do?" she said. "But you leave it to me. I'll knock some sense in him." She grinned at him as she trundled out of the office.

Jules watched her waddle away from his shop. He scooped the bracelet and rings in an envelope, which he locked in his desk drawer.

On his way out, he tossed the locket in a wastebasket.

Chapter Two:
The Family Jewels

Edna Norquist was on her deathbed in Needles, California, which meant Ryan Campanella needed to act fast before the old bat kicked off.

* * *

The Norquist estate consisted of a large ranch house and an acre and a half of green grassy lawn and red rose gardens next to the brown desert on the south end of Needles.

Ryan Campanella turned in to the driveway, early on a Tuesday morning. He parked and spotted a groundskeeper, a middle-aged Hispanic man, on a riding mower in the front yard. Ryan waited for the man to drive the mower around the back of the house before he killed the engine and picked up his briefcase from the passenger seat. He gave himself a look in the rearview and got out of the car.

A petite fiftyish woman in a maid's uniform answered the doorbell. "*Sí?*"

"Hello," Ryan said. "I'm from the insurance company of Overarching Underwriters LLC Inc. of Los Angeles, and I'm here to see Mrs. Norquist." He handed the woman a business card. "I have an appointment."

"*Sí?* Mees Norquist?"

"Yes, ma'am. *Muy importante.*"

The maid examined both sides of the card. "*Sí señor*, Mees Norquist is in her room. She is very sick." She motioned Ryan to come inside, removed a surgical mask from her apron pocket and handed it to him. "You put this on you face, *por favor*, and come with me."

The maid led Ryan down a hallway lined with framed black-and-white photos of a young Edna Norquist and her late husband, Hubert, with people Ryan recognized as important back in the 1960s and '70s—Spiro Agnew, Nelson Rockefeller, Barry Goldwater. In one picture, Hubert Norquist shared a laugh with Richard Nixon and Henry Kissinger over highballs in the Oval Office. In another, Hubert and Edna played horseshoes with Dwight and Mamie Eisenhower.

Based on his painstaking research, Ryan knew Hubert left his factory job in Minnesota sometime after World War II and he and Edna headed West. He went on to amass a minor fortune through expansive real estate holdings in six states and an interstate trucking company, which he sold months before his death in the mid-1980s.

But Ryan didn't give a damn about all that. What interested him instead was Edna's impressive jewelry collection: loose diamonds and other gemstones, and others mounted in fabulous gold settings, many of them custom-made.

Nobody knew the collection's true value, but according to Ryan's more knowledgeable sources, it was a shitload.

All he had to do was get his hands on the rocks, and then pass them along to his buyer, a guy who'd called in his marker on an impressive and quite overdue poker debt.

The maid opened a door at the far end of the hall. Inside the room, Ryan got his first glimpse of the bedridden Edna Norquist. He held his breath.

Edna, tubes up her nose, stared at the ceiling. Bottles of prescription medications sat atop a small bedside table. Sunlight filled the room through two windows. The only sounds were the ticking of a clock on a fireplace mantel and the beep-beep-beep of Edna's EKG machine.

The room had a certain depressing cold feel—Ryan knew death was hanging around, biding its time. The scene reminded him of the nursing home back in Philly where his grandfather spent his last few years.

Edna blinked. Once. Twice.

Ryan exhaled. He slipped the surgical mask over his nose and mouth.

"Mees Norquist, she spends all day in bed. Her doctor comes today."

"Well then," Ryan said, "I'll make this *muy rapido.*"

The maid motioned toward an ancient leather wingback chair at Edna's bedside. "*Señor,* is okay for me to tell you Mees Norquist likes to talk a lot. But she don't make no sense since her brain, it is all gone." She offered him a tired smile as she exited, closing the door behind her.

Ryan pressed his ear to the door and listened as the maid padded down the hall. He locked the door and searched for hidden security cameras. Finding none, he double-checked the locked door and returned to Edna's bedside. He lifted a pair of white cotton gloves from his jacket pocket and slid them on his hands as he sat in the old chair. "Good morning, Mrs. Norquist, I'm here for our appointment. You remember, about your precious and valuable gemstones."

Edna squinted at him. "Ohmygarsh, Hubert, you haven't worn that suit in *years*." Her voice was soft and scratchy. "Don't you think it's time you get a new one? It smells musty, for heaven's sake."

Ryan cringed. The threads cost a bundle, retail, in Beverly Hills. "Mrs. Norquist—may I call you Edna? I'm not Hubert. My name is Kenny and I'm here on behalf of Overarching Underwriters to care for your valuable jewelry collection."

Edna hawked mucus into a tissue. Ryan winced. "My doctor's coming by today. He's such a nice man, don'tcha know." She looked at Ryan's gloves. "Hubert, it must be cold outside for you to wear those mittens. But I am glad you shoveled the driveway. Maybe I can have Lupe make you some hot soup."

Ryan waited a moment. "No thank you, Edna. All you have to do is tell me where your jewelry collection is stored, and I will make sure it is safe and well cared for."

He took note of Edna's glassy-eyed expression. Although he lacked expertise on dementia and its symptoms, despite having witnessed what his grandfather endured in his final years, Ryan knew enough to realize the tenor of their odd conversation indicated the gas tank fueling Edna's mind was running on fumes. He wondered how long she would stay that way before sudden lucidity blew his plans all to hell.

There was only one way to find out.

He said, "And here ya are, and it's a beautiful day, yah?"

"Youbetcha, Hubert," Edna said.

"You're darned tootin'. And maybe we can have a hotdish and pop for supper, and we'll listen to the Twins game on the radio there."

"Oh yah, the Twins," Edna said. "Hubert, you know I love you to pieces, don'tcha know, but that Tony Oliva fella is awful handsome for a dark-skinned Puerto Rican man."

Ryan checked his watch. *Enough of this bullshit. The old lady's lost it and my timetable's getting screwed.* He rose, triple-checked the locked door, and said, "Yes, good to know, Edna. So, back to business—where do you keep the jewels?" *You wrinkled-up prune.*

Edna raised her hand and pointed with a gnarled, chalk-white finger to a four-drawer dresser across the room. "Now you know I keep that deal in the drawer over there. As much as I love Lupe, you can't trust those Spanish people. They're different."

Before she could finish the sentence, Ryan dashed to the dresser and pulled on the top drawer. But it was locked. So was the second one, and the third. "Dammit." He pulled on the fourth drawer but it, too, refused to budge. He gave up when he felt beads of perspiration form above his brow.

"I just know she took my best hat, the one I wear to church every third Sunday. You know the one, it has the green—"

"Edna, darling, where the hell's the key for this thing?"

"Oh no, Hubert, you silly goose. Not *that* drawer"—she pointed to a highboy on the other side of the room—"the other one, kitty-corner from it, top one on the left. You should know after all these years."

Ryan licked his lips as he glanced at the locked bedroom door. Then he gave the drawer a tug. Inside he found monogrammed lace handkerchiefs and an antique black lacquer box with a mother-of-pearl inlay scene of pagodas, geishas, and cranes. Ryan opened it, grinned, and pumped his fist.

He also found cash in the drawer; stacks of bills held together with rubber bands. Had to be at least twenty large, Ryan figured. He distributed the money between his pants and jacket pockets and carried the jewelry box back to his bedside seat.

"Okay, Edna, now we'll have you sign a document giving us permission to take your jewelry into safekeeping." He took an official-looking form from the briefcase and slipped a pen in her veiny hand. She scrawled a signature, little more than a straight line with a couple of bumps.

Like it mattered. Ryan reclaimed the pen and placed the paper in the briefcase. He took out a large, padded clasp envelope, opened the jewelry box, and dumped its contents into the envelope. He sealed the envelope and placed it back in the briefcase.

"Hubert, let's go out to dinner this evening, after the nice doctor leaves," Edna said. "Maybe we should give Lupe the night off so she can spend time with her Spanish friends."

Ryan returned the empty jewelry box back to the drawer, and then sat at Edna's bedside. "Edna," he said as he picked up his briefcase, "on behalf of Overarching Underwriters, I thank you for your time and your generous business. You may now die."

"Aw, bless your heart, Hubert."

Ryan met the maid at the front door, pleased at being ahead of schedule. Combined with his brother Frank's probable delayed departure from another debauched weekend in Las Vegas, this meant he could swing by the house and change before his meet with Tommy Chunks.

He removed the surgical mask and stuffed it in a pocket. "Say, *abuela, tu eres Lupe?*"

"No, *señor*. Lupe, she pass away twenty year ago. *Me llamo* Roselia." The maid squinted at the gloves on his hands. "Mees Norquist, she okay?"

"Well, Roselia, I'm no expert, but I think she's gonna pull through just fine."

Roselia smiled and crossed herself.

Ryan grinned as she opened the front door. "*Hasta la vista,* baby."

"*Vaya con dios, señor.*"

* * *

In the Omelet House restaurant on West Charleston Boulevard in Las Vegas, Tommy "Chunks" Lohmiller answered his cell phone.

"Texaco, two hours," said Ryan Campanella, who hung up.

Tommy looked at his half-eaten huevos rancheros—eggs over easy, sauce red and tangy, pinto beans, globs of melted cheese. A few dashes of hot pepper sauce made it interesting.

"Right."

Tommy placed his cell on the table. He set his fork aside.

How wonderful. Yet another breakfast interrupted long-distance from Arizona by one Campanella or another.

This is it. This is the last job I do for either of those morons.

I'm done.

* * *

Thanks to an anonymous phone tip, federal immigration agents arrived at the Norquist estate and took Roselia and the gardener into custody.

Moments later, Edna Norquist breathed her last. Her final words, to her doctor: "Hubert, make sure Lupe doesn't overcook the walleye. It'll dry out, don'tcha know."

In the foyer, one of the immigration agents picked up a business card from a side table. "Huh." He handed it to a colleague. "I knew the guy's career was in the shitter, but I never thought it'd come to this."

The second agent read the card:

Overarching Underwriters LLC Inc.
Insurance/Investments/Bankruptcies
Certified and Bonded
(323) 555-1218
Kenny Loggins, Agent

Later, a San Bernardino County sheriff's deputy called the number on the card. Whoever answered said something profane in a thick accent. He repeated the call and got the same response. The deputy then did a reverse-411 and traced the number to a Vietnamese fish market in Alhambra called Phúc Yu.

* * *

At the Texaco station about an hour up US 93 from Kingman, in northwest Arizona, Ryan Campanella opened his briefcase on the hood of Tommy Chunks's black Trans Am.

"Bunch of diamonds, some sapphires, rubies, a few emeralds." Ryan handed a brown leather toiletry bag to Tommy. "Shitload of diamond and sapphire rings in there, too—gold, white gold, some silver. Empty settings, the whole nine yards."

Tommy, a cigarette dangling in his mouth, accepted the bag. At the same time, he hoped Ryan's briefcase wouldn't scratch the car's hood. Last time it cost him a couple hundred to get it buffed out.

"Don't, I repeat, do not transfer the stuff from the kit until you get there," Ryan said. "The bag's a prototype, new technology. It has this thin layer of high-opacity lead built inside. Totally TSA-proof."

"Let me guess."

"This guy I know's doing R&D for the cartel in Reynosa."

Tommy said, "Is it what you expected?"

"Not bad. I almost felt sorry for the old broad, but hey, better me than probate." Ryan handed him a sealed envelope. "Here's a couple grand. It's all the cash she had, so Merry fucking early Christmas."

Tommy exhaled cigarette smoke, which a hot desert breeze caught and blew toward Ryan.

He stepped aside to avoid it. "Easy, man. New shirt."

Tommy dropped the cigarette and mashed it with his shoe. "Who's this I'm going to see?"

"Jean-Jacques Fontainebleau. Me and him, we go back— he'd never screw me over. He's expecting you."

Tommy nodded.

Ryan retrieved another envelope from the briefcase and handed it to Tommy. "Plane leaves Vegas tonight. It's a red eye. Sorry about that. There's a connection in Miami, and then it's on to Barbados."

Tommy placed the toiletry kit, cash, and the airline ticket in a black backpack and zipped it shut. "You flew solo."

"Hell yeah, I did. Dumb ass passes up a score like this to screw around Vegas for a long weekend? I'm taking advantage." Ryan removed his sunglasses and wiped them with a handkerchief. "Call me when it's done, which means, save the poon and the piña coladas for *after* you conduct my business."

Tommy responded with a nod. He climbed in the Trans Am and hit the road, northbound, back to Vegas.

Ryan slipped his shades back on and checked his watch. He figured he had plenty of time until Frank would return home.

* * *

Ryan entered the house in Kingman he shared with his brother and hung his keys on a hook inside the front door. He went to his room and thought, because he was in a good mood and it was a beautiful day, he'd have a dip in the pool.

Until he smelled something gross and felt a hard object press against the base of his skull.

A voice said, "Okay, where the fuck's he going?"

Chapter Three:
The Campanellas

The gross smell, as best as Ryan Campanella could tell, was a mix of bourbon and cheap cigars. The hard thing, he learned, was the business end of his brother's gun.

*　*　*

This wasn't the first time Ryan found himself staring down the muzzle of Frank's nickel-plated SW1911. But with his brother in a foul mood, he sure as hell hoped it wouldn't be the last.

"Goddammit, you took the old broad's jewelry." Frank straddled Ryan's waist, pinning him to his bed. He stuffed the muzzle up Ryan's left nostril. "You went to Needles behind my back and you took her jewels, and now she's dead. I bet you killed the old broad, too."

"Frank, shut up," Ryan said. "Besides, you're the one decided to screw around in Vegas even though I told you about the stones months ago. What was I supposed to do?"

Sometimes, as a professional courtesy, Ryan gave Frank first right of refusal to participate in a score. Not his fault Frank blew him off in favor of a four-day, money-is-no-object bender in Sin City.

Frank sneered. "What was this bullshit at the gas station, you and Tommy Chunks? Helluva long way to go to suck each other's dicks, fruitcup."

Enough's enough. "Listen up, fat boy, I'm not gay."

"Look at you in your pink shirt. No real man wears a pink shirt."

"This thing cost me a wad. And you're wrinkling it."

"Yeah, uh huh, and I caught you shaving your chest the other day, too."

"It's called 'manscaping' and it wouldn't hurt you to try it once in a while."

"You say that with a straight face." Frank snorted. "See what I did there?"

"Listen," Ryan said, "if I was gay, like you say I am, then I wouldn't have screwed Rhonda Tutwiler, in her room, with her parents downstairs, in the den, watching *Cheers*, three times in one night." Back in junior high.

"What, 'Old Butterface'?" Frank snorted again. "Don't know how to tell you this, little bro, but that was sloppy seconds."

"All I'm saying is, you could take lessons in style from me, and that's all I'm gonna say. Just look at yourself for once."

Frank did. On his head, a pure black New York Yankees cap, its flat bill slanted over the right side of his forehead. He wore a red hoodie, baggy black jeans halfway down his wide butt, and unlaced, pure white, low-cut sneakers.

"Back on point, numbnuts." Frank held up his smartphone, showing a picture to his brother. "So, what's this you're giving Tommy? I bet there's no toothpaste and floss in the ditty bag."

Based on the angle, Ryan figured Frank took the pic around the corner of the Texaco station, behind and to the left of Ryan and Tommy, out of their line of sight. Ryan hadn't seen Frank or his convertible Corvette when he scouted the area twenty minutes before Tommy Chunks arrived.

Frank advanced to the next picture. "Here you are giving him some envelope." The next picture showed Frank, beer in hand, lying on a sidewalk, the Stratosphere Tower in Vegas rising from his crotch. "Shit." He clicked on the next pic. In it, Frank hoisted a giant martini in a nightclub while a pair of young girls engaged in a full lip-lock beside him.

He stuffed the phone in his hoodie pocket. "So, yeah, I'd be right about all this, huh?"

Ryan nodded. The gun's muzzle in his nose followed the motion of his head. "Yeah, dipshit," he said, his next move in place.

"So, where'd you send him?"

"I think you already know."

Frank slipped the gun into the back of his jeans. "Here's the deal, one-time only offer. You listening?"

"Speak."

"You get those jewels back. Call Tommy Chunks and get them back, or else I put your ass on a plane and you fly to him and go get my share and bring it back to me. And if you don't, I'll hunt both your sorry asses down."

"You realize how pathetic you sound."

Frank picked up a phone from a nightstand. "Call his ass.

Now."

At home in Vegas, Tommy Chunks checked caller ID and, recognizing the incoming number, let the phone ring.

After returning from his meet with Ryan, Tommy shredded the ticket to Barbados and began packing a suitcase. He left the jewels and rings in the toiletry bag, unopened since the hand-off, which he tucked away in his black backpack.

The phone rang again and Tommy continued ignoring it, knowing Yolanda, his platonic, non-multitasking housemate, wouldn't answer it, either.

Downstairs, Yolanda sat at her computer, focused on her seventh Facebook update of the day. This time, she wrote something about collagen injections and how they didn't hurt as much as she thought they would. But she figured she deserved them considering she just sold another overpriced condo. Oh, and she ate a chicken Caesar salad for lunch.

The phone kept ringing. Yolanda glanced at the caller's number and yelled up the stairs, "Probably for you."

"Probably," Tommy yelled back.

Yolanda shrugged, muttered, "Whatever," and resumed documenting her interesting day.

"He's not answering," Ryan said.

"Try his cell," Frank said. "As for me, I'm going to my room to dump my shit. Dial my man's number."

The phone stopped ringing. Moments later, Tommy Chunks watched his cell vibrate. He turned his attention to packing clean underwear in his suitcase.

Ryan hung up when nobody answered after ten rings, and then opened his door and peered down the hall. Frank's door was closed, so he shut and locked his and took a suitcase from his closet.

In his room, Frank tossed dirty clothes from his Vegas trip

on the floor and piled fresh jeans and hoodies in his duffel.

Ryan removed pressed shirts and coordinating pants from his closet and arranged them in a suitcase.

Finished packing, Tommy grabbed his suitcase and backpack. He dragged them downstairs, where he found Yolanda in her office.

"I'm heading out. A trip," he said. "Don't wait up."

Yolanda stopped typing and spun her chair around to face him. "That was a joke."

Tommy stared at her mouth. "What happened to you?"

"Condo, on the Strip. You like them?"

"Carly Simon know you have her lips?"

"Who?"

"I thought you were getting those evened out first."

Yolanda peeked down her blouse. Her left breast was a cup size larger and much firmer than the right. "Well, I would have but the boob doctor had to go to his step-father's funeral back East—Ohio, I think. But some offers just came in on a house Dean Martin or some other famous dead person once slept in. By this time in a week or so, I should be balanced in front. If the boob doctor's back by then."

"Good to know," Tommy said. "I'm leaving."

Yolanda turned to the computer and picked up where she left off. "Cool for you. Where to?"

"Away."

"Have fun."

Frank picked up his bag and looked down the hall. He tiptoed to his brother's door. "I hope you're still dialling away in there, precious."

Ryan coordinated a selection of belts with his pants. "He's not answering, cheese brain. But I'll keep trying. In the meantime, make yourself useful. Take a nap or something."

"Genius idea," Frank said. "I think I'll just sit my tired ass down and relax." He ran down the hall and bolted out the front door to his Corvette, which he'd parked around the corner from the house, where Ryan couldn't see it. Frank threw his bag in the back seat and peeled out.

Hearing the car roar away, Ryan sprinted outside in time to see his brother race from view. His timeline accelerated, Ryan ran back inside, slammed his suitcase shut, dashed to the garage, jumped in his Impala, and took off after Frank.

In Vegas, Tommy Chunks met a cab outside his house and directed the driver to take him to the airport.

* * *

That evening, a knock at the door interrupted Yolanda as she again updated her Facebook page. This time, she announced her plans to pursue thigh liposuction and a butt-lift if she sold a McMansion to the executive producer of the reality TV ratings bonanza, *Celebrity Paintball Wars*.

She opened the front door and found a well-dressed man with highlighted brown hair on the porch. "Yes, can I help you?"

The man pushed her back inside. As her lungs emptied, Yolanda thought, *Wait, I know this guy.*

He kicked the door closed behind him and forced her against a wall. "Where the hell'd he go?"

Yolanda felt her heart pounding behind her uneven breasts. *Now* she knew who he was: Tommy's friend from Kingman. The one with the nice teeth and the slob brother who always hit on her.

With both hands gripping her shoulders, he leaned back and examined her chest with a puzzled expression. Then he squinted at her mouth.

"Jesus Christ, Yolanda," he said. "What happened to your lips?"

* * *

When the Airbus A330 reached cruising altitude, Tommy Chunks, in coach, reclined in his seat. He looked up at the overhead storage compartment, which held his black backpack.

Ahead, a brief layover in Honolulu, then a quick stop in

Kona, on the Big Island, via the cheapest inter-island airline he could find on the internet. He figured he'd spend two days, max, finishing this business.

Minutes later, he heard a woman, a couple of rows ahead, talking to her seatmate. She was loud, overcompensating for the cabin's incessant hum, and her voice carried.

"My best cousin lives in Hilo. Been a long time since I seen her, like seven years, so I told her she ought to play tourist with me in Kona. I grew up there. So, this is your first time going to Hawaii?"

After a few moments, Tommy tuned out the woman's melodic speech.

Then, he closed his eyes and dreamed of Fiji.

Chapter Four:
The Dream Couple

On a Tuesday afternoon at a baseball field next to the ocean on the Kona Coast, Dean Pahukoa, eager to display his awesome home run hitting skills, prayed for Jordan Lono to strike out.

After all, Jordan was only eighteen and had his whole baseball future ahead of him, what there was of it. On the other hand, Dean was twenty-six and, in spite of the hype and years of help from his boss, he was running out of time.

A pair of teenage girls lounged in the bleachers behind the Kona Diamond Kings' bench. They drank sodas and stretched their brown thighs in the sun. He smiled at them. They giggled and waved in return.

As he took several warm-up swings in the on-deck circle, Dean scanned the dozen or so faces in the metal bleachers. He saw the usual suspects—old folks, and Jordan's mom, kinda hot for an older sistah. Guys he knew from the auto shop where he got oil changes, taking another three-hour lunch. And some dude in a yellow tank top and plaid shorts.

What Dean failed to see in the stands were Major League scouts. Not even anyone who looked like a scout. At least what he figured a scout should look like. He'd heard rumors about guys from most of the West Coast clubs being on the island, including a few from Los Angeles and San Francisco.

Dean took another practice swing. *If there were big league scouts here, Jules would've told me. Because Jules, he wants me to be in the majors as much as me. Maybe even more.*

At the plate, Jordan Lono swung and missed for strike two. The pitcher for the Kona Diamond Kings' cross-island rival, the Hilo Hardware Hammerheads, walked off the back of the mound and rubbed the ball.

Dean rested the bat on his muscular right deltoid. *Come on, brah, get it over with already.*

On the next pitch, Jordan obliged. Strike three.

Bottom of the ninth, one out, runners on first and second, score tied, 4-4.

All right, Dean thought. *Showtime.*

As he strolled to the plate, he heard scattered applause,

while a man yelled something about a missing wallet.

Dean knew the smart move for the Hammerheads was to walk him intentionally and pitch to the next batter, a bruddah who'd hit into more double plays than anyone else in the league. Besides, Dean already smacked a home run and three doubles in the game. But this pitcher was cocky; Dean knew the guy would come at him with his heat, try to show him up, all because he was Dean Pahukoa.

Pops Brimley, the Diamond Kings' manager, clapped and paced in the dugout. "Okay, Deano, just stroke it, little base hit babe, hit wins the game, all we need. Good speed out there, no need to kill it, just find grass and we're winners."

Taking another practice cut, Dean spotted team sponsor Jules Matsumoto, his business and baseball mentor, standing behind the bench. He nodded toward Jules, and then stepped into the batter's box, dug in, and stared down the pitcher.

Despite Pops Brimley's belief in common sense baseball fundamentals, Dean hated singles. Home runs were cooler—they impressed the babes. Maybe not his wife so much, because she never went to his games, but still. And they meant more for his quest to make the majors. That's what Jules always told him.

The ballpark next to the ocean had odd dimensions, but the only part Dean worried about was the distance from home plate to the fence in left field. No one anywhere seemed to know how far it was but Dean walked it off one time and estimated it at about 375 feet away. To knock a home run that far proved impossible for every player on every team in the league. The big-talkers from Hilo couldn't do it; neither could those wannabes with the Waimea Steak & Brew Bulls or the losers with the last-place Windward Realty Evictors.

The powerful Dean, well, he was the exception. He'd cleared the fence this season, counting the homer he blasted in the first inning, sixteen times.

Dean cradled the bat handle in his bare hands and settled into his stance. He watched the kid pitcher nod to the catcher. Then the kid, swear to God, he grinned at Dean—big-time arrogance—before he wound up and unleashed a fastball.

Dean swung.

The ball cleared the far-off left-field fence by a good fifty feet. It bounced a few times on a neighboring field until it rolled to a stop in the middle of a junior soccer league game.

Fans clapped. The teenage girls in the bleachers called out their phone numbers. Jordan Lono searched for a pen and paper. The rest of the Diamond Kings mobbed Dean as he crossed home plate.

Pops Brimley spat a river of tobacco juice. "Attaway Deano, game winning tater there. Dialed eight when a single would've done the job, but a dinger works, too."

Dean thanked Pops as Jules approached him with a smile and an extended hand, each finger adorned with a garish diamond ring. "Nice hit, Dean."

They shook hands. "It's all good," Dean said. "But you know I'd rather be on my way to the Major Leagues. It's the only thing that'd be better."

"Don't worry, we'll get there." Jules lowered his voice to a near-whisper. "So…Veronica still out of town?"

"She's shopping in Honolulu for her birthday. She gets back tomorrow."

Jules chuckled. "Oh, that wife of yours, she sure does like to spend your money."

"It's mostly hers but no worries."

"Next thing I know, you'll be asking me for a raise to keep up with her."

"Well, no, boss," Dean said. "I mean I don't want to be taking advantage—"

"Come over tonight, huh?" Jules arched an eyebrow. "We'll work on…*it* some more."

Dean felt his face get warm. "Uh yeah, okay. No way I'm gonna miss it."

He hoped Pops and his teammates couldn't hear their conversation, because what Jules and Dean did when they got together, alone, was a secret. No one, he hoped, would ever find out.

* * *

Wearing a blue floral-patterned blouse and white skirt, and with her luxurious jet-black hair flowing in a breeze, Veronica Keawe knew she embodied Hawaiian feminine pulchritude.

Sashaying through the Ala Moana Mall in Honolulu, Veronica drew all kinds of attention—not only because she was gorgeous but also, from the knees down, she wore long white socks and steel-toed combat boots.

And if anyone dared ask why, she had a reasonable explanation: She had to. For protection.

Slung over her shoulders, a black backpack contained her digital camera and boxes of Dean's favorite gourmet Oahu chocolate truffles. Along with a shiny new pair of 14-karat, white-gold-and-diamond hoop earrings, a present to herself. Well, one of them anyway, as she had one last stop on her annual birthday shopping extravaganza before she'd reconnect with her sister for an expensive sushi lunch.

Then, the next day, she would fly home to the Big Island and Dean. She missed him but bad. He treated her well and allowed her to spoil herself since she knew he knew she deserved it; in turn, she adored him. Well, what she truly loved about him were his many hard muscles.

God, Dean was hot.

She remembered he had one of his baseball games today. She missed it as she did almost all of his silly games. Despite Dean's many positive traits, Veronica was unconvinced his baseball hobby would evolve into anything lucrative—in spite of Jules Matsumoto's claims. Jules, Dean's boss at the jewelry store and his team sponsor, gave Veronica the creeps—what with the way he acted around Dean, filling his head with wild notions about playing in the big leagues and making millions for doing it.

Although the prospect of her husband one day hauling in truckloads of dollars stimulated her, Veronica nonetheless considered Jules's interest in Dean's athletic future as, well, unhealthy.

But she banished those thoughts as, in the middle of the mall, Veronica found Piedi Felici, the finest shoe store in all of Hawaii. She walked in and zeroed in on a pair of black patent leather Jimmy Choos.

"I'd like to try these in a six, please." She handed the display shoe to the salesman, sat, unlaced her boots, and removed her socks.

"Yes, ma'am, I'll be right back." The salesman retreated to a back storeroom. He returned a few moments later with the shoes. "Let's see how these fit you."

When Veronica lifted her bare left foot onto the bench, the salesman gasped.

She smiled. "Anything wrong?"

He stared at her pedicured foot, her nails bright red, a gold ring wrapped around the second toe. He took a moment to catch his breath before he jumped up and ran to the cash register, where he grabbed a sales brochure.

Veronica recognized it right away, as she had several copies in her portfolio.

The salesman looked at the photo on the brochure's cover, flawless feet in a pair of high-end leather thongs from Spain. With trembling hands, he showed it to Veronica.

She said, "I see you're familiar with my work."

"Oh my God," the salesman said, "oh my God, you're…you're…you're *her.*"

* * *

Dean Pahukoa parked his car outside of Jules Matsumoto's house on Manukai Street in Keahou, south of Kailua-Kona.

Dean liked visiting there after games the Diamond Kings won. The backyard featured a built-in barbecue island, a cabana with a teak dining set, and a pool.

Jules often invited the players and their wives and girlfriends over for a cookout with free beer. Dean enjoyed the parties, but he never understood why Veronica hated them and why she never said anything nice about Jules. This made Dean wonder whether he should quit the jewelry store job. But he also knew if he did, Jules would kick him off the team. No matter if he was the best player in all the islands.

Dean killed the engine and looked at Jules's house. These visits over the last three years—he knew what they meant for his career. But they still gave him chicken skin. Like what would happen if anyone found out. Jules always told him, *It's our secret. Don't tell anyone.* Dean understood, but he also believed hiding this from Pops Brimley and the team—and Veronica—was dishonest. However, Dean also knew he'd never play big league ball if word leaked out, no matter how awesome he was.

It had to stay that way. As long as Jules was helping him, Dean could punch his ticket to stardom and big bucks in the Show. He loved Veronica, with all his heart—God she was hot and wow, did that girl like to have sex. And he'd do anything to help her always have the expensive stuff she liked, even if it meant doing whatever he needed to do to sign a multi-year contract with a huge signing bonus.

Dean took a deep breath, wiped his sweaty palms on his jeans, and got out of the car. He walked to the front door and rang the doorbell.

Jules greeted him, a glass of wine in his hand. "Hey, Dean, come on in," he said. "Can I get you some merlot?" Kylie Minogue played on a stereo in the background.

When it came to alcohol, Dean was a beer guy. Wine gave him headaches and made him fart, which he discovered at his wedding reception. "Uh, no, but thanks."

"It's cool." Jules sipped his merlot. "Say, I almost forgot, and you know I hate to mix business with pleasure, but I wanted to give you a heads-up."

"Okay."

"I'm expecting a good friend tomorrow, a close friend coming in from the mainland. He has a delivery for me and not much time to waste."

Dean blinked but said nothing.

"If he shows up and if I'm not around the store," Jules said, "be sure you call me on my cell immediately. Okay?"

"Shoots, no worries."

"This is important because this delivery is the biggest one we've ever handled," Jules said. "It's critical for our next edition of Island Creations. I can trust you on that, of course."

"Yeah, boss." Dean didn't think twice about it. He was used to being ready for these deliveries, whether from the mainland or Honolulu or wherever.

"Make sure the melter's ready to go. It's going to be quite a job." Jules smiled and peered over the rim of his wine glass. "Anyway, all of that's for tomorrow. For now, why don't you have a seat and make yourself comfortable? I think you earned it."

"Yeah, hey, wish I could, but I can't stay long," Dean said. "Veronica gets back tomorrow and I need to get the place clean.

I got crap all over the place and she hates messy stuff big time." He shrugged his broad shoulders.

"No problem, we'll make it quick." Jules sipped more wine. "Let's do it in the bedroom."

He led Dean to his master suite, with its king-sized bed and panoramic ocean view. "Just get ready and relax."

As Jules opened a drawer in his nightstand, Dean unbuckled his belt and dropped his jeans and underpants. He bent over the bed, elbows tucked under his chest.

"Hey, boss," he said, "now don't go getting no weird ideas back there."

"Dean, you'd think after three years you would have a better line."

"Just saying."

"I mean, you know me better."

His face buried in the bed, his bare ass in the air, Dean clenched his fists. "Boss, just *do* it, okay?"

"All right," Jules said. "Now hold on, this won't hurt a bit."

Then Jules plunged a syringe in Dean's butt.

Chapter Five:
The Arrival

On a sunny Wednesday, a conflicted Noelani B. Lee made the long drive from Hilo across the island to the Kona airport.

On one hand, she looked forward to seeing Wanda Tess Fong for the first time since she'd left Vegas. Wanda was her favorite cousin and Noelani long considered her more of a sister than her own aloof siblings. But at the same time, she was a bit miffed; Wanda's surprise visit forced her to postpone several profitable jobs. In desperation, she handed a couple to another private investigator who lacked any sense of professionalism or ethics, and hoped she wouldn't live to regret it.

Noelani parked her Nissan Sentra at Kona International and looked up at an incoming plane. A relic from another era, it had four loud propeller-driven engines belching black exhaust.

Geez, something so old should be in a museum instead of flying around with people in it.

But when she made out the airline's name—ISLAND SKIPPER—painted in block letters on the plane's fuselage, it hit her: *Oh my God, Wanda's on* that *thing?*

Alarms began going off in the former Air Uzbekistan Douglas DC-6 as Island Skipper Airlines pilot Dax Lancaster began the long descent toward Kona, on the last leg of a Honolulu-Maui-Honolulu-Kauai-Honolulu-Kona milk run.

"Jesus," he said, "what's happening?"

"Dude, how should I know?" His friend and first officer, Andrew, gulped a Coors Lite. "You're the pilot. Besides, anything bad happens and the feds start asking questions, *I was never here.*"

As they watched the DC-6 pierce the clear blue sky, Orestes and Sabina Zamora held their breath. On board was their son, Benjie, coming home for a weeklong visit from the University of Hawai'i-Manoa, where he majored in general studies and idle pursuits.

Standing a few feet away, the stoic Dean Pahukoa, awaiting the arrival of his wife, the beautiful Veronica Keawe, felt a sudden chill.

Not far from him, Noelani sensed something about the plane looked wrong as it drew closer to the runway.

A moment later, it dawned on her.

"It's the landing gear," Dax Lancaster said. "It's not coming down."

"Well, brah, all I can say is, you better *make* it come down already." Andrew looked out the window. "Land's getting awful damn close."

As Dax felt sweat roll down his forehead, he took a deep breath and toggled several switches. One turned on windshield wipers; another, an overhead fan emblazoned with a red Soviet star. Still another filled the cockpit with the sounds of the Tashkent National Men's Choir singing "Copacabana" in Uzbek.

In the plane's cabin, Wanda Tess Fong, full of whiskey sours, gazed up at the overhead compartment. She wished she could take the phone from her black backpack and maybe call Noelani and apologize for screwing things up. Instead, she threw up in an airsickness bag.

Across the aisle, Benjie Zamora looked out the window with saucer-sized eyes as the coastline and ocean below drew closer. He so much needed the warmth and comfort of either his Mom's home cooking, or Ozzie, his stuffed koala. But Ozzie was tucked out of reach in Benjie's black backpack in the overhead compartment above him. Sensing the inevitable, Benjie peed his pants.

One row forward, Veronica Keawe stared down at her feet—steel-toed boots and the thickest cotton socks available. She glanced up at the overhead bin. A tear rolled down her cheek as she thought of her black backpack; inside it was her new earrings, which cost her plenty and which, dammit, she hadn't even worn yet.

Across the aisle, Tommy "Chunks" Lohmiller felt the plane

dropping fast. *Well, shit*, he thought, resigning himself to certain death. He looked up at the overhead compartment and figured if he were a goner, his black backpack and its valuable contents were going down with him. The ultimate "screw you" for the Campanellas, even if it meant his retirement ended before it even started.

He sipped bottled water and closed his eyes.

"Island Skipper 2, this is Kona Tower," a mission-control type voice said over a speaker in the cockpit. "You're coming in pretty hot."

"Yeah, I know, Einstein," Dax said. "I can't get the wheels to go down and bells and buzzers are going off like crazy up here."

"Uh, Island Skipper 2, how about you take your bird on another lap and try to get your gear down on your next pass?"

Dax noted the fuel gauge was closing in on empty. "Tank's tapped, bro. Got any other bright ideas?"

"Island Skipper 2, flip the appropriately marked switch and you should have no problems at all there, over."

"Dude, I've done every…" Dax realized he'd neglected one last switch. So, he flipped it. This ejected the cassette with the Tashkent National Men's Choir, just as they began singing about how the now-older Lola discovers her beloved Copacabana is a disco.

"Oh man," Andrew said, "about freaking time."

"Island Skipper 2, this is Kona Tower; your gear is still not down."

Dax wanted to say, *No shit, Sherlock.* But as he looked down and saw emergency vehicles mustering on the airport's tarmac, he realized it was a bad time to be a total smart ass.

Noelani Lee shuddered and held her hands over her heart as the plane dropped hard and steep from the sky.

Sabina and Orestes Zamora started with the Hail Marys.

Dean Pahukoa willed his wife to lift her feet from the plane's floor.

The aft end of the airliner's fuselage skimmed the runway in a shower of sparks.

Snapped back to reality, Dax remembered something he learned while piloting a dive-bomber in a World War II video game.

He pulled hard on the controls. The plane jerked up and overshot the end of the runway. It almost nicked the ocean's surface. Waves licked at its underbelly as the DC-6 gained altitude.

"Well okay, you have my full attention," Andrew said, "but now what?"

Dax considered his available emergency landing options—ditching in the sea as the immediate choice—until he remembered the runway at the old Kona airport. Long ago condemned and converted to a parking lot for a beach park, it was just down the coast, a few miles south.

Dry land or water: either way, he knew this wasn't going to end well. Dax nudged the aircraft to port and lifted its nose upward until he had the fuselage level with the ancient black lava flows of the Big Island's leeward coast. When the abandoned runway, with big yellow *X*s painted on it, came into view, Dax knew he had just one shot to land the plane without killing everyone aboard.

He said to Andrew, "Hang on, bro, this shit's about to get serious."

The DC-6 belly-flopped onto the pavement with a thunderous *wham*. In the cabin, overhead compartments flew open. Carry-ons fell out, pelting passengers and piling up in the aisle. Buried among them, between rows 15 and 16, were four almost identical black backpacks.

Leaving an enormous spray of sparks in its wake, the DC-6 rocketed down the old airstrip. It smashed through a guard rail fence and slid closer and closer to an open-air roller hockey rink, where a group of adolescent boys fired slapshots at an empty goal.

With his eyes glued shut and his fingernails dug into the controls, Dax couldn't bear to watch what was about to happen. Which was, the plane came to an abrupt stop, its nose mere inches from the rink's outer fence.

Dax opened his eyes. The first thing he saw was a sign: "CAUTION FLYING PUCKS." The next thing he saw was a flying puck. It bounced off the cockpit's windshield.

He heard a young male voice call from the rink, "Fool, you screwed up my concentration."

As the reality of the situation sank in—they all just survived an epic crash-landing—the rattled passengers and flight attendants took a collective breath before they cheered and fist-bumped and Tweeted and recorded the aftermath with their smartphones.

Among them, Wanda Tess Fong wiped the corners of her mouth. She reached into the aisle and tossed aside purses and laptop cases until she found a backpack, which she picked up as she let out a loud belch.

In his seat across the aisle, Benjie Zamora grabbed the closest black backpack and placed it over his wet crotch. He decided he'd tell Mom and Dad something spilled on him.

Ahead of him, Veronica Keawe pulled a black backpack from under a pile of jackets and camera bags. She then instructed emergency responders to be careful of her feet. She also demanded a bottle of chilled Evian, as she had a tendency to parch when under extreme stress.

And across the aisle from her, Tommy Chunks admired the black backpack on his lap. Like untold thousands of other people, he purchased the pack cheap several months earlier, when an Oregon-based sporting goods chain—anticipating a Canadian rival's hostile takeover attempt—liquidated its inventory and flooded the market with them.

As rescue workers arrived on the scene and began helping other passengers off the aircraft, Tommy waited for his turn.

He held the pack close, at ease with the knowledge that the impending sale of its precious contents would soon put six-thousand permanent miles between him and those moron Campanella brothers.

Chapter Six:
The Black Backpacks

Early Wednesday evening, her overnight bag in her left hand and a plain white canvas tote on her right shoulder, Noelani B. Lee stopped short of the threshold of the King Kamehameha Hotel in Kailua-Kona.

Wanda Tess Fong chose the hotel as the headquarters for her visit because of its central location in the heart of Kona's tourism vortex. But this place was foreign turf for Noelani. As a Big Island native and a local, she made it a point to avoid the Kona side of the island unless a job required her to be there.

Surrounded by too many loud aloha shirts and bright red sunburns to count, she said, "I can't believe I let you talk me into this."

Standing next to her and gripping a wheeled suitcase, Wanda beamed. "Yeah, cool, huh?"

As they stepped inside, Noelani picked up a faint whiff of stale 1970s nostalgia seeping through the hotel's décor. Aside from the slight yet perceptible aroma of mildew, the first thing to grab her attention was a full-scale outrigger canoe, displayed atop a large platform. Photo-taking tourists swarmed around it.

Entering the lobby, Noelani and Wanda passed display cases filled with ancient artifacts, portraits of Hawaiian monarchs, and numerous paintings depicting island life before the white man's invasion. With each step, Noelani became convinced she'd taken a wrong turn somewhere and, instead of entering a hotel, had wound up in an ersatz Hawaiian museum.

Wanda said, "What do you think, Miss I Don't Hang With Tourists?"

Noelani weighed her response before she said, "This is what Hawaii would be if Vegas did Hawaii."

Wanda beamed. "You know it, cuz."

As they approached the registration desk, Noelani said, "Sweetie, I wish you'd just flown into Hilo and stayed with me at my place."

"Noe, Island Skipper Airlines only charges like thirty dollars one way between islands. Besides, they don't fly into Hilo."

"And I wonder why."

The crash landing was a few hours past, allowing sufficient time for Noelani's heart rate to stabilize and for the alcohol level in Wanda's bloodstream to achieve a state of near normalcy.

"I just figured," Wanda said, "you must be bored sitting around with your ukulele and being the funny spinster cat lady way before her time." When she smiled, dimples cratered her plump cheeks. Though several inches shorter and much rounder than her older cousin, Wanda long ago developed an innate knack for turning up the charm in certain circumstances. Especially when she wanted her way.

Which Noelani conceded. This time. "Watch it."

"Think of it this way, too—you get time off from your job. Everyone needs a break, even you."

"Ah, you've been talking to my mother again. She put you up to this."

"Geez, Noe, no way," Wanda said. "I mean yeah, Aunty Coco says you work real hard and you need time off. What's this she said, you don't sleep most of the time?"

"Only when I'm working, which is what I should be doing now. In Hilo." Noelani stepped aside so a family of five—walking abreast—could pass her. "I hope you didn't forget I live on this island."

Wanda Tess Fong said, "Yeah? And?"

"Well, you live in Vegas and I know for a fact you never go to the Strip."

"Noe, just last week, I went down to this casino, it's called the Kremlin, to see the new Cirque du Prétentieux show, *Merde d'avant-garde.*"

"I know the only reason you went was because Aunty Opal came from Seattle to visit. She told me all about it."

Noelani studied Wanda for a reaction, which turned out to be a simple tight-lipped smile. She could tell, though, her cousin's brown eyes were hiding something.

"But," Noelani said, "I am glad you're here. Even if here, is *here.*"

"Me too, Noe. Big time."

At the registration desk, they fell in line behind a tall man with gray hair. Noelani saw a suitcase at his side, and a black backpack hanging on his shoulder.

"You know," Wanda said, "maybe you'll get hooked up with

someone this week." She tilted her head toward the man.

Noelani looked at him, then at Wanda, "Why not you?"

"Because you're the pretty one."

The man thanked the front desk clerk as he picked up his key card. He turned and nodded at the women. "Ladies," he said, as he wheeled his suitcase toward the elevators.

As he walked away, Noelani noticed he kept a tight grip on his backpack's shoulder strap.

She also thought he looked familiar.

* * *

Tommy Chunks rode the elevator alone to the fourth floor of the hotel's West tower. When the doors opened, he hesitated before he exited the car, taking a moment to look down the hallway. Seeing nobody else around, he went to his ocean-view room.

He slid the key card in the door and entered, leaving the suitcase in the hallway but clutching the backpack to his side. Once inside, he flipped on all the lights before he inspected the bathroom and closet, peered under the bed, and opened the sliding glass doors to the lanai. He paused to watch workers preparing the grounds below for the hotel's luau before he dropped his backpack on the floor next to the bed. Then he returned to the hallway and retrieved the suitcase, locked the door behind him, took his cell phone from his pocket, and hit "1" on speed dial.

"I'm here," he said to a voice mail. "See you tomorrow."

He ended the call and picked up his backpack. He placed it on the bed, unzipped it, and looked inside.

His mouth went dry. He clutched his chest and felt woozy.

This can't be happening.

* * *

After checking in, Noelani and Wanda boarded the elevator to their room on the sixth floor of the hotel's West tower. As the doors closed, Noelani said something smelled funny.

"Hey, wasn't me," Wanda said.

"No, you goofball." She sniffed her cousin's backpack.

"Chocolate?"

* * *

Lounging in bed in her house on Ho'omama Street, Veronica Keawe propped her head on one hand and ran the fingertips of the other through Dean Pahukoa's hair. She detected a wispy smile on his lips as he picked up a TV remote and changed channels from a Lifetime movie starring Jaclyn Smith to professional wrestling.

It wasn't the big dopey grin she'd hoped to see, though, after all she did to get him going. She'd used her lips, tongue, breasts, hands, teeth, a feather boa, and half a bottle of baby oil; but no amount of sucking, licking, rubbing, stroking, biting, teasing, or lubrication got him hard.

Veronica realized he'd been like this for—what, a couple of years? She wondered what was wrong; when she first started dating Dean several years ago, she soon discovered he was the only man she'd ever slept with who could satisfy her insatiable demand. He could handle any new, strange, exotic position she wanted to try, sometimes four or five times a night.

But she noticed over time, as his muscles expanded and got harder, his once unstoppable, perpetually stiff penis shrank and stayed limp longer. And she also realized, it all started when Jules Matsumoto, his boss, began feeding Dean all kinds of garbage about him becoming a rich and famous big-league baseball star.

She looked at his flaccid dick, and then at her own taut body—naked except for knee-length black socks.

Still young and hot, she did everything possible to stay that way; she watched her diet, did Pilates several times a week, and used generous amounts of lotion to keep her skin soft and supple.

Still, Dean's interest in sex had waned in the past year or so, and no matter what she did to help get him excited, he could only muster a half hard-on at best. Even then, he didn't last long. This wasn't enough for Veronica, who suffered bouts of grumpiness if she failed to achieve at least three orgasms a day.

For that reason—plus the fact Dean's loyalty to her equalled his devotion to hitting baseballs—Veronica convinced herself he wasn't cheating. *If he can't screw me, he can't screw anyone else,* she thought. *So what the hell is it?*

She said, "Dean, baby, are you okay?"

"Yeah, sure, Roni. You know I'm glad you're home, yeah."

"You missed me, huh?"

"Big time." He glanced down at his crotch. "It's just I… You know, been working hard and all, the shop and the baseball. Sorry."

"It's okay," Veronica said. She thought about her favorite double-headed dildo hidden in her bra drawer. "I know you'll make it up to me one of these days." She dawdled with his hair. "Anyway, I have a surprise for you from Honolulu."

He smiled. "Oh, yeah? What is it?"

"Stay right here, I'll get it for you." She kissed him on the cheek, climbed out of bed, and padded to the living room.

Thanks to her earning power as the Pacific Rim's premier foot model, their home brimmed with every builder upgrade she could afford.

Her work for a high-end resort on Moorea—its glossy brochure featured her flawless feet in a hammock, with the blue sea and a snow-white beach in the background—paid for new granite kitchen countertops. A weeklong catalog shoot in Sydney locked up new bamboo hardwood floors in the living room. Another in Tokyo for a line of plastic sandals with snap-on manga characters yielded a hot tub in the backyard.

Still, the home was incomplete. Veronica wanted to remodel the master bathroom to give it more of a luxurious, spa-like feel. She also wanted to add a big family room onto the kitchen. As far as she could tell, though, Dean remained indifferent to both projects, even though he once told her they'd be on Easy Street once he made a Major League roster and got paid serious cash for whacking his trademark long-distance home runs. The family room addition was cool, he once told her, because he could throw big parties for all his ballplayer friends. As for the spa-like bathroom, he once said he didn't know what that was; he was sure their existing master bath worked just fine for all the reasons he needed to use it, which, he said, had nothing to do with massages or cucumber slices on his eyelids.

Veronica knew it didn't matter. If she wanted a huge family room and a luxurious master bath with a spa-like feel, then she'd get them.

All of this meant a major outlay for her. But she was about to turn thirty. Despite her toned thighs, tight abs, and perky boobs, not to mention her collection of protective combat boots and thick socks and her thrice-weekly pedicures, she knew in foot model years, she was just about on her last legs.

In the living room, Veronica found her black backpack on the corner of a tan leather sofa. It contained her gift of exclusive Oahu chocolates for Dean, along with the crazy expensive earrings she'd bought herself for her birthday. *The night isn't a total loss*, she thought.

But when she opened the backpack, she did not find the precious candies or the high-priced gold hoops. Instead, she found inside a cell phone, a smashed, half-empty bag of Funyuns, a bottle of water, a Big Island tourist guidebook with several dog-eared pages, and a keychain with a brass fob shaped like a hammer and sickle.

She pulled out the cell phone. It beeped a couple of times before its battery died. She dropped it back in the pack.

An object in the bag sparkled, catching her eye as only sparkly things could. She held up a necklace with a strange gold-plate-and-cubic zirconia pendant to the light. "What the fuck?"

She froze. *Oh my God, where are my earrings?*

Veronica caught her breath and stormed back to the bedroom. "Dean, turn that crap off and get up," she said. "Somebody stole my backpack and *you* need to find it *now*."

Chapter Seven:
The Sponge

Fifteen hours after the Island Skipper Airlines emergency landing, Benjie Zamora took full advantage of his mother's every indulgence.

"Benjie, you still look hungry," Sabina said on Thursday morning, as Benjie finished his second plate of bacon and eggs. "I know a plane crash has to take something out of you. You need to eat some more."

"Mom, I'm good," Benjie said. "I've had plenty."

"You better listen to what your mother says," said his father, Orestes. "Remember, she's the one who changed your diapers. She knows for everything goes in you, something else comes out."

Sabina rinsed dishes in the kitchen of the family's modest home on Olua Place, east of downtown Kailua-Kona. Orestes sat at the eat-in bar with the morning paper. Benjie occupied a stool beside him, nursing a glass of orange juice.

Sabina worked at the Kona Winds Timeshare Village on Kailua Bay. Orestes owned a successful car wash near the intersection of Route 11 and Palani Road, which happened to have the longest waits of any traffic light on the island. Together, they pulled in enough money to send their only child to U-H, often reminding him of their hope he'd go on to become a lawyer, doctor, something important.

But Benjie long ago determined his post-graduation plans included a move back home, where he'd take a few years off from the grind of college so he could figure out what to do with the rest of his life.

Madagascar played on the TV in the adjoining family room. Benjie watched it from the corner of his eye. It was his all-time favorite movie. He wished, though, his parents had a bigger TV—forty-two inches diagonal was too small. Plus, a kick-ass surround sound with a hi-def DVD player and a top-shelf game system would be way cool.

"I washed your jeans," Sabina said. "The wet spot in the front, from the drink that flew up and landed in your lap? It's all gone."

"Thanks, Mom."

"It had a funny smell, like pineapple or grapefruit juice."

"You know," Orestes said, looking up from *Dilbert*, "you gave us a big scare with your landing yesterday."

It was the eleventh time his father said those exact words since the incident. "I know, Dad," Benjie said, "but there wasn't much I could do about it."

Sabina rinsed the last plate in the sink and dried it by hand. "Are you sure I can't make more eggs for you before I go to work?"

"I'm sure, Mom."

Orestes folded the newspaper and rose from his stool. "I'm going to work, too. I have a new shipment of air fresheners coming in today direct from India. They're called 'French Lilac Fields.'" He slapped his son on the shoulder. "You'll take care of the back lawn today, right?"

It wasn't what Benjie wanted to hear.

"Now, Father, you know Benjie lived through a terrible ordeal yesterday," Sabina said, as she stowed the clean plate in a cupboard.

"Well, true, Mother, but I just thought seeing how he has time on his hands today—"

"What he needs," Sabina said, "is time to relax. It's not every day your only son has a near-death experience in a fiery plane crash."

"Son," Orestes said, "is it true in those situations, you see your life flash before your eyes, or there's a light at the end of the tunnel with angels and trumpets?"

Benjie shook his head. "Nah, it wasn't so bad."

Orestes nodded. "Uh huh." He grinned at Benjie, the same grin Benjie had seen innumerable times before in his youth. A toothless half-smile Benjie knew meant, *Your mother won this round, but the next one's mine.*

Sabina picked up her purse and car keys and kissed her son's forehead. "You just rest and do your reading homework for college and relax, and we'll see you later."

Then both of his parents were out the door and gone.

Except for the movie on TV and Sabina's parakeet chirping in the living room, the house was quiet. Benjie picked up his orange juice and wandered out to the backyard.

Dad was right. The grass was getting deep.

He heard the neighborhood rooster crow two doors down. He drank his juice, gave the yard another passive glance, and went back inside.

Benjie walked down the hall to his room and grabbed his backpack. Still a little hungry, he returned to the kitchen and raided the pantry. He snatched the last snack-sized bag of Fig Newtons from its box, and took it, his juice, and the backpack to the family room.

Benjie sat in a rattan chair with floral print upholstery and placed the juice and the Newtons on a side table. He opened the backpack and reached in to pull out Ozzie, the stuffed koala, and his botany textbook.

But there was no Ozzie and no boring text.

Instead, the pack contained an airline ticket and a toiletry bag. Benjie didn't own a toiletry bag and he knew he'd left his boarding pass somewhere on the plane.

He took the kit from the backpack and opened it. He felt his lungs empty and his eyes pop wide open. He shivered.

Inside the kit, Benjie saw rings and bracelets earrings and clear stones he assumed were diamonds. He didn't know what the red and blue ones were but even if they weren't diamonds, they still had to be worth a lot.

He zipped the bag shut and read the boarding pass. It belonged to somebody named Thomas Lohmiller, who'd flown from Las Vegas to Honolulu and then from Honolulu to Kona. Paperclipped under the first ticket was another, for Thomas Lohmiller to fly from Kona to Honolulu, and then on to Suva, Fiji.

Benjie tried to distract himself from his rapid breathing with a Newton. Chewing the cookie, he studied the boarding pass. He didn't know who Thomas Lohmiller was, except someone else on his plane. And this Thomas Lohmiller no doubt wanted the toiletry bag, and all the stuff inside it, returned. Like, real soon.

He watched the movie for a couple of minutes. The animated meerkats sang their stupid "I like to move it, move it" song Benjie often could tolerate only after several Jaeger shots.

He washed the Newton down with juice and wondered what he should do. Sabina always taught him to be honest. Orestes always taught him to be resourceful. *But, I can't tell them about this. No friggin' way.*

Benjie drained the rest of his OJ in one gulp. He placed the toiletry bag and the airline tickets back in the pack, which he threw over his shoulder. Then he stepped outside, climbed on his bike, and made his way toward downtown…

…where a man in a yellow tank top and red-and-blue plaid shorts walked down Ali'i Drive, Kailua-Kona's main drag, and sized up his next mark, while listening to "Holiday in Cambodia" on an 80-gig iPod which did not belong to him.

Chapter Eight:
The Loco Moco Mama

Because she could cook and because her cousin Herman a few years back became the second person she ever killed by accident, Esther Halekealoha wound up owning a restaurant called the Loco Moco Mama.

* * *

"Girl, quit flirting with that *haole* boy and pick up this order here."

Esther Halekealoha made sure her voice boomed out from the restaurant's cramped kitchen. The target of her wrath, a teenage waitress—in the midst of trying to tease a sweet tip out of a bushy-haired surfer—gave Esther stink eye.

"Hey, lady," the surfer called back, "I ain't *haole*. My great-grandparents came here, like, uh, a real long time ago."

"Oh, so they was some of the original white folks subjugated my people, so shut up," Esther said. She looked at the waitress. "And you—how many times I got to tell you, no cleavage at work? It ain't professional."

Ignoring two middle fingers raised in her direction, Esther turned to face her cook, Mr. Lim—the only person small enough to share the kitchen with her and still have room to do his job. "What is it with girls showing their boobies all the time? Girl do that I was her age, we get the business end of Daddy's belt, sometimes worse."

Mr. Lim mumbled something in Hokkien and resumed preparing an order of Portuguese sausage and eggs over easy.

"Go easy on the rice," Esther said. "We running out fast." She left Mr. Lim to his work and wandered to the dining area. She assumed a position next to the cash register, behind a display case filled with Loco Moco Mama logo tee shirts and ball caps and surveyed her dominion.

Tucked in a shopping center called the Ali'i Sunset Plaza across from Kailua Bay, the Loco Moco Mama drew throngs of locals and tourists alike. Esther took pride in her breakfasts, which early risers who worked in the town's tourism industry devoured every morning. Meanwhile, her lunch menu featured

Hawaiian-style plate lunches, including the namesake loco moco—two beef patties atop a huge pile of rice and hidden under a couple of fried eggs, all drowning in thick gravy.

Esther revelled in the rave reviews she received from food critics and a loyal clientele, some of whom on Thursday morning said they'd return for lunch.

But by the time she took a break from overseeing Mr. Lim, the breakfast crowd thinned. A local woman who worked at Costco sat at the counter, while two tourist couples sat at a table, pointing at a map. Another couple at a neighboring table ate in silence. Meanwhile, their bratty kid—a boy about seven who Esther caught stealing mints from a dish next to the register— used his knife and fork to play a loud game of "swordfight" against himself.

Then there was the surfer boy, alone at a table for two. He sneered at Esther and in return, she glowered at him, her wide nostrils flaring and her clenched teeth visible between thick lips. Her carotid artery throbbed under several layers of fat. Long, frizzy gray hair flowed down either side of her broad face and over her deep brown, tattooed arms. Her mammoth shoulders rose and fell with each inhale and exhale.

She laughed under her breath as the kid's smirk withered, and he turned to look outside at nothing in particular.

About then she saw another young man, about the same age as the surfer boy, enter the restaurant. A Filipino kid, he sat at a corner table, holding a black backpack real tight to his scrawny chest.

Esther watched as the kid, acting nervous, looked around the room and dropped the pack to the floor. He stuffed it against the wall and planted his right foot against it. Esther's other waitress, more modest than the first and dressed right for work, approached him with a glass of water and a menu.

Esther looked at a clock on the wall.

She thought, *Where the hell is he?*

* * *

Noelani B. Lee emerged from the King Kamehameha Hotel's elevator and turned a corner to find her cousin, Wanda Tess Fong, babbling in Hawaiian.

"Sweetie, calm down," Noelani said. "I'm sorry I'm late getting down here but I needed to call this guy who's helping me with—"

"Noe, it's okay."

"Oh. Well then, why are you so upset?"

Wanda held up the black backpack. "This." She jammed it in Noelani's face. "This has got me *real* pissed."

Noelani lowered the bag with her left hand. "I thought you liked chocolate truffles, not to mention diamond hoop earrings."

Wanda unzipped the pack and pulled out a stuffed koala.

Noelani blinked at the toy. "Oh. What happened to the other one?"

After getting off the elevator, Wanda said, she stopped to clean her sunglasses. When she finished, next thing she knew, the backpack with the earrings and the chocolates became a bag containing a stuffed animal and a book about plants.

Noelani opened it and found, tucked inside the cover, a receipt from the University of Hawai'i bookstore for $52 and a handwritten note on steno paper. Noelani read it aloud: "'Buy beer, buy pizza, ask Dad to paint room (red or black), ask Mom for money.'" She looked at Wanda. "Do you remember any college-age kids on the plane with you?"

"There was this one real skinny dude got on in Honolulu. He had a black backpack looked a lot like mine."

"Did anyone else on the plane have packs like this?"

Wanda said, "There was so much happening with people all freaking out when we crashed, I kinda had other things on my mind."

Noelani nodded as she tried to figure out how her cousin wound up having two backpacks, neither of them hers, in the space of just a few hours.

"I really wish I had mine," Wanda said. "See, the necklace Daddy got custom-made for me for my birthday is in it. It's a one-of-a-kind thing."

Noelani noted a faint green line around her cousin's neck. "Tell you what—I'll see if the airline will help us track down who else was on the plane. Maybe we can find the college kid. He might have your necklace by mistake."

She asked Wanda whether she'd seen any suspicious people near her in the lobby. Wanda said no, she just set the pack down next to her before she started cleaning her shades. "But you know the tall handsome man in line ahead of us last night? He bumped into me."

"He did?"

"Yep. He just came up behind me and said 'sorry' and I said 'no problem.' Then he split through those doors over there." She pointed toward the hotel's main entrance.

Noelani looked at the glass doors. "Was he carrying the pack he had with him last night, or anything else?"

"Nope. But he was walking real fast and looking all around at people," Wanda said. "Kinda like he was in a big hurry to catch up with someone."

* * *

The young man caught Tommy Chunks's attention when he swiped a black backpack from a short, round woman in the lobby of the King Kamehameha Hotel.

As a seasoned professional, Tommy appreciated the art of common street thievery. He started the same way back in Buffalo; his alacrity in lifting wallets and snagging purses from unsuspecting victims caught the attention of others up the criminal food chain. Through time, he graduated to more important and enriching felonious endeavors. Although, and much to his chagrin, his skills dulled since he moved to Vegas and attached himself to those idiots from Arizona, the Campanella brothers.

Part of it was age, considering he had about ten years on them. Plus, they thought of him as little more than a glorified errand boy on twenty-four-hour call. The morons.

In the lobby, Tommy pretended to admire a painting of an old Hawaiian village as he observed the thief slip around a corner and out of view. Tommy then stepped away from the picture and bumped into the woman, replacing her pilfered backpack with the one in his possession.

"Sorry," he said. "You okay?"

At first taken aback, she smiled and said, "Oh hey, no worries."

"All right," Tommy said, "have a good day," and followed the young man into the warm Hawaiian morning.

* * *

Gerald Kapono MacTavish perused the contents of the black backpack he nicked from the fat chick in the hotel. Inside he found half-melted chocolate truffles and a cheap digital camera, with pictures of people he didn't know, including a hot babe. Full-body pics showed her wearing boots and long socks. But there were no pics of the fat chick. He figured she was the one who took them.

What caught his attention in the pack, though, was a blue box with fancy silver printing on the outside. It made a design of weird-looking eagles. He stopped and opened it.

The box contained a pair of hoop earrings. The price tag, still on them, said they cost $1,500. Esther would be proud of him. But, he wondered, could she get what they were worth from Jules? The jeweler cheaped out on her last time, which pissed her off in a big way, to the point she told Gerald she'd never do business with Jules ever again.

Gerald closed the box and wondered whether he ought to hang on to the earrings for himself—hide them from Esther until Jules asked for more stuff or was willing to pay a decent price. He'd stand up to her for once, eliminate her as the middleman, and get the money he deserved for all his hard work, instead of Esther's trickle-down change.

Gerald paused beside the seawall on Ali'i Drive and slipped the box in his pocket. He left the camera—a crappy old 4-megapixel thing—on the seawall, at a spot where he knew a wave would drench it. Besides, he had better cameras, including an awesome, brand-new Canon SLR he picked up the night before from a dude who left it unattended in a tee shirt shop.

* * *

Several paces back, Tommy lit a cigarette as he followed the younger man into the Kona Inn Shopping Village. There, he watched the guy snatch wallets from oblivious tourists and drop them in the backpack. At the far south end of the shopping center, he swiped a BlackBerry from a woman who set it aside as she bent over to tie her shoe.

Tommy marvelled at the guy's proficiency. What made it even more fascinating was he did it all amid crowds of tourists, in broad daylight, while wearing a yellow tank top and bright red-and-blue tartan plaid shorts.

A minute or so later, the young guy looked over his shoulder and made eye contact with Tommy. Then he cut across the street, dodging minivans and pick-up trucks.

Tommy waited for a break in traffic and jogged after the younger man, but he was no match. He settled back and watched as the guy entered the rear of a business in a shopping center.

Tommy knew the place well. He had scheduled a meeting with a contact there anyway, so he figured he'd cross paths with the younger man later.

As he entered the shopping center, he passed a shoe store and a coffee shop and peered into the large window of a restaurant called the Loco Moco Mama. Inside, he saw several people eating breakfast under the watchful eye of an enormous brown woman.

But the young man in the plaid shorts was nowhere in sight. So, Tommy continued to his appointment, a couple doors down.

Chapter Nine:
The Business

A musclebound young Hawaiian, mid to late twenties, was wiping down a glass display case when Tommy Chunks entered Jules's King of Diamonds.

"Aloha, sir," he said, "but sorry, we don't open till ten."

"Mr. Matsumoto in?" Tommy looked at the wares on display—rings, bracelets, cuff links, and pendants shaped like tropical flowers and sea creatures, many with precious stones set in them.

The buff dude hesitated before he said, "Sure, lemme go get him." He set aside his cleaning rag and a can of glass cleaner and passed through an open doorway next to the showroom, into Jules Matsumoto's office. Tommy heard him say, "Boss, some guy out here wants to see you." Tommy heard Jules tell the young man to show him in.

Jules shook Tommy's hand as he entered the office. Jules said to the buff dude, "Dean, if you want to get some breakfast, I can hold the fort for a while."

"Sure, boss." Dean picked up a black backpack and exited the shop.

Tommy focused on the pack as he said, "Seems like a nice kid."

Jules invited Tommy to sit. "He's the best baseball player in all of Hawaii. I'm telling you, remember the name Dean Pahukoa because he'll be a star in the majors soon. We're working on it."

Tommy sat. "Okay."

Jules closed a ledger book on his desk. "There's a game Saturday in Waimea—perhaps you could come along and watch if you're still on the island?"

"No."

Jules nodded. "Well, ready to get down to business, I see. You have the stuff?"

Tommy examined the fingernails of his right hand. "Jules, we need to talk."

* * *

His mom's breakfast an hour old and still heavy in his stomach, Benjie Zamora ordered a ham-and-cheese omelet, hash browns, and a glass of guava juice. He eyeballed the other patrons in the Loco Moco Mama as he kept the bling-filled backpack pressed between the restaurant's wall and his right foot.

Benjie had an hour to kill before Jules's King of Diamonds opened. He figured, if anyone would buy the stuff, it would be Jules. Everyone in town knew the jeweler's reputation.

The waitress delivered his breakfast. Benjie prepared to flood his potatoes with ketchup when he looked up to see a big, ripped bruddah enter the restaurant—carrying a black backpack, just like the one under Benjie's foot.

* * *

Dean Pahukoa sat at an empty table, next to one with a bushy-haired surfer. He placed his backpack on a chair and looked up as a cute waitress approached him with a menu.

"Hi, Dean," she said, batting her eyelashes. "You want coffee, tea or—"

"What I tell you, girl?" Dean heard Esther Halekealoha bellow across the room. He knew Esther and liked her, even if she sometimes scared the crap out of him. He also knew she had a close business relationship with Jules.

The waitress froze. From the corner of his eye, Dean noticed a kid drop a ketchup bottle in his hash browns.

The girl opened her mouth to say something to Esther but instead looked at the surfer. "Can I get you anything else?"

He showed her a slip of paper. "Touch you later?"

She shrugged and gazed at Dean, eyelashes fluttering. "Your usual, Dean?"

"The ham and eggs over easy—sure sounds good."

The waitress handed Dean's order to Esther.

"You knock off the attitude now, girl," Esther said, as she relayed the order to Mr. Lim in the kitchen through the pass-through.

Behind the cook, Esther saw Gerald Kapono MacTavish,

waving to her and holding up a black backpack.

Well, it's about time.

* * *

Jules rubbed his chin. "A stuffed koala bear."

Tommy said, "Technically, they're marsupials. Not bears."

Jules propped his feet on the desk and leaned back in his chair, hands clasped behind his head. "Do you think Ryan or Frank have figured things out yet?"

"No. They're too stupid."

Jules and Tommy were longtime business partners, though not what either would call "friends." Still, Jules planned to pay big for the goods Tommy swindled from Ryan, in part because Tommy was at long last cutting ties with the Campanellas. Not that it mattered so much to him, but Jules figured helping fund Tommy's retirement also would pull one over on the brothers. But because Tommy'd lost the stuff, Jules now faced unavoidable delays in filling advance orders for his newest line of Island Creations.

It also meant he wouldn't get the added cash infusion he needed to continue financing the next critical steps in Dean's promising baseball career.

The jewelry Esther Halekealoha brought him of late was both of inferior quality and insufficient quantities. This stuff Tommy brought from the mainland, well, if it was as good as Tommy figured, then Jules needed it in the worst way.

Jules said, "You can imagine how hard it'll be to track down a backpack with all these tourists around here."

"I know."

"They call it the Big Island for a reason."

"You think?"

"Pretty much impossible."

Tommy stared at him.

"If someone opens it and finds the stuff," Jules said, "then you and me, we're in deep doo-doo."

"I know," Tommy said.

Jules remembered Tommy was a man of few words. He also knew Frank Campanella nicknamed Tommy "Chunks" because, during their usual business dinners, he took oversized bites of food so he'd spend more time chewing and less time talking.

Jules said, "How long till you go to Fiji?"

Tommy picked at a cuticle on his right thumb. "Depends."

"On?"

"When we find the stuff."

We. "If you need help, I can ask Dean to work with you. He pretty much does what I say, anyway. He's big enough to frighten the bejeebers out of anyone, although he's as gentle as they come. The only thing is, his wife…"

Tommy sniffed and looked at him sideways.

"Let's just say," Jules said, "she has a firm grip on a short leash."

"I'll let you know. After breakfast."

Jules recommended the Loco Moco Mama. Tommy stood. Jules wished him luck and escorted him to the front door.

Tommy turned and said, "Question."

"Yes?"

"Weird kid around here, wears plaid shorts?"

Jules laughed. "His name's Gerald. He's not a kid. He's about thirty going on fifteen. As for the shorts, well…he used to wear a kilt."

"A kilt."

"He thinks he's a Hawaiian Braveheart."

Tommy arched an eyebrow.

"His mother owns the Loco Moco Mama," Jules said. "Trust me, he's nuttier than a macadamia grove. But he's also one heck of a thief and a pickpocket."

"I noticed."

"I'm sure he got me once. I was about to pay for a cappuccino one day and reached for my wallet and—poof, gone. Why do you ask?"

"No reason," Tommy said.

"Just one word of advice," Jules said. "He's good for nothing."

* * *

"For starters, why you always gotta be on Hawaiian time?"

Esther slapped Gerald upside the head as they stood outside the restaurant's service entrance. She reasoned she was within her rights to abuse him, considering he was illegitimate. "What's the matter with you—always gotta be late?"

Gerald rubbed his head. "You don't got to get all *huhu* on me."

"You want crazy? I'll show you crazy, babooze."

"Too late, I already know."

Esther shoved the backpack in Gerald's face. "So, this all you got? I send you on one errand and all you get is three wallets and a couple hundred cash money."

In an affected Scottish brogue, Gerald said, "Beggars canna be choosers."

"Enough already talking like that," Esther said. "I told you, you ain't all Scottish." She looked at his plaid shorts. He wore them every day. "You and them nasty-ass shorts and them loud horns you play."

He dropped the brogue. "Don't spoof the pipes. And I washed the shorts two days ago."

"Whatevahs," she said. "You say this all you got, but I know you holding back from me. You always holding stuff back from me all the time."

Gerald shook his head. "No, it's all there."

"Well, it ain't enough." Esther took the cash from the wallets and stuffed the bills in her bra. She pitched the wallets in a trashcan. "Besides, last bunch of crap you got me to give Jules the jeweler man? He said it was garbage."

"I kinda liked the watch myself."

"Next time you get one, keep it," Esther said. "Don't give it to me to sell to him because he ain't buying. Makes me look bad." She tossed the backpack to Gerald. "Now fill this thing by supper or else get something good I can sell. No junk, neither."

In his brogue, Gerald said, "It's an ill bird that fouls its own nest."

"Stop the shit." Esther raised her hand to slap him but Gerald backed away. "Now move it, I gotta help Mr. Lim with the grinds. I look for you laters and you ain't here, I find you and you ain't gonna like it."

Esther shuffled back inside the restaurant. As the door slammed behind her, Gerald hummed a couple bars of "Loch Lomond" and thought, *If that's what she wants, then that's what she'll get.*

He grabbed a couple of rocks from a pile near the back door and dropped them in the backpack. Then he wandered toward the street.

*   *   *

Noelani Lee, surrounded by pale mainlanders, sighed as she and Wanda Tess Fong meandered along Ali'i Drive.

"Now come on, cousin," Wanda said, "it's all good."

At one point, Noelani stepped into traffic to pass a family of four. The move earned a dirty look and a honk from a man driving a rental car. "You know, if this was Hilo, I could find out who he was and make his life miserable."

"Yeah, but then you'd be miserable instead of having a good time with me."

A minute or so later they arrived at a shopping center on the *mauka*, or inland, side of the street. It consisted of three single-story buildings shaped like an inverted capital E, with the open ends facing the ocean.

"It's up here," Wanda said, pointing past a coffee shop. Red umbrellas cast shade over tables on the shop's lanai, where tourists sipped their drinks.

Wanda looked at the blue water of Kailua Bay behind them and said, "Hey, Noe, lemme take your picture with the ocean in the background."

Noelani wanted to protest but decided to play along. It was Wanda's vacation, after all. *Stop whining and lighten up*, she thought. *She'll be back in Vegas in a week and who knows when you'll see her again.*

Wanda dropped the backpack with the textbook and stuffed koala on the ground and took a point-and-shoot digital camera from her pocket. Noelani turned on her best smile, even though she hated having her picture taken, and Wanda clicked the shutter. She looked at the pic in the camera's LCD screen, and then grunted as she picked up the backpack.

"Wanda, are you okay?"

"Wow," Wanda said, as she struggled with the pack, "this thing got heavy all of a sudden."

Noelani zipped it open and reached inside. "Oh. Here's why."

* * *

In the corner of a nearby parking lot, somebody dumped a black backpack containing a college textbook and a stuffed koala into a large wooden box.

Later in the day, volunteers from a local charity collected the box's contents and took them to a thrift store, where other volunteers inventoried them and priced them cheap for resale.

* * *

Sabina Zamora was restocking boxes of laundry detergent in the Kona Winds Timeshare Village office when a man entered. "Aloha, welcome to the Kona Winds," she said. "Do you have a reservation, Mister…?"

"Uh, no," the man said. "See, I just wanna know if a motherfu…if a friend of mine got here, yet."

"What is your friend's name?"

"Tommy Ch… Lohmiller."

Sabina checked the computer records for Mr. Lohmiller, owner of a two-bedroom ocean-view unit. "No, sorry, he has no reservation this week. And it looks like we're not expecting him any time soon, as far as I can tell."

The man nodded. "Huh. Well, that's weird."

He poured sweat, no doubt because he wore a black hoodie, a black leather ball cap, black jeans, and a pair of black-and-gray sneakers, on a hot, humid day.

"Yes," Sabina said. "I suppose you could say it's weird."

The man nodded. "So, uh, you know a place around here where I can get some chow?"

Chapter Ten:
The Business (Cont'd)

Noelani Lee said, "There's something weird going on with these backpacks."

"Maybe someone picked it up by accident," Wanda Tess Fong said.

Noelani removed a large stone from the pack. Round and smooth, it was gray except for a white blotch of bird crap. "Wanda, can you tell me who walks around town with a bag full of rocks?"

* * *

Benjie Zamora wolfed down his breakfast, placed one of his dad's twenty-dollar bills on the table, and left the Loco Moco Mama. On his way out, he almost ran into a tall gray-haired man in a maroon polo shirt and khaki shorts.

"Excuse me," Benjie said, pressing the backpack to his chest as he walked toward Ali'i Drive.

* * *

Dean Pahukoa looked up from his ham and eggs to see the man who just visited Jules entering the restaurant. He watched the man's eyes follow a kid, who left the place with something under his arm. After a moment, the man approached him.

"Good morning," the man said.

"Eh, howzit?" Dean said.

"You work for Jules." He motioned toward an empty chair. "May I?"

"Go for it."

The man sat with his back to the door. The waitress with the cleavage delivered a menu and a glass of water. She looked at Dean and said, "Can I get you anything else? More water?"

"I'm good."

"Coffee, black," the man said.

The waitress looked at him. "I'm sorry, you said something?"

"Coffee, black; one egg, easy; wheat toast, margarine." The man handed her the menu. She repeated the order as she wrote it down, smiled at Dean, and walked away.

The man extended his hand across the table. "Tom Lohmiller."

"Oh, uh"—Dean dropped his fork and shook the man's hand—"*aloha*, I'm Dean Pahukoa. Nice to meet you."

"How long have you worked for Jules?"

"About five years now," Dean said as he resumed eating. "I play baseball for him, too. He sponsors a team in this one Hawaii league."

"Any good?"

"We're in first place. And see, not bragging or nothing, but I'm the best player in the whole league, yeah."

"Interesting."

"Jules says I got da kine chance to be in the majors. Not bragging, like I said, but we're kinda working on a plan to get me to the Major Leagues."

Tommy sniffed but said nothing.

"Yeah, Jules got me... I'm working out a lot," Dean said. "Lots of weights. Doing it natural, is what he says."

"I can tell," Tommy said. "Is that your backpack?"

"No, and it's not my wife's neither. See, she was on the plane crash landed yesterday. She's got one just like it but it's gone." Dean stuffed a forkful of egg in his mouth.

Tommy nodded. "What's in it?"

"Bunch of crap."

"Like?"

"Tourist book, a funny-looking keychain, dead cell phone, a cheap necklace."

"Sounds like crap."

Dean laughed. "Ho brah, lemme tell you, my wife—her name's Veronica—she opened this one last night? She got all insane pissed off, like big time."

"Uh huh," Tommy said. "What's in hers?"

"She went to Honolulu for her birthday and got herself this expensive present." Dean leaned across the table and lowered his voice. "I can tell you, right?"

"Please."

"I mean, I don't want no one else knowing, since they're lost."

Tommy nodded.

"She told me they were these earrings, with lots of diamonds on them, yeah."

Tommy said, "Huh."

"She said they cost her way more than a thousand dollars." Dean sat back. "But we can afford it. I mean I had to stay here and work but she's a big-time foot model."

"A foot model."

"She goes all over—people take pictures of her feet for da kine advertisements and catalogs." Dean scarfed his ham and eggs. "Oh, almost forgot, she had her little camera in there, too."

Tommy slid his hand in his pocket and felt the camera.

The waitress arrived with Dean's check. "You sure I can't get you anything else, Dean? Maybe a glass of passion-orange-guava juice? I know you like that because—"

"Dammit girl, why you not *listen* at me again?" Esther Halekealoha turned to face Mr. Lim through the pass-through. "Remind me I gotta fire her ass."

Mr. Lim yawned and flipped eggs on the flattop.

Dean wiped his mouth and tossed the paper napkin on his plate. "Hey, listen, Mr. Tom, can't talk story no more, I gotta get to work." He left money on the table and picked up the backpack. "'Kay den, see you around."

Dean stepped outside and almost reached Jules's King of Diamonds when his cell rang. He put the backpack on the ground and answered.

Veronica Keawe: "So, did you find it yet?"

"No, baby," Dean said, "but I been looking."

"All right, well, I have an appointment at noon for a mani-pedi and then I'm having lunch with the girls. And when you get off work, start looking again."

"Okay. But, baby, if I don't find it, what happens then?"

"Then I expect you to sneak one of Jules's things home to make up for my earrings," Veronica said. "Something awesome, of equal or greater value, and with huge stones." She hung up.

Dean stared at the phone. *No way I can steal from Jules. Not with my baseball career riding on my job and those visits to Jules's house.*

He needed to find her backpack.

Dean took a deep breath and entered the shop. As he did, he forgot he'd left the pack with the tourist book, the funny-looking keychain, the dead cell phone, and the cheap necklace sitting on the ground.

* * *

Benjie Zamora felt a knot in his stomach.

Pressing the backpack to his chest, he thought about Jules's TV and radio ads, Jules saying he'll buy anyone's unwanted gold and jewelry for a fair price.

Big time cash in exchange for the backpack would be cool. But more than anything, Benjie wanted Ozzie.

He scuffled along the street, head bowed. He thought about going back to his bike, locked to a rack in a parking lot behind the restaurant. He'd jump on it, ride home, and hide the jewelry deep in his closet. Maybe take more time to think about this situation. Or else he'd just suck it up and sell the stuff to Jules and walk out with the money he needed for, whatever. Or he could use more of Dad's cash and buy a smoothie or something, or he could—

He walked straight into someone's chest. Benjie looked up to see a wide, sweaty man dressed in black.

"Hey yo," the man said, "watch where the fuck you're going."

"Sorry, sir." Benjie clutched the pack tighter and continued down the street.

* * *

Wanda elbowed Noelani as they entered the Loco Moco Mama. "There he is, cousin." They sat, Wanda taking a chair with her back to Tommy, which forced Noelani to face him.

"Wanda, can you just chill about the old guy already?" Noelani said.

"He's not so old."

"He's as old as Uncle Leonard, easy."

"No way, not even."

As a waitress brought water and menus, Noelani saw a diminutive Asian man wearing an apron enter the dining area. He approached a table where an even tinier Asian woman sat drinking coffee.

In subdued tones, the woman gave the man an earful. She

spoke in what to Noelani sounded like a Chinese dialect. She couldn't hear them but the man's body language indicated he was in trouble about something. Still, he nodded as the woman spoke but said nothing in response. The woman took one last gulp of coffee and left the restaurant. The man wiped his hands on his apron and returned to the kitchen.

Noelani thought, *This is why I shall remain forever single.*

Wanda held up her menu. "Look at the righteous local grinds they got here, cuz."

Noelani perused the menu, with photos of chicken katsu, kalua pork, huli huli chicken, saimin noodles, and the house specialty, loco moco. "This reminds me," Noelani said, "how's Uncle Arthur coming along since the heart attack?"

"Daddy's way better now he's got the stents in," Wanda said. "So, I'm surprised you never heard of this place."

"I don't get out much."

Wanda pointed at the restaurant's slogan on the menu: "Great Luau Food Without the Big Time Luau Prices." She said, "The weird spiky-haired dude on the Food Network said this is the best plate-lunch on the whole Kona Coast." She nodded toward the cash register. "See the sistah there?"

Noelani looked at the massive woman ringing up a customer. "I think it's impossible not to."

"She's got one great story, about how she got this place and what makes it so great."

"Okay, Wanda, tell me—what's her story?"

Chapter Eleven:
The Lines of Communication

"Her name's Esther Halekealoha," Wanda Tess Fong said. "Story is, she kinda inherited the place when her cousin died. He called it something else but the *tita* there changed the name. So, she starts making all kinds of *ono* local grinds and this place gets popular in a hurry. She's got a rep for being an awesome cook, like, there's nothing she can't make."

A waitress took their orders—scrambled egg whites with spinach for Noelani B. Lee and fried Spam, fried eggs, and rice with beef gravy for Wanda.

"You see, Noe," Wanda said, "the sistah's one big-time food legend in Hawaii. A real celebrity. I should take her pic and get her autograph."

Just then, Noelani's smartphone buzzed.

Wanda glared at the phone. "Noe, swear to God, don't you even *think* about answering it."

Noelani looked at the incoming number. "Just give me a second. I'll be quick, honest." She walked outside and answered the call.

At his table, Tommy Chunks looked out the window and saw the weirdo in plaid shorts walk past the Loco Moco Mama, a black backpack slung over his shoulder.

* * *

Inside Jules's King of Diamonds, Dean Pahukoa panicked when he realized he forgot the backpack with the pendant and tourist book. He stepped outside and looked around. But it was gone.

Just then he saw the Tom man, Jules's friend, following the crazy dude in the plaid shorts—the restaurant lady's *lolo* son—toward the street.

Dean returned to the shop in time to hear Jules on his phone: "Yes, they're missing…A black backpack…It's worth a lot to me, too…I need them, like, yesterday…You're that close?…All right, but I can be assured of confidentiality?…Sure, I can get you one…Thanks, see you then."

When Jules ended the call, Dean flipped the "Closed" sign on the front door to "Open." By then, the crazy bruddah and Mr. Tom were way out of sight.

Dean thought about what he just overheard. He had no idea who Jules was talking to, but he figured it must have something to do with the raw materials Jules was expecting. And they must've been in a black backpack.

Okay, so that's why the haole *Tom was here.*

Dean handled a lot of those "raw materials" in the last couple of years, ever since Jules taught him how to make rings, bracelets, and pendants as part of the shop's exclusive Island Creations. Dean never asked where the stuff came from. It was none of his business. He just did what Jules told him.

Dean decided, when he had a chance, he'd call Veronica.

Jules poked his head out of his office. "Dean, I need your help with something."

Noelani ended the call and stepped back inside the Loco Moco Mama.

Wanda said, "What was that all about?"

"I just need to take care of something in town since I'm here," Noelani said. She spread a napkin on her lap.

"Yeah, right."

Noelani noted her cousin's pout and said, "It'll only take a few minutes. Honest, sweetie, I'll be quick."

* * *

Gerald Kapono MacTavish whistled "Scotland the Brave" as he strolled down the breezeway of a building next door to the Ali'i Sunset Plaza, with several shops on the ground floor and condos on the six stories above.

Standing in the shadows at the breezeway's far end, his back turned to the street, he opened the backpack and rummaged through its contents. But there was nothing worth keeping—just a book about the island, an old cell phone, and a funny-looking keychain.

Then, at the bottom of the bag, he saw a shiny necklace and

pendant. He took it out and held it up for a good look, and then slipped it over his neck. It was ugly but different. It had character, just like him. So, he decided this, he'd keep.

Somebody grabbed his shoulders, spun him around and pushed him up against a wall. It was the tall, gray-haired man wearing the maroon polo shirt and khaki shorts—the same creepy dude who'd followed him from the hotel.

The old guy gripped his shirt with both hands, his fists pushing into Gerald's throat. Gerald felt lightheaded. "Hey, easy brah," he said, fighting for air, "you want it, it's all yours."

The man blinked. "Want what?"

"This." Gerald held up the pendant. "You want this, right?"

The man blinked. "Shut up and listen."

* * *

On the tarmac in Honolulu, in the cockpit of a de Havilland DHC-6 Twin Otter—which Island Skipper Airlines rented in a pinch from a skydive club—Dax Lancaster said, "Pop me another one of those."

Andrew handed him a beer. "Bro, I can't believe they got you flying all over the eight-oh-eight already."

"And yet they do."

"You pulled some serious shit yesterday," Andrew said. "I mean, I figured they'd give you a week in Cali, like as a reward."

Dax was back on the job less than a day after his lifesaving heroics in Kona led to fawning news interviews and three marriage proposals on Twitter.

He opened the beer and took a swig. "Well, I'm our only pilot and these babies don't fly themselves. Besides, I *did* get a raise."

"Sweet." Andrew watched a 747 taxi past the little plane. "This is a non-stop?"

"It better be."

Inside the terminal, an Island Skipper gate agent announced pre-boarding for Flight 3 with service from Honolulu to Kona.

Sitting among the waiting passengers, Ryan Campanella disconnected a call on his cell and checked his watch. *Nice,* he thought, *we're five minutes ahead of schedule.*

He stood and examined an object in his right hand—a brass

key attached to an oval-shaped white plastic fob. On one side was a number written in permanent marker. On the other, embossed in metallic red, were the words, "Kona Winds Timeshare Village."

Chapter Twelve:
The Connections

Gerald Kapono MacTavish lifted his hands in the air. "Man, whatever you want, I can get you. Word."

Tommy Chunks released Gerald's shirt but stood close enough to discourage him from escaping. "I'm counting on it," he said.

Gerald lowered his arms and blinked a few times. "Say again?"

Tommy dropped his voice to a low growl. "Where are they?"

"Who?"

"Not *who*, you idiot. *What.*"

"What, what?"

"The earrings."

Gerald smirked. "Not my style, you know what I mean, dude?"

"Do not call me 'dude.'" Tommy glanced over his shoulder, toward the street. He plunged his left hand in Gerald's right pocket and pulled out a cardboard box. Printed in silver script on its blue lid were the words "N. Romanov & Sons," above the Russian coat of arms—a two-headed eagle with a bejeweled crown on each head. A third, larger crown hovered above the eagles.

He showed Gerald the box. "Ring a bell?"

"Oh yeah," Gerald said, "*those* earrings."

"Uh huh."

"How'd you know about them?"

Tommy said, "We need to talk. But not here."

* * *

Standing outside the Loco Moco Mama, a pack full of rocks on her back, Noelani B. Lee said, "This will only take a few minutes."

"Some bruddah calls you in the middle of breakfast," Wanda Tess Fong said, "and you tell him you're gonna meet him and you don't even invite me along."

"You know your matchmaking doesn't work with me, even if that was the case, which it is not. But for the record," Noelani said, "I did get the name of the kid who might have your necklace, didn't I?"

To do so, Noelani endured an excruciating series of calls to Island Skipper Airlines in Honolulu.

A woman who answered the phone put Noelani on hold for ten minutes before hanging up. Noelani called back and asked the same woman for a flight manifest. She explained she needed to find a passenger who may have taken another passenger's property amid the confusion following the crash landing in Kona. The woman said she didn't know what the heck a flight manifest was and hung up.

On the third try, as she wandered from the restaurant and down Ali'i Drive, Noelani asked the same woman if she could talk to a supervisor. A man came on the line and identified himself as the airline's owner. Speaking with a pronounced drunken slur, he told Noelani the manifest was official airline property. He claimed he could not release it to anyone without a notarized, court-ordered subpoena in triplicate. Then he hung up.

On her fourth and final call to the airline, Noelani lapsed into her best R. Lee Ermey imitation from *Full Metal Jacket*. She said her name was Hartman, a senior investigator with the National Transportation Safety Board.

As Hartman, she said the NTSB needed the manifest ASAP, if not sooner, as part of its investigation into the crash of Island Skipper Airlines Flight 2. Hartman then told the numbnuts maggot airline owner if he didn't grow a pair and turn over the manifest in three fucking seconds, he would unscrew the man's head and shit down his neck.

Seconds later, a PDF copy of the manifest arrived on Noelani's smartphone.

As she returned to the Loco Moco Mama, Noelani glimpsed a heavyset man dressed in black hip-hop gear jaywalking across the street. He flipped off drivers who honked at him and suggested they perform unnatural acts on themselves. When he made it across, he slowed as he climbed a set of stairs and slunk up against a building, where he peeked around the corner of a souvenir store.

With her hands in her pockets, Noelani ambled past the guy in black. With a quick sideways glance, she saw a man in a maroon shirt and khaki shorts at the far end of a hallway. He was talking with someone shorter than him, who wore something plaid. A black backpack sat on the ground beside them.

Noelani stopped at a shop window and pretended to check out realistic displays of fake orchids made from clay. When she turned and retraced her steps, the man in the black outfit saw her, leaned against the wall, and said, "Hey there."

Noelani smiled as she strolled past him. About then, she noticed a slender kid sitting on the seawall across the street, holding a backpack the same way a mother cuddles a newborn.

She stopped and looked over her shoulder but the guy in black was gone. Turning around, she saw the skinny kid left his perch atop the seawall and crossed the street, where he disappeared among clumps of tourists.

Noelani said, "How about I meet you in the room at noon? You'll have some time to check out the stores."

"Sounds like more than a few minutes," Wanda said, "but okay, I'll see you at noon."

They split up after a hug. As Wanda meandered toward Kailua-Kona's myriad tourist-trap shops, Noelani walked two doors down, to Jules's King of Diamonds.

As she entered the store, a tall, muscular young man greeted her with an "aloha." She noticed as his gaze settled on her backpack. "Hey, howzit?"

Before Noelani could answer, Jules Matsumoto entered the showroom from his office and grabbed her arm. "It's okay, Dean, she's here to see me. Miss Lee?" He escorted her into the office, and closed and locked the door behind him.

Noelani sat down and plopped the backpack on the floor. "Nice shop you have here, Mr. Matsumoto.

Seated behind his desk, Jules hunched forward in his chair, elbows on his desk. "You come highly recommended. Some people I know in Hilo give you high marks for your work. But this, can we keep it between us?"

"I appreciate the compliment," Noelani said. "How can I help you?"

"Miss Lee, I need you to find a missing shipment of gold

and gems. By way of background," Jules said, "my Island Creations—are you familiar with my collections?"

She thought of the square white box, in her overnight bag at the hotel. "I think I've heard of them."

"Be sure to take a look on your way out. We have an assortment of bracelets that complement your complexion perfectly. Plus, I've slashed prices on my current inventory."

"I appreciate the offer—"

"Better yet," Jules said, "you help me with my dilemma and you can have the piece of your choice, at no charge."

"Well, I—"

"You name it, it's yours."

Noelani blinked at the rings on Jules's fingers; some adorned with solitary diamonds, emeralds, or sapphires, other with settings combining small diamonds with black, red, or white stones she could not identify.

Jules held up the back of his right hand and pointed at his pinky. "Perhaps the man in your life would like one of these, made with real coral."

"Mr. Matsumoto," Noelani said, "could you give me some more details about your dilemma?"

"It works this way," Jules said. "After I design a piece of jewelry, my apprentice, Dean, and I use a variety of raw materials to bring it to life."

Noelani watched Dean replace a man's watch battery with the same focus he had when he eyeballed her backpack. She also thought his hair looked greasy and made out, from a distance, stretch marks on the insides of his elbows.

Jules said, "In many cases, I have suppliers, intermediaries, who purchase gold, silver, diamonds, what have you, at auctions or estate sales. I think of it as a recycling program for precious metals and gemstones."

"It must be more economical that way for you, too."

"They get the stuff cheap. I pay them a modest mark-up, and then I…well, you know."

Noelani nodded.

"But my Island Creations are worth every penny," Jules said. "Anyway, I was awaiting delivery of some materials from one of my suppliers who had handed them off to a courier. They were from the estate of an older lady who passed away recently."

"I see," Noelani said. "And the courier didn't show up."

"Oh, he did. The problem is, he brought these items to the island in a backpack. Just like yours. And now it's gone."

Noelani hefted the pack from the floor to her lap. She opened it and placed one of the gray rocks on Jules's desk. "Not the stones you're looking for, I bet."

"Is that bird poop?"

"You wouldn't believe me if I told you," Noelani said.

"Anyway," Jules said, "this courier flew in yesterday. Somewhere between his arrival on the island and when he came here, his backpack and its contents vanished."

"How well do you know this delivery man? What's his name?"

"I'm not sure," Jules said. "It's not like we spend time chatting."

"When he makes his deliveries, which is, how often?"

"Once or twice a month."

Noelani said, "You trust him?" *Even though you don't know his name.*

"I have no reason not to."

"The way I understand how it works is, he brings the jewelry from your supplier and you give him the money."

"Typically, yes," Jules said. "And no, he's never skimmed any cash from us."

Noelani returned the rock to the pack. "If I could talk to him, maybe we could narrow down when and where he lost the bag."

Jules shook his head. "He couldn't stay on the island. He flew back to Honolulu last night."

"Oh," Noelani said, "well, I bet your supplier must be pretty steamed with this guy."

"Well, I didn't want to get him in trouble," Jules said. "I called my supplier and explained everything, you know, to let the kid off the hook. He did nothing wrong."

"Except he lost a bunch of jewelry, which is worth how much?"

"Plenty. Maybe he won't be making any more deliveries, but at least I kept him from getting into anything worse."

As Jules talked, Noelani studied him. "Slick" was the least snarky description she could apply to him. "How about your intermediary—what can he tell me?"

"Well, see, he's in an incredibly…" Jules hesitated. "I guess I should say he's in an intensely competitive business." He smiled. "He keeps a low profile, if you catch my drift."

Noelani nodded as she continued analyzing Jules.

"He never wants me calling him. Just the other way around—he initiates the business. I mean, he's legit but our relationship is such that I cannot disclose his identity. I hope you understand."

Noelani asked Jules whether the courier could retrace his steps from the airport to the shop. Jules said the man caught a taxi instead of renting a car, because he planned on being in Kona for only a few hours. Jules said he told him he couldn't see him right away due to his business, so he suggested the courier get some dinner. The courier then asked the cabbie to drop him at a restaurant. But when he paid his tab and prepared to leave, he discovered the backpack was gone.

Noelani said, "Like someone just took it?"

"The tourism people wouldn't like me saying this but we both know, there's an active criminal element on this island," Jules said. "But he said something else, something about plaid."

Noelani leaned forward. "Plaid? Like clothing, you mean?"

"He said he saw someone wearing a plaid shirt or shorts. He wasn't sure which."

"And he didn't call the police."

Jules shook his head. "Poor kid was scared to death."

"You called him a kid," Noelani said. "Your courier's a young guy, college-age maybe?"

"I call a lot of people 'kid' but only because almost everyone's younger than me. Why do you ask?"

"No reason," Noelani said. "Except if he's young enough, and maybe needs the cash, who knows, maybe he ripped you off. Maybe he sold the jewelry to someone else."

"Ah, he knows better. Besides, there's nobody else…" Jules stopped himself.

Noelani waited a beat. "Yes?"

"Anyway, I went out and looked for the backpack myself, every restaurant in town, it felt like. But no luck. So, I contacted a few Chamber of Commerce friends and they all suggested I call you. They all said you're very discreet with your investigations."

Noelani's gaze settled on a carved wooden tiki-like figurine on Jules's desk. It had a distended belly and an exaggerated penis and sat atop a matching wood base etched with the words, "Cook Islands." She pointed at the statuette and said, "I'd say I'm a bit more discreet than your friend there."

"He's Tangaroa, a fertility god."

"I see."

"I used him as a model for my Legends of Polynesia line of pendants and charms few years ago. If you want one, I think I may still have a few—"

Noelani held up a hand. "Um, no, but thank you, though."

After a moment, Jules said, "Miss Lee, I get the feeling you don't think much of me."

She responded with a close-mouthed smile. "I'm not sure I understand."

"You don't care for my business, what I do for a living." He sat back in his chair.

Noelani looked at items hanging on the wall—certificates from gemological organizations, plaques recognizing his Better Business Bureau membership, and framed magazine and newspaper articles. "Well, you're a jeweler. It's not like you're a lawyer or a politician."

"No, how I do it, I mean," Jules said. "How I get my materials and what I do with them, my methods."

"Mr. Matsumoto, your business is your business. The point is, you've asked for my help, which means you're willing to pay me for a job. Speaking of which, I charge seventy dollars per hour plus mileage and other expenses."

Jules laughed. "My friends in Hilo were right."

Noelani tilted her head.

"They warned me, advised me is a better way to put it, what you lack in social graces you more than make up for with an *attitude*."

He had a point there, with the way he stressed the last word. The various chips on Noelani's shoulder had instilled in her a healthy aversion to other humans, family excluded. "I make it a point not to let my emotions interfere with my work."

"Oh, and the way you do your job," Jules said, "fast and thorough. And smart."

"The way I approach a case is, I like to think everyone else isn't too bright. Then I work my way up from there."

Jules beamed. "You and I should get along just fine."

He asked if she would accept a retainer of five hundred dollars. She agreed, so he cut her a check. When they finished their business, Noelani left Jules's office and entered the showroom, now empty of customers. Dean stood behind the display case. He pretended not to pay attention to her or her backpack. She stopped to peruse of Jules's wares.

Dean approached her and said, "Can I help you?"

Even from a couple of feet, Noelani could tell he had awful breath. "I've never been in here before and I just wanted to see what you have."

Dean nodded, his eyes on her backpack. "Okay, well, let me know if you need anything, yeah?"

When Noelani left the store, Dean watched her walk toward Ali'i Drive. He then looked through the window separating Jules's office from the shop—and saw Jules on the phone. Again.

* * *

Ryan Campanella deplaned at Kona International Airport, rented a white pearlescent Chrysler 300, and drove to Jules Matsumoto's house in Keahou.

He arrived six minutes earlier than he'd anticipated. Jules invited him in and motioned toward the living room. Bette Midler played on the stereo.

Ryan plopped into a leather sofa, which he rated the most comfortable squat he ever copped. "Jules," he said, "what you're telling me is, the son of a bitch flies over here with my stuff, gets in a plane crash, and now he says he doesn't have them anymore."

"He said something about a mix-up on the plane," Jules said. "He grabbed the wrong bag but didn't know it at the time. Now he has no idea where they are."

"Which means, thanks to him, some tourist has my rocks."

Jules shrugged. "What can I say?"

"How much does he want for them?"

"We haven't agreed on, uh, a figure."

Ryan handed Jules a pen and fished a scrap of paper from his wallet. "All right, if you *did* have a 'figure' in mind, what would it be?"

Jules wrote something on the paper and handed it to Ryan, who folded the note in half and slipped it in his wallet. "You know, if all this bullshit works out in my favor, I'm going to consider this a binding contract," he said.

Jules nodded.

"And no one else brought them to you yet?"

"Not before I left today," Jules said. "I'm sure Dean—he's my apprentice—would have called me if someone did."

"Yeah, uh huh."

"Anyway, I imagine you would want to know," Jules said, "seeing as he stole them from you."

"Mighty damn thoughtful of you." Ryan checked out Jules's house, filled with fancy-ass furniture and useless, dust-catching crap—including a full suite of antique samurai armor standing in a corner. *Who the hell needs such shit?* "You said he leaves at the end of the week for where, Japan?"

"Fiji."

"Whatever."

"He said this is his last gig for you and Frank. He has money socked away in offshore accounts, but he figured whatever he got for the—your jewels would help him out in his retirement years."

Ryan ran his right hand over his chin. He needed a shave and a facial. Maybe even a peel. "Tell me again. He just shows up out of no-fucking-where and says he has the stones for you."

"I didn't know he was coming until you called from the airport in Las Vegas," Jules said. "I bet you just missed being on the same plane with him to Honolulu."

"What a co-inky-dink."

"Last night, he left me a voice message saying he was on the island and he wanted to meet me. He came by the shop this morning and told me the whole story."

"Apparently it wasn't the whole story, Jules," Ryan said. He looked out a huge picture window at the panoramic ocean view. *A salt scrub would be nice, too.* "You are well aware, such shit doesn't sit well with me, when people play me like this."

"Ryan, I'm just wondering," Jules said, "we've had a good professional relationship for, what, ten years?"

"Closer to eight, if anyone's counting."

"Why didn't you just bring the jewels to me?"

"Because I never planned on bringing them to you, period."

Jules cocked his head.

"I'll explain it like this: I'm in serious arrears to another acquaintance, and if I don't pay up and I mean pronto, I'll wind up *taking it* in the rear."

Jules held up the palms of his hands. "Thoroughly understandable."

Ryan asked Jules where Tommy was staying. Jules said Tommy didn't tell him. "You figured out he was coming here, though."

"Just a hunch." Ryan recalled Tommy, between undercard fights preceding a light-heavyweight championship bout at the MGM Grand, told him about the timeshare he bought in Kona. Finding the timeshare's key in the house Tommy shared with the compliant, surgically enhanced Yolanda was too easy. It made Ryan wonder how Tommy could be so sloppy. He also wondered why Tommy never bragged about banging Yolanda, because he must have at one time or another.

Jules said, "What about Frank?"

"What about the dumb ass?"

"Do you think he's figured it out yet?"

Ryan remembered Frank missed the conversation at the fights because he chose instead to hit on a *muy caliente* Mexican babe at a concession stand. And because Tommy considered Frank was a moron and, consequently, rarely spoke to him, Ryan figured it was a safe bet Frank knew nothing about Tommy's timeshare. Which, Ryan reconsidered, meant he *did* know about it.

"All I'm saying is, I'll worry about the dipshit when I need to, and that's all I'm gonna say." Ryan checked his watch. He had things to do. "All right, so you told me you can get me a piece. Let's see it."

Chapter Thirteen:
The Beautiful Relationships

After her meeting with Jules Matsumoto, Noelani Lee sifted through her mental notes as she lugged the rock-filled backpack.

Aside from the sketchiness of Jules's story, she wondered if she'd regret taking the job. While she was proud of her ability to track down missing or stolen property and had pulled through for numerous clients, almost all of those cases had been in Hilo. Over there, she knew the turf and cultivated relationships and valuable contacts with the locals. On the other hand, doing a job like this in Kona—where tourists and their stuff went home after about a week—posed all kinds of challenges.

He's assuming it's still here, she thought. *Lotsa luck, Noe.*

At the same time, as she passed souvenir shops and galleries selling over-priced local art, she tried to figure out the true reason for Wanda Tess Fong's impromptu visit.

She loved Wanda to pieces, despite their polar-opposite personalities; Noelani was reserved and calculating, while Wanda and unpredictable and passionate. But Wanda had stayed in touch over the years, which was more than Noelani could say about her uncommunicative sisters: Anela, who found God and joined a convent in Missouri; and Okalani, who found a girl named Athena and opened a lesbians-only tattoo parlor in suburban Boston.

Noelani wondered, *Why does Mom think* I'm *the weird one?*

* * *

When Coco Lee was pregnant with her third "and this is it, no more kids" child, she picked what she thought was the perfect name if the baby was a girl.

Her husband, Quan Lee, prayed for a son—"come on, we have two girls already"—and chose the name of his all-time favorite movie star in case it was a boy.

So, when the baby was born and the doctor said, "Congratulations, it's a girl," Coco agreed to a compromise.

They named their youngest daughter Noelani Bruce Lee.

As they grew up, Noelani and her sisters didn't know much about what Quan did for a living. Yeah, he owned an Asian curio shop in Hilo but it seemed to them as if he spent little time there. Except, Coco once explained to the girls, Quan's *real* job as she knew it had something to do with imports and exports.

One evening when Noelani was eight, Quan did not come home from work. It was then Coco added the words "conspiracy," "racketeering," and "life without possibility of parole" to Noelani's vocabulary. It happened when he got popped in a massive RICO investigation involving L.A.'s Korean mafia and sex-slave smugglers in Honolulu. Quan left his unsuspecting wife and three young daughters on the Big Island with almost insurmountable debts and a family reputation in shambles.

By the time she was twelve, Noelani began displaying physical traits that concerned Coco. For starters, she could lower her voice, way, way, down. Not just in a dusky Kathleen Turner manner, but so low she often fooled telemarketers into believing she was the man of the house.

Meanwhile, Coco developed other concerns about her youngest child as she matured. Notably, Noelani barely developed.

By the time she was fifteen, Noelani had what Coco figured was the flattest chest on the island. It never got much bigger. And while Noelani had great legs—her best attribute, by her own admission—her hips were quite narrow.

Coco dragged Noelani to the doctor to figure out why her daughter didn't seem to be a total, well, girl. The doctor ordered some tests and found Noelani had a mild form of something called hyperadrenalism. He explained it was a hormonal imbalance, which resulted in her underdeveloped bosom and sometimes-masculine voice. An unfortunate side effect was she'd never have children. But, the doctor told Coco, Noelani had none of the nastier symptoms associated with the condition.

"You mean, like mustaches?" Coco said.

"No facial or excessive body hair," the doctor said. "Well, not *too* much, at least we can hope."

A relieved Coco watched her youngest grow up normal in all other respects. Noelani earned good grades in high school and after graduation enrolled at a community college in Hilo, where she studied court reporting. She hoped it would lead to a career as a lawyer. The closest she came to achieving her dream was when she began dating an attorney. But a few months later, the state disbarred him for "failure to act with reasonable diligence in representing a client." As in, he spent a week on the slopes in Park City with his partner's smoking hot niece instead of defending his mechanic *pro bono* against a manslaughter charge, as he'd promised he would.

When a second lawyer/boyfriend dumped her a year or so later for a professional ballroom dancer from Australia, Noelani—disillusioned with law and the men who practiced it—quit her job. But when she discovered how difficult it was to find work in Hawaii in the midst of an economic downturn, she told Coco, "Maybe what I need is a change of scenery."

It wound up being a move to the mainland. Noelani packed a bag and kissed Coco good-bye. She bought a one-way ticket to Las Vegas, where she sublet a room from Wanda.

It didn't take Noelani long to hate Vegas. The palm trees were ugly, chunky things, not the pretty coconut palms like those back in Hawaii; and it never rained there. She'd loved rain since childhood and even as an adult, she'd stand in it as long as it kept falling, face skyward and arms outstretched. She believed it had cleansing, purifying effects for the mind, body, and soul.

Still, she tried to make the most of her new life in Vegas. She got a job as a keno runner at one casino and waiting tables at an über-exclusive seafood restaurant in another. For three years, she lived frugally, sending whatever disposable income she could spare back home to Coco.

Until the incident in the casino parking garage with the governor of Nevada and her follow-up shut-up visit from James Vartoogian.

Returning to Hilo, Noelani used some of James Vartoogian's hush money to help Coco repay debts resulting from Quan's incarceration.

Soon afterward, a grateful Coco told Noelani she was moving to the solitude of Kauai. She explained she'd grown frazzled by the "hectic big-city life" in Hilo with its forty thousand inhabitants. On sleepy Kauai, she settled into a tiny bungalow, learned *ikebana*, and struggled to write her memoirs.

Then one day, Noelani told her mother she planned on

going back to school, this time, to study Criminal Justice. After graduation and four years doing investigative work for a prestigious law firm in Honolulu, she obtained her private investigator's license and relocated back to the Big Island.

She soon made a name for herself on the spurned spouse circuit; local businesses hired her to suss out fraud committed by opportunistic customers. And she worked for angry customers pissed about dishonest merchants ripping them off.

In the back of her mind, she knew it was an important first step toward giving former Nevada governor and now Senator Joe Whatever and his pal, James Vartoogian, their long-overdue comeuppance.

* * *

Noe, she thought to herself, *think like a detective*.

Strolling along the seawall toward the King Kamehameha Hotel, Noelani wondered if Wanda's out-of-the-blue visit truly had anything to do with "staycations" or relaxation. Something about this seemed off.

She hasn't been on the island for years, and all of a sudden, she just decides to come for a visit?

Noelani confirmed her suspicions when returning to their room, she found Wanda sitting on her bed, leafing through an apartment finder magazine.

"See, it's like this," Wanda said, "Vegas just isn't the same without you, since you moved back to Hilo."

Noelani placed the rock-filled pack on the floor and sat cross-legged next to her cousin. "Well, it *has* been seven years."

"Still. Then a couple months ago, a doctor I work for got into trouble for reusing syringes. And another one got sued big time for malpractice, and the other two might leave for Utah because they're Mormons, and—"

"You are *seriously* homesick."

"Yep, big time."

Noelani said, "Why didn't you just tell me in the first place, about wanting to move back?"

"I wasn't sure, when I first decided to come visit," Wanda said. "But my landlord in Vegas, he said I can get out of my lease any time. He's *kanaka*, too, so he knows what I'm thinking. I can move when I quit work but I need work here and since—"

"You figured because I know a lot of people, I can help you find a job."

Wanda nodded.

"Okay," Noelani said, "I have a client, Mrs. Hanratty, who owns a housecleaning service in Hilo. She might have an opening. And don't roll your eyes, it's honest work and will help get you on your feet." After a beat, she said, "I guess this means you're okay with me taking a job of my own."

When Wanda relented and said she was, Noelani detailed her discussion with Jules, about the so-called courier and the lost gems in a black backpack, and someone wearing plaid and another someone dressed all in black. She also said she spotted a Filipino kid on the street with a similar backpack.

"He might be the Benjie Zamora who was on your plane," she said. "We should pay him a visit."

Wanda said, "You think maybe I can help you?"

Noelani hesitated for a moment before she said, "Wanda, I prefer to work alone. Plus, there's a ton of legal and liability issues involved, if you get hurt or worse."

"There's gotta be stuff I can do that won't get me or you in trouble," Wanda said. "Besides, you can't be everywhere all at once. Looking for these backpacks, it's gotta be a lot different than sitting in your car, taking pictures of someone's husband doing the nasty with a skanky ho."

Wanda raised a valid point. Noelani also thought, *Oh how I wish I'd hung on to the earrings we found in the first pack. I could've used them.*

* * *

After their breezeway confrontation, Tommy Chunks forced Gerald Kapono MacTavish to Gerald's Saturn Ion, parked in a lot behind the Loco Moco Mama.

Tommy took Gerald's keys and demanded directions to his house. It turned out to be a small outbuilding in the backyard of a home in Holualoa, just south of Kailua-Kona.

Tommy surveyed the interior: The furniture consisted of mismatched lawn chairs and a Coleman cooler, which doubled as a table. A small refrigerator—like those college kids have in their dorms—and a microwave comprised the kitchen. Cans of soup and tuna and a stack of paper plates sat atop the nuker.

Tee shirts hung on old dry cleaner hangers from a wire strung across the back of the space. A single open window on the east wall, along with two battery-operated emergency lamps, provided light.

A faded yellow flag, with an ornate red border surrounding a red lion, hung on one wall above an Army surplus cot.

Out of place, as far as Tommy was concerned, was a slick new 32-inch flat-screen LCD television and an attached Wii gaming console. The components rested atop a white, gold-trimmed lacquer coffee table, which reminded Tommy of one he owned in the 1980s.

Without air-conditioning, the place reeked of sweat and soiled underwear. Tommy covered his mouth with one hand. "This explains a lot."

In his brogue, Gerald said, "He goes long barefoot that waits for dead men's shoes."

Tommy stared at him. "Why do you do that?"

Gerald told him:

In her post-high school dropout youth in Honolulu, his mother, Esther Halekealoha, made a living by getting men drunk and rolling them for whatever cash they had. One of her victims was a merchant seaman, who Esther got loaded and lured to a fleabag hotel. When he passed out, she separated him from more than three-hundred dollars, slipped out of the room, and caught a taxi home. The next day, about twenty nautical miles off Oahu, the still-inebriated seaman fell overboard and got sucked into the ship's propellers.

"His name was MacTavish," Gerald said. "He was my father. She finally told me about him after I bugged her for years, since I was but a wee lad."

"The fake accent?"

"Pride in my heritage. I got bagpipes and I had this kilt, ordered it all the way from Glasgow. But Esther, she told me not to wear it when I'm working the streets. She said it's not a good idea."

"Go figure."

"She got me these shorts, MacTavish clan tartan. Says to me it's a compromise."

Tommy blinked at him.

"It's the only thing she ever got for me," Gerald said. "See, I'll get me a big score, one day. Then I'll leave the hogbeast Esther and go to live forever in Alba."

Figuring he was as acclimated as he could be to the shed's rank odor, Tommy uncovered his mouth and nose. "All right. It's time to talk business. Sit."

Gerald did, on the cot. Tommy sat on a lawn chair and held up the N. Romanov & Sons box. "You do good work."

"I got some mad skills. I'm the real deal."

"Jules's man, Dean—he knows you have them?" Tommy detailed his breakfast conversation with Dean Pahukoa, about the expensive jewelry Dean's wife bought in Honolulu but lost during the crash landing. "She had these in a backpack. Like the one you took from the chubby woman in the hotel."

"It was easy, candy from a baby easy."

Tommy pocketed the earrings. "How many packs did you grab?"

"Today?" Gerald thought for a moment. "Three, I think. Dumped a couple with crap in them. Why, you want one, too?"

"Yes. A special one. But I need your help. Do it right, you get a reward."

"Rewards are good. Big ones. Benjamins."

Tommy said, "First, I need to trust you. Because if I can't, if you screw this up, I will kill you."

Gerald felt his stomach hit the floor. "No need for killing. Serious."

"You wouldn't be the first."

Gerald shivered. "Can I have the earrings back?"

"No."

"See, there's a complication. It's called Esther."

Tommy said, "Does she know about them?"

"Not yet," Gerald said. "There's lots of things she don't know."

"Keep it that way." Tommy sat back. "Now pay attention. This is important."

* * *

Armed with visual confirmation that Tommy Chunks was in

Hawaii—although he wondered, *Who's the faggot with him in the plaid shorts?*—Frank Campanella skipped breakfast.

Instead, he went to visit a family friend. Someone who could lend him a much needed helping hand.

* * *

For Benjie Zamora, the items he found in the black backpack belonging to a person named Thomas Lohmiller were no longer a lucky discovery. Instead, they'd become a source of worry and paranoia.

Benjie was sure people were watching his every move, wondering when he would set the pack down and take his eyes from it even for a moment. Then they'd grab it and run off with the stuff. Either that, or someone, maybe even Thomas Lohmiller himself, would find him and kill him and *then* take the pack.

He needed Ozzie real bad.

Just as he approached Jules Matsumoto's shop, he saw a man dressed in black, the same one he'd run into earlier in the morning. Dripping sweat, the man grabbed the door handle and sneered at Benjie as he entered the store. Benjie hesitated for a moment before he followed him in.

Inside, the sweaty man approached the display counter and said, "Hey yo," to the ripped Hawaiian dude who worked for Jules.

"Howzit," the Hawaiian dude said.

They both ignored Benjie, who lingered by the door.

The sweaty man said, "Jules around?"

"No, he had da kine appointment, said he was meeting a friend flying in."

"Oh, is that right? Who's he meeting?"

"He didn't tell me," the ripped dude said. "He just said he's gone for the rest of the day, yeah."

The sweaty man wiped his forehead with a sleeve.

"I can tell him you were here," the Hawaiian dude said. "Who are you?"

"Tell him Frank's in town and wants to say hello. Maybe take his ass out for a beer or one of them sissified umbrella drinks."

"Okay," the ripped dude said. "I'll let him know."

"Cool." The sweaty man turned as if to leave but stopped. "Hey, you see some old guy around here, in a dark red shirt and shorts?"

Benjie watched the ripped dude think for a moment. "Sounds like Jules's friend, the Tom man. I forgot the bruddah's last name."

"Ch…Lohmiller," the sweaty man said.

Benjie felt lightheaded.

"He was here, yeah," the ripped dude said. "He talked story with Jules for a while this morning and then left. If I see him again you want for me to tell him you were here?"

"Hell no," the sweaty man said. "What I mean is, I see him, I'll say 'hi' myself." He nodded at the ripped dude. "Later." He turned to leave but stopped and stared at Benjie. "What the fuck're you looking at?"

Benjie clung to the backpack. "Uh, um, nothing."

The sweaty man pointed at the pack. "What's in there?"

"This, it's nothing. Just a—my backpack. For school."

"Whatever. Out of my way, shithead." He brushed Benjie aside and left the shop.

"Help you, brah?" the ripped dude said to Benjie's backpack.

In Benjie's arms, the light backpack felt like a load of bricks. "No, ah. I remember, maybe I can come back later."

"You need to see Jules, too?"

Benjie then had a moment of clarity: Why not make a deal with the ripped dude? Jules wouldn't have to know a thing about it. He and the ripped dude could sell them to another jeweler, but they'd both get decent coin for them, and Benjie would still get home in time for dinner.

But the sweaty man in black who knew Jules *and* Thomas Lohmiller—this spooked Benjie and gave him chicken skin. If he was looking for Thomas Lohmiller, then he was looking for Thomas Lohmiller's jewels. And Thomas Lohmiller must be looking for them, too, which explained his visit to Jules.

Benjie backed up toward the door. What he wanted to tell the ripped dude got stuck in his brain before it could reach his mouth.

Instead, he heard his voice say, "I'll come back tomorrow."

* * *

Sitting in the passenger seat of Noelani Lee's car, Wanda Tess Fong opened the rectangular white box and whistled.

Noelani drove from the King Kamehameha Hotel onto Palani Road and toward Queen Kaahumanu Highway. "If you're into that sort of thing."

"Which I know you're not," Wanda said. "But dang, girl, you been holding out on me big time."

Noelani had just finished telling Wanda the whole sordid tale about how she came to own the jewelry, while confessing why she moved back to Hawaii from Las Vegas.

Wanda absorbed Noelani's story. "The old man tried to rape you?"

"Another few seconds," Noelani said, "and he would have gotten away with it."

"Then they paid you off." Wanda bowed her head. "Dang, that ain't right."

"The funny thing is, I get the feeling this James Vartoogian would've made me the same offer either way."

"But he never sent you the rest of the money."

"They had no reason to. Once I left Vegas, I was twenty-seven hundred miles out of sight *and* mind."

"You think you'll ever get money?"

Noelani waited a beat, her attention focused on the road. Then she said, "One day, Wanda. Perhaps one day."

A few more moments passed. Wanda said, "Does Aunty Coco know this happened to you?"

"She never will, sweetie." Noelani gave her cousin a closed-mouth smile.

Wanda again examined the box's contents. "You keep these in your safe all the time? Don't even wear them?"

"You know me. Plain and simple."

"Plain's kind of a stretch, cuz, and there's no way you're simple." Wanda closed the lid and handed the box back to Noelani. "What're you going to do with them now?"

Noelani slid the box under the driver's seat. She said there was a way to make good use of the jewelry, even if it meant she might lose them.

Wanda held up her hands and shook her head. "No way, you

do *not* lose stuff like this on purpose."

"Considering where they came from, much less how Jules made them, I have no problem letting them go," Noelani said.

"Even if it means helping the sleazy Jules dude?"

"Ironic, huh?"

A couple minutes later, they parked in front of the Zamora home on Olua Place. Wanda rang the doorbell but there was no response. Noelani peered through a window but the only living thing in sight was a parakeet in a cage.

Wanda rang the doorbell again. "There's no one here."

Noelani checked the house number. "Well, this is the right address."

"You saw him in town," Wanda said. "Does he even look like a diamond-carrying courier-type dude?"

"A college boy who wants money on the side might do something like this."

"But didn't Jules tell you the kid went back to Honolulu last night?"

"Well, it's what he *told* me."

Wanda rang the bell a third time.

Noelani said, "When you saw this boy at the airport and on the plane, he only had one backpack, right?"

"Yep, just like mine."

Noelani wrote a note on one of her business cards. She slipped it in the crack of the door, just above the deadbolt. "All right, let's get out of here."

* * *

Gerald gazed at the backpack containing the tourist book and dead cell phone and said to Tommy, "What do I do with this?"

After a lengthy discussion in Gerald's shed, they drove to a strip mall at Palani Road and Kuakini Highway, uphill from the King Kamehameha Hotel.

In the passenger seat, Tommy said, "Give it to me."

Gerald handed it over. "Like I told you, Esther wants me to get her stuff, too."

"I don't care."

"Well, what do I tell her when she gets all up in my bizness, all like saying I'm not bringing her enough things because you got me looking for the diamonds?"

"Like we talked about," Tommy said, "you don't tell her shit about the diamonds."

"But if I'm looking for your stuff and I don't deliver her stuff she wants, she'll mess me up. Not lying."

"Do what you need to do for her. But also do what you need to do for me."

"Okay."

"Then you won't have to worry about her," Tommy said. "And you won't have to worry about me. Got it?"

"Aye."

Tommy rolled his eyes. "If you find them, you will call me. Immediately."

Gerald nodded.

Tommy got out of the car. He leaned in the open window and stared at Gerald again. Then he walked downhill toward the hotel.

As he watched him walk away, Gerald wondered if he'd ever see Alba before this Tommy killed him.

Feeling a lump in his throat, he started the car and drove away.

* * *

Benjie took the business card from the front door.

Great. Thomas Lohmiller's hired a detective.

On the card's backside was a handwritten note: "Please call or text me ASAP."

Mom and Dad weren't home. Good thing, too, because if they'd gotten there first, they'd probably ask him about the detective. He figured it was better if they came home and instead asked how he spent his day and what he wanted for dinner, without knowing about anything else.

Benjie looked at the backpack and realized he couldn't bring those jewels back into the house. No way.

Then he remembered a place where he could hide the pack and its contents, a place from his childhood so far off the beaten path he was sure no one would ever find it.

He ran around the side of the house, climbed on his bike,

and rode down the street.

At the same time, a car began following him.

* * *

Hoping to center himself, Tommy took a walk on the beach adjacent to the King Kamehameha Hotel. It was on Kailua Bay, between the luau grounds and the pier which served as the starting point for the swim portion of the Ironman Triathlon every fall.

Above him, the tropical sun blazed down. Not a cloud in the sky. He looked down and saw a handful of tourists in various shades of red, scattered on the sand.

With the backpack over his shoulder, Tommy thought about his deal with Gerald. He wondered whether he'd been desperate to include the plaid-loving Scotsman wannabe in his search for the missing jewels. But he was convinced he had no choice. And besides, the moron did have a decent skill set.

No sane person wants to live in a shed, he reasoned. Not even Gerald, who believed he stood to gain a few bucks in exchange for helping Tommy. Which in reality he'd never see, as Tommy would have no problem getting rid of him. It was just a matter of how soon he or Gerald could get their hands on the gems.

Tommy had to get the pack with the tourist book out of play. He could follow the easy route and toss it in the trash. Better yet, he could return it to its owner, the round little Hawaiian woman from Vegas.

Tommy stopped and lit a cigarette. *Why did I do this? If I'd just taken the stuff to Barbados, I could've dumped it, taken my cut, and then told both Campanellas to kiss my ass.*

He inhaled the smoke and released it in a slow, steady stream. A woman sitting nearby on the beach gave him a dirty look. He turned his back on her.

They just aren't worth the headaches anymore. Sticking my neck out for them all these years and getting squat in return.

He sighed and looked down at the sand. He saw something that caused him to drop his cigarette. "Oh, great."

It was a footprint, made by someone with only three toes.

Chapter Fourteen:
The Tube

Under the surface of the Big Island of Hawai'i is a honeycomb of ancient caves and tunnels called lava tubes. Dozens, perhaps hundreds of these tubes date back generations to eruptions on the Mauna Loa, Mauna Kea and, in contemporary times, Kilauea volcanoes.

Lava tubes develop when a crust forms over flowing lava as it channels through the earth. When the lava rivers run dry, they leave behind underground tunnels, which often emerge as holes from a sea cliff on the ocean.

Throughout the centuries, various arthropods and other tiny invertebrates have adapted to the dark world of the tubes and thrived in them. Man, meanwhile, has discovered lava tubes can serve many practical purposes—some as tourist attractions, others as subterranean personal storage units.

*　*　*

Although he wasn't accustomed to tailing people, Dean Pahukoa got the hang of it as he followed the bike-riding Filipino kid with the black backpack.

After the kid left his house on Olua Place, Dean followed him to Nani Kailua Drive. The kid went east to Hienaloli Kahului Road, and then left to Keolani Drive.

At one point, when the kid looked right back at him, Dean almost took out a mailbox when he turned into a driveway. After waiting a few beats, he pulled back onto the street and continued his snail's pace chase.

His mind wandering as he drove, Dean weighed the idea of running the kid off the road and jumping out and taking the backpack. He gave up on the thought, though, when he remembered how angry Veronica Keawe would be if he wound up in jail.

Although the trip was uphill all the way, the bike-riding kid handled it with no problems. *Little buggah must have some serious quads on him.*

About a half-mile up Keolani Drive, the kid pulled his bike off the road and locked it to a small tree.

Dean stopped on the shoulder and watched the kid wander into the brush. He waited a few seconds before got out of the car and continued following the kid on foot.

A few years had passed since Benjie Zamora hiked this path, just before he graduated from high school. But it all came back to him in a rush.

The stillness and the hot sun were the same. The smells of earth and plants, and the sounds of mynah birds singing and the doves cooing in the trees. This was semi-rural Hawaii, or at least as rural as the eastern reaches of Kailua-Kona could get.

Benjie followed a path next to a line of trees until he came to another area of thick growth—and found what he was looking for.

When he stubbed his toe on a large rock, Dean realized his flip-flops weren't designed for hiking through undergrowth. But he ignored the pain and stayed a decent distance behind the kid without losing him—until the kid stopped at what, from a distance, looked like a hole in the ground.

During Benjie's teen years, the lava tube had served as a quiet refuge from the harsh realities of life. Like the time Dad wanted him to clean the garage, top to bottom. And the day one fall when Mom asked him to deliver apple pies to all their neighbors. Thankfully, they both did those jobs themselves.

He never told anyone about the tube; it was his private haven. He read comic books, napped, and snuck nudie magazines there—he just hung out in the tube from the time he was old enough to ride a bike alone, until the time he went off to college.

Benjie looked around him, over both shoulders and into the nearby brush. He got spooked a couple of times when he saw a silver car trailing him and wondered whether the sweaty man or Thomas Lohmiller was chasing him in a rental. He scratched behind his right ear and figured, well, they would have jumped him by now.

He heard what sounded like a twig snapping.

He peered into the general direction of the noise and, even though he didn't see anything, called out, "Hello?"

The only reply came from birds.

After several seconds, Benjie convinced himself the coast was clear. He dropped the backpack down the hole, and then he squeezed himself in after it. He landed on a low sloping path, which led into the heart of the cave. The tube was about six or seven feet underground at its deepest, ten feet wide at its widest, and extended about forty or fifty yards at the most. Sometime in the course of natural history, part of the tube's roof collapsed. When it did, it sealed the cave off from the distant Pacific.

He felt a modest wave of nostalgia as he entered the cave, yet something was different about his underground hideout. Something about it was way out of place.

Enough light entered the hole so that when Benjie's eyes adjusted to the darkness, he saw things he'd never before seen in the tube.

Dean stared at a twig under his foot and stifled a sneeze at the same time. When the kid said "Hello?" Dean hunkered behind a flowering ʻilima bush, maintaining visual contact with the kid while doing all he could to camouflage himself.

After the kid slipped into a hole in the ground, he figured all he had to do was hide in the trees and wait for him to leave. Then it would be clear sailing to go into the hole, grab the backpack and—

His cell phone rang.

All around, Benjie saw boxes and plastic shopping bags.

A shoebox contained at least a dozen watches. He found several iPods and one of those electronic book-reading things he'd seen on Amazon, all in an old Priority Mail box. He discovered a laptop in a plastic shopping bag, and at least a dozen point-and-shoot digital cameras in another bag. He picked up another box and found—

Somewhere outside the tube, a phone rang.

Dean backtracked until he was sure he was out of the kid's earshot and checked to see who was calling him.

It was Jules Matsumoto. "Hi, boss."

"Say, Dean, I called the shop but there was no answer. Everything okay there?"

Dean wished he'd done more cardio as he tried to get his breathing under control. "Uh huh, yeah, everything's cool here. I mean, well, see, I'm not at the shop."

After a moment, Jules said, "Where are you?"

Dean was awful at making up stories, even little white lies. The problem was, his loyalty kept him from ditching work when Jules was away, because Jules was helping him to be the greatest Hawaiian-born baseball player of all time.

Then he remembered breakfast.

He said, "I think I ate something made my stomach feel bad."

"Oh?"

"Yeah," Dean said, "see I went down, I'm like, at the pharmacy place to get some of the pink stuff. I don't know, it might've been bad ham in the omelet, yeah."

After a beat, Jules said, "Well, shut down the shop and go home if you need to. I won't be in the rest of the day, anyway."

"You won't?"

"Besides, we need you healthy by Saturday. We have that game up in Waimea and I know Pops and the team will be counting on you."

"Huh," Dean said. "Yeah, the game. Gotta be ready for the game, sure thing."

"The reason I called," Jules said, "is because Mrs. Bankhead wondered if she could drop off a necklace. It needs a new clasp. But don't worry about it. I'll pick it up from her personally. You just take care of yourself."

Dean looked toward the hole in the ground. He figured the kid had to have heard the phone. The only thing left for him to do now was leave, which of course meant Veronica would demand he come back later.

"Yeah, I'll do that, boss," Dean said. "No worries."

Benjie popped his head through the hole and again surveyed the surrounding landscape but saw no one around. As far as he could tell, he was all alone.

Just to be on the safe side, in case someone had followed him—he again pictured the silver car—he decided to stay put for a while. Maybe until about an hour or so before Mom would get home from work.

Besides, his legs were tired from the long bike ride.

He turned to face the collection of bags and boxes in the lava tube. All of them were open, their contents exposed.

One at a time, he framed them in the viewfinder of a Canon digital SLR he found and started taking pictures.

* * *

Fresh from a mani-pedi and a late lunch with a pair of friends who both happened to be former Miss Hawaii second runners-up, Veronica Keawe peered out the window of Jules's King of Diamonds.

She said, "Where's your boss, the...*Jules* person?"

"He had to meet someone, said he won't be back today," Dean said. "I told him I was sick, but well..."

"Yeah, you can't really leave this place, can you?"

Dean asked a couple of tourist ladies, admiring rings in a display case, whether they needed help. They said no.

"Thank God for that." Veronica leaned across the display counter. She whispered, "Did you find my backpack yet?"

"No, but I need to—"

"Geez, Dean, don't you do anything I ask you to do?" The ladies looked at Veronica. She apologized and lowered her voice to a whisper. "What have you been doing all day instead of finding my birthday earrings?"

"Baby, try wait, I need to tell you something." He motioned toward the women, who browsed clearance-sale pieces from a discontinued line of Island Creations. After a few moments, they left the shop without buying anything.

Dean came around the counter, flipped the "Open" sign to "Be Back in 15 Minutes," locked the door, and led Veronica to Jules's office.

"Dean," she said, hands on her hips, "what's going on?

You're acting all kinds of weird."

Dean spent the next few minutes explaining how he overheard Jules's phone call earlier in the morning, and his own conversation over breakfast with Tom Lohmiller. Then he told Veronica about the visit from the sweaty white dude wearing black clothes who said he wanted to see Jules.

Veronica said, "You're telling me there's a backpack just like mine somewhere on this island, and it's filled with cool things that are even more valuable than my birthday earrings."

"Jules needs them for the da kine Island Creations," Dean said. "I mean he didn't say so to me direct, but he did tell me yesterday he was expecting this one big delivery. That's kinda what I'm thinking they're for, yeah."

Veronica bit her lower lip. "Well, not anymore."

Dean shuddered. "Baby, there's no way I can cheat Jules like that."

Veronica arched a freshly plucked eyebrow. "Listen up, Dean. I love you. But if you want to keep on loving *me*, you'll do everything you can to find the jewelry and you'll keep Jules out of it. Understand?"

Dean felt sweat forming in his pits, a common physical response when Veronica got aggressive. "Roni, you know, my job and the baseball—"

"I know the baseball thing is important to you and yes, I know you have a game this weekend and blah-de-blah, blah, blah," she said. "But just this once, I wish you'd try thinking about us and our long-term stability. Priorities, Dean—we have priorities."

Dean said, "But Jules, he says I got a real good shot of being in the majors one day, I keep playing like I do and I don't wanna mess it up." And just as Veronica was about to respond, he said, "I think I know who's got the backpack, the one with the jewels."

Veronica squinted at him. "Run that by me again."

"I don't know who the bruddah is, this dude on a bike. But I know he's got them and I know where he put them."

She tilted her head. "You do?"

"He hid them in da kine cave, up in this field." Dean grinned. "You know I'm telling the truth, Roni, I always tell you the truth."

"When are you going to get them?"

"Tonight, when it's all dark out. I'll just need a flashlight, yeah."

Dean watched as Veronica's expression changed. She had the same look in her eyes as she always did, just before she would try to get him to have sex with her.

She said, "You'll do that for me?"

"Damn straight. But after I get them and if we don't give them to Jules, what'll we do then?"

Veronica didn't answer. Instead, she unbuckled his belt and unzipped his pants. She reached into his boxers. "Baby, just leave that to me."

Dean gulped. "Roni, be careful, customers might come in."

"You locked the door. Remember?" She kissed him, plunging her tongue to his tonsils. Then, with her free hand, she reached over and swept Jules's desk clear.

Dean panicked as he watched Jules's phone and Garfield desk calendar and World's Greatest Dad coffee mug full of pens tumble to the floor. "I don't think this is a good idea. This is all Jules's stuff."

"Yeah, well, pick it up when we're done." Veronica pulled his pants to his ankles, stood, and then ripped off his shirt.

Dean noticed her staring at his chest. He looked at his pecs; they were a little rounded and not as solid as they once were, but he figured it was because he wasn't as young as he used to be. "What, Roni?"

She leaned in close. "Dean?"

"Yeah?"

"Are these zits on your chest?"

Dean examined the acne. "I guess, but no big deal, yeah."

"Okay, well, whatever." Veronica backed up and peeled off her skirt. Dean caught a glimpse of her pink thong—his favorite. She lay back on the desk and pulled him close, stroking him with both hands.

As she worked on Dean, Veronica spotted Jules's wooden Cook Islands tiki carving on the desk. She picked it up and said, "He has a penis. Why's this thing got a big penis?"

"He's some kind of fertility god," Dean said. "Jules told me."

Veronica looked from the statuette to Dean's limp member. "Well, let us pray," she said, and began rubbing the souvenir all over her husband's pecker.

He backed away. "Geez, Roni, that's way too weird."

"I'll try not to give you splinters. Now get back here."

She noticed, to her surprise, it was working; he'd popped up to about half-mast. She pulled him closer and continued massaging him with the wooden god until he was about two-thirds erect. "This is as good as it gets?"

When he shrugged and said, "Yeah, I think so," she set the god aside.

"He's going home with me."

"Wait, Roni, he belongs to Jules. You just can't steal him."

"Well, it's not like Jules is using it for anything. Now shut up and screw me."

She jumped on him and slid down his shaft. She knew from recent experience she'd have to make the most of this rare and no doubt short-lived opportunity.

As Dean laid her back on the desk and grabbed her ankles, raising them level to his shoulders, Veronica said, "Careful with the toes, baby. That pedicure was expensive."

* * *

Gerald Kapono MacTavish delivered a brand new hi-def digital camcorder to Esther Halekealoha.

She beamed. "Damn, boy, you done good this time."

"I did?"

She reached over and Gerald steeled himself for a slap to the head. Instead, Esther put her hand behind his neck, pulled him close, and buried him in her chest with a hug.

Stunned and struggling for air between his mother's enormous boobs, Gerald couldn't figure out how to react to this display of affection—because to that point in his life, Esther had never shown him any.

She released Gerald and held the camera to the light in the Loco Moco Mama's kitchen. Behind them, Mr. Lim—sweat dripping from his forehead onto burgers he grilled on the flattop, a lit cigarette dangling from the corner of his mouth— did his best to ignore his boss and her son.

"This is a good one, too," Esther said, "da kine new one from Panasonic."

"True, it is."

"I know a guy's gonna like this and pay big money for it." She looked at Mr. Lim, toiling over the hot grill, and then grabbed Gerald's arm and led him out through the back door. "What else you got?"

From a black plastic trash bag, Gerald removed an iPod, two checkbooks, and three wallets. Esther dispatched the checkbooks to a trashcan. She emptied the wallets of about five hundred dollars. From the bills, she pulled a twenty and handed it to Gerald. "There. You get a reward."

Andrew Jackson stared up at Gerald. He didn't know whether to thank her or recite another Scottish proverb about wealth and happiness.

"You can have the music thing, too—I got too many of them now." Esther grinned. "Finally, you procure some good shit I can get good money for. You know what? Take the rest of the night off."

"Yeah, well, there's something else."

"Where? What you got?"

"No, not with me," he said. "I'm not supposed to tell you because the *haole* will kill me."

"What *haole*?" Esther grabbed Gerald by the shirt and pulled him close. "Wait, you holding out on me again? Or this time you gonna tell me the whole story for once?"

He looked up into her bloodshot eyes. Yet he felt an odd calm as he said, "I'll tell you if you promise to go halves with me."

Esther released her grip. "Only if it's good."

Gerald smiled. "It's real good. Win-win, me and you and no one else."

She folded her arms over her chest. "'Kay den, boy, talk. I'm listening."

* * *

After Veronica coaxed an orgasm out of Dean, she got dressed, kissed him deep and hard, stuffed the fertility god statue in her purse, and left the shop.

With the "Closed" sign still in the window, Dean sat in Jules's chair and nodded off. When laughter outside of the shop stirred him awake about a half-hour later, he tried to replace the items on Jules's desk just as his boss had them. He also hoped Jules wouldn't notice the fertility god's absence.

When he got home about an hour later, he found Veronica in bed, wearing a black teddy she'd bought in Honolulu. The Cook Islands statuette stood propped against a pillow beside her. She baited Dean, reminding him about their romp in Jules's office and saying there was more where that came from.

"But only if you're a good boy," Veronica said, "and bring me the backpack with the jewelry."

Relieved because he didn't have to try and work up another hard-on, Dean drove to the lava tube.

This time wearing sensible tennis shoes instead of flip-flops, Dean stumbled along the same path he'd followed earlier in the day when he stalked the Filipino kid. But now, in the darkness, he had to rely on a flashlight with failing batteries to see where he was going; he barely made out the trail through the underbrush, and twice banged his shin into stumps and fallen trees.

After several minutes, he emerged into a clearing and found the hole in the ground. The lava tube's entrance was narrower than Dean anticipated. He stared at it for a moment and wondered whether his well-developed upper body may not squeeze through. Figuring there was only one way to find out, he slid his legs in and although rock scraped his triceps, he wriggled his torso and shoulders in with only minor difficulty.

Once under ground, Dean scanned the cave with the dim flashlight, which was just bright enough for him to see a bunch of open boxes and bags. On closer inspection, he found most of them were filled with electronic stuff.

Dean knew a little about lava tubes, but he never dreamt they had all kinds of slick things like this in them—including a nice watch with the glow-in-the-dark face, which he wrapped around his wrist and admired in the flashlight's dull beam.

Getting back to business, he resumed his search for the backpack. But after several minutes of looking under every box and every plastic shopping bag and kicking rocks aside on the tube's floor, he got a queasy feeling.

The pack, which he could swear he saw the kid take to the cave earlier in the day, was gone.

Dean stopped for a moment and wondered if he was in the right lava tube, unsure how many there might be in the area, or if the Filipino kid came back and took the pack somewhere else.

He lost himself in concentration. He closed his eyes and wondered whether the kid figured out he'd been followed and maybe moved the stuff.

His mind wandered and he envisioned Veronica, at home with the Cook Islands statue, wearing her new teddy, her toenails all red and perfect, waiting for him to deliver the gold and diamonds. And when he got there, she'd tell him to drop trou and then she'd grab the statue and start rubbing his—

An unnerving shriek wailed through the cave.

Snapped from his trance, his eardrums rattling and his heart pounding, Dean aimed the flashlight in the direction of the sound. In the darkness, he made out some sort of creature—it had three headless necks connected by a red ribbon, and a belly that inflated and deflated as its screams filled the cave.

Dean yelped and dropped his flashlight as he scrambled from the tube, pulling himself out of the hole with all his might. Ancient rock scraped his arms and snagged his shirt. The creature's shrieks followed him, as if it were hot on his heels. He ran, somehow avoiding further damage to his lower legs, until he reached his car.

Sitting on a three-legged stool in the lava tube, Gerald Kapono MacTavish finished tuning his bagpipes. Then he launched into a full-throated version of "Mull of Kintyre."

As he did, he wondered (a) what happened to his Canon digital SLR camera, and (b) what the big strong dude from Jules's jewelry store was looking for in his lair.

* * *

Inside one drawer, the man found folded shorts and some underwear; in another, jeans and leather belts, rolled and held together with rubber bands.

In a closet, he perused short-sleeve cotton shirts in patterns and solid colors, which hung next to pressed linen pants, one pair white and the other, khaki; the clothes hung above two pairs of black shoes and a pair of brown leather sandals.

Satisfied with his inspection, the man returned to the condo's living room, where he had a seat. He looked through the sliding glass doors leading to the lanai and its panoramic view of Kailua Bay. But otherwise, he sat still.

When the last of the sun's rays dispersed and stars appeared in the heavens, he got up and made sure everything was as he'd found it before he exited the condo.

He went downstairs to his car, got in and locked the doors, and slumped in the driver's seat.

In another car at the far end of the parking lot, a second man watched the first one, checked his watch, and waited.

* * *

Wanda Tess Fong said, "Geez, Noe, that's a gun."

At her little house on Iwalani Street in Hilo, Noelani Lee removed the Ruger and a spare clip from her closet safe. She and Wanda had driven there to, in Noelani's words, "stock up" on things she'd need—like men's tee shirts, old jeans, and theatrical make-up. And the gun.

"Wanda, we can't be too careful." She shut and locked the safe. "We don't know who we're dealing with here."

Earlier, she researched her client, Jules Matsumoto. She found his shop's website and a newspaper article detailing Jules's contributions, among others, to the election campaign of the island's current mayor.

Through a background check, Noelani learned Jules was twice divorced and had three grown kids scattered across the mainland. But his record was spotless—no arrests, nothing out of the ordinary. The only blemish was a traffic ticket he picked up in Hilo a few years ago for running a red light.

Other articles outlined Jules's co-founding of a Big Island baseball league. They included pictures of him with Dean Pahukoa, the star player he claimed he discovered and who also worked for Jules at his shop.

In one article, Jules said something about Dean being the top Major League prospect in all of Hawaii. In some of the older pictures, Dean was downright scrawny. In more recent ones, he looked like Mr. Olympia.

Further research revealed Dean was married to a Veronica Keawe. According to the Island Skipper flight manifest, she was on Wanda's flight when it bounced its way onto the Kona Coast. An archived newspaper article mentioned she was a model of some sort.

"You're thinking the old white guy might be dangerous," Wanda said. "Or maybe the sketchy dude in the black?"

"Hard to say." Noelani clipped her gun's leather holster to her belt. She double-checked the contents of an overnight bag— various tools of her trade, like lock pick kits and GPS trackers and listening devices. "But it never hurts to be prepared, just in case."

Wanda rubbed Master Po behind his ears. The cat purred. "All that stuff—you're like totally serious about all this."

"I have to be. Mr. Matsumoto is a paying client."

"I bet you got a plan worked out already, to find the jewelry."

Noelani picked up the bags. She didn't want to admit she had no idea where or how to begin.

"Let's get back to Kona side. Tomorrow's going to be a busy day and you'll need your rest."

Wanda said, "What about you?"

"Well, since I started doing this for a living, I refuse to let sleep interrupt work."

Noelani slid her closet door closed and gave Master Po a quick rub under his chin. "I'm ready if you're ready."

"I'm ready."

"Let's go."

Chapter Fifteen:
The Situation

For Dean Pahukoa, a bad Friday morning followed a rough Thursday night—when he withstood various phases of Veronica Keawe's wrath, from name-calling to name-shouting, to the throwing of breakable objects.

He explained what happened in the lava tube, telling Veronica how he couldn't find the backpack containing the jewelry, and about how some weird animal scared him away. But she didn't believe him, for what Dean figured was the first time ever.

The conversation came to an abrupt end when Veronica slammed the bedroom door. She emerged a minute later, no longer clad in her teddy but instead decked out in an oversized, faded purple tee shirt and unsexy, baggy gray sweatpants. She tossed him a pillow and told him he'd be sleeping on the sofa until he came home with the gems.

Dean didn't see her again until the morning, when she went to the kitchen. She ignored him as she made coffee. Dean knew, when she wanted to be, Veronica was an expert at the cold shoulder thing. He rolled over and pretended to sleep.

Minutes later, he felt a slap across his butt. "Get up, Dean," Veronica said. "It's getting late and you have work to do." She stood above him, a cup of steaming coffee in her hand. For a brief instant, Dean thought she might be mad enough to pour it on him.

"You have missing jewelry to find," she said. "We need it. We have plans, Dean—a spacious family room and a luxurious master bathroom with a spa-like feel." She walked across the room in her thick socks, picked up a telephone, and returned. She stuck it in Dean's face. "Call your buddy Jules and tell him you're sick and won't be coming to work today."

Then her tone changed, and she smiled. She put the coffee cup on the floor and sat next to him. "You'd do that for me, wouldn't you, baby?"

Dean wasn't sure he could. Not after he lied about his upset stomach the day before. He couldn't bail on Jules two days in a row. "Well, Roni, you see…"

Veronica slid her hand inside Dean's boxers. "Pretty please?

Call him? For me. Please."

"Yeah, sure." Dean sat up and dialed the number. As he did, Veronica pulled down his shorts.

* * *

Under a gray Friday morning sky, Jules Matsumoto backed out of his garage and drove north from his home in Keahou toward Kailua-Kona.

Across the street, Noelani Lee—wearing a wig with long, black hair—started her Nissan Sentra and followed him.

He drove a convertible Lexus with the top down, which allowed Noelani to see him talking on his cell as he took Kamehameha III Road and turned left on Queen K Highway. From a distance, she watched him disconnect the call then dial another number. He stayed on the second call until he turned left on Kuakini Highway and rolled downhill, toward the heart of town.

Noelani parked several spaces away in the lot behind the Ali'i Sunset Plaza, and waited as he got out of his car. She adjusted her wig, donned oversized sunglasses, picked up a clipboard from her passenger seat, and followed him into the shopping center.

But Noelani saw that instead of going to his shop, Jules beat a path to the Loco Moco Mama. Pretending to leaf through papers on her clipboard, she watched as Jules reached for the restaurant's door, someone came outside and started talking to him.

Jules Matsumoto cowered when Esther Halekealoha stepped out of the Loco Moco Mama and positioned herself between him and the restaurant's entrance.

"Hey, it's my good buddy, Jules the jeweler bruddah," she said. "Howzit, man?"

"Hello, Esther," Jules said. "Good to see you, but I'm meeting someone here in a couple of minutes, so I don't have time to talk."

"Well, *mahalo* for the patronizing," she said. "But first things first. I have news to share with you, brah."

"And what news would this be?"

"The news about da kine big-time delivery you told me about. You get it yet?"

Jules swallowed. "Why, yes, I have. Why do you ask?"

Esther laughed. "Oh man, you don't lie too good."

Jules felt hollow. "I, uh, I'm not sure what you mean."

She stepped closer to him. Esther stood five inches taller than Jules, and with her hands planted on her hips, was twice as wide. "Since you seem to forget," she said, "the *hapa* boy told me all about your friend went and lost the jewelry on the plane."

"Um, did he now?"

"He says this *haole* wants him to find them for him and not for me to sell to you. I'm missing any details so far?"

Jules snickered. "Your son has a way with telling tales."

"Oh, you ain't kidding," she said, "but this time I believe the *hapa* boy, cuz he got no reason to be spreading the bullshit. Unlike *some* people I know."

Jules ran a hand through his hair. "Esther, this is neither the time nor the place to discuss this."

"This is as good a place as any, you ask me." She almost said something else but stopped and stared at something behind him. Jules peered over his shoulder and saw a woman in a yellow shirt and sunglasses standing several feet away. The woman turned the page of a tourist magazine and wrote on a notepad attached to a clipboard.

Esther said, "You ever seen that sistah?"

"She looks official, but no."

"Whatevahs. 'Kay den, since you acting all nervous and you supposedly meeting someone, how about I drop by your store bumbye and we'll get down to the business?"

"Fine," Jules said.

"But first, something I'm curious about," Esther said. "What's your friend asking for the stuff?"

Jules shifted his weight from foot to foot. "Really, Esther, it's none of your business."

She grinned. "It is now, because me or the Scottish boy find them first before the *haole* does, I'm gonna be knocking on your door. And since you don't pay me for nothing last couple times I bring you stuff, you're gonna have some making up to do. Which means, you're gonna do better by me than for your friend. You feeling me, Jules?"

Jules reached into his pocket and took out a pen. "Understand," he said, "this is a mighty generous offer and it is the absolute best I can do. Give me your hand."

Esther extended a meaty paw and Jules wrote something on her palm.

She read it and smiled. "We got da kine fresh pork today," she said. "Cousin went and shot a boar. Try it with the rice."

Noelani watched Esther step inside her restaurant. Then she slunk past Jules, hiding her face from him. As she stopped and pretended to check out a pair of shoes in a nearby store window, she caught another person's reflection behind her.

It was a round man wearing a plain white tee shirt, an oversized gray hoodie, and drooping blue jeans with the waistband around his butt.

She watched him shake hands with Jules before they stepped inside the Loco Moco Mama.

* * *

Jules poured milk into his coffee and said to Frank Campanella, "How was your flight?"

"What's to say, it was a long plane ride," Frank said. "Stewardess wasn't hot at all, the seat made my ass numb, and the movie sucked. But the good thing is, we didn't crash."

Jules sipped his coffee but didn't respond.

Frank said, "A meet with you like this, it's freaking early for me, seeing as I'm still on Arizona time."

"Well, then," Jules said, "you should have no problem being awake by now."

"Not based on my typical daily routine." Frank skimmed the menu. "What, you guys got no McDonald's around here?"

"This place is convenient to work. Besides, the food is terrific."

"Just saying, there's nothing wrong with an all-American Egg McMuffin for a real breakfast."

"Frank," Jules said, "they serve good breakfasts here."

"Yeah, well, look at this shit—Spam, hamburgers… Who

ever heard of fish and eggs at this hour?"

Seated nearby, an Asian woman stopped reading papers inside a manila folder long enough to give Frank a dirty look.

"Keep it down, Frank." Jules tilted his head toward her. "She happens to be the cook's wife. I should add, the *award-winning* cook's wife."

Frank applied his most sincere smile. "Hey, no offense, lady. Except for tacos, I don't eat much foreign food."

Mrs. Lim ignored him and continued studying her paperwork.

"Sorry I wasn't around when you dropped by yesterday," Jules said, "but when Dean called me, I knew I had to meet you as soon as possible."

"No biggie. Now, tell me, you seen any familiar faces lately?" Frank smirked.

Jules feigned reading the menu. "A couple. I'm sure I don't need to name names."

"True, but maybe you can tell me their sad stories."

Jules set the menu aside. He then outlined the visits by Tommy Chunks and Ryan Campanella. He described how Tommy lost the gems in a backpack during the plane crash. In the course of his recap, however, Jules withheld how he helped Ryan purchase a gun. And that he had hired a private investigator to find the lost jewels.

Frank said, "Tommy's retiring—where, Samoa?"

"Fiji."

"Same thing."

"He leaves by the end of the week. You can imagine, he needs to find those jewels as soon as possible." Jules leaned across the table. "Before someone else gets them first, I mean."

"Right." Frank tore open four sugar packets and dumped their contents into his coffee. "I'm assuming you got a price for the stuff."

Jules wrote a number on a napkin and slid it across the table.

Frank picked it up, read it, and smiled.

"Is that reasonable?"

Frank nodded. "Hell to the yeah." He folded the napkin and slid it into a pocket of his black hoodie. "Hey, is homie there the cook?"

Jules watched Mr. Lim walk across the restaurant toward his

wife's table. "Yes, he's a real nice guy, too."

Mr. Lim and his wife exchanged greetings in Hokkien, which Mrs. Lim punctuated with a sneer at Frank. She showed something in the folder to her husband.

Jules said to Frank, "Now you know what's happening. Just wondering, though, how'd you know Tommy was here?"

"'Fraid I can't tell you, Jules," Frank said. "Trade secret. All you have to know is I'm here now and I'm not leaving till I got the goods and you're buying them from me."

Jules watched as Mr. and Mrs. Lim parted ways. The cook returned to the kitchen and his wife gave Frank another dirty look as she picked up the folder and left the restaurant.

"Damn, Jules," Frank said, "please tell me what I said to piss that old broad off."

From her vantage point in the kitchen, Esther Halekealoha peered into the restaurant's dining room, where Jules Matsumoto and a fat white guy in hip-hop threads talked like they were long-lost buddies.

When she saw Jules pass a note to the other guy, and when the other guy smiled and stuffed the note in his pocket, she thought, *That's how it's gonna be, huh?*

* * *

Noelani Lee called Wanda Tess Fong, who was staking out the King Kamehameha Hotel lobby.

"Nope, haven't seen him," Wanda said.

Thanks to the Island Skipper Airlines flight manifest, they knew the tall older man staying at the hotel was named Thomas Lohmiller. He sat across the aisle from Wanda on Flight 2 from Honolulu.

Noelani said, "You sound jittery. Everything okay?"

"Just killed my fourth triple latte. You kept me up late."

"You haven't seen him at all?" Noelani pressed. "Are you sure? Maybe he left the place, like he slipped past you."

"I'd know the dude, like, a million miles away," Wanda said. "Besides, this Tom man, he's got a lot of handsome to be sneaking around without nobody seeing him. But enough about me—what are you doing?"

Noelani told her about the meeting underway at the Loco Moco Mama between Jules Matsumoto and a mystery man. She peeked at them through the diner's plate glass window as she sat on a bench outside of the restaurant.

"Well, if I see him, I'll call you right away," Wanda said, "but you owe me big time for this, cuz, you know."

"Understood."

"Like a big greasy lunch and I mean a lot of it, too. I mean I'm getting hungry here. Hey, I gotta go pee." Wanda disconnected the call.

As the line went dead, Noelani looked through the window and saw a waitress in a way-too-small tee shirt deliver the check to Jules and the other man. But she didn't stick around long enough to see which one paid the tab.

* * *

Standing outside the restaurant, Frank unleashed a low, rumbling belch. "Don't worry, I'll get them for you. Hell, Jules, you've given me thousands of damn good reasons to find the stuff."

"I figured as much," Jules said. "Listen, if you need any help, my man Dean is available. He's an even-tempered fellow even though he's strong as an ox and—"

"If Tommy or my douchebag brother gets to you before me, I'm the first person you call, am I right?"

Jules nodded but didn't say anything. Frank clamped a hand on his shoulder. "Correct answer. I'll call you later unless shit rolls on your end. In which case, you know how to find me."

As Jules turned for his shop, Frank stuffed his hands in his pockets and strolled down to Ali'i Drive. There, a woman wearing huge dark sunglasses and a bright yellow tee shirt with the logo of the Big Island Tourism Bureau, her hair in a long, black ponytail, approached him. She held a pen in one hand and a clipboard and a black baseball cap in the other.

"*Aloha*, sir," she said, "*e komo mai* to the Big Island."

Frank sized her up. Nice skin, kind of easy on the eyes, but too bad—real small titties. *What is it with these flat-chested Hawaiian chicks?* "Hello there yourself," he said.

"My name is Lani and I'm conducting random visitor surveys and if you'd like to participate, you'll be entered to win a sunset cocktail cruise—"

"I don't got the time but yeah, you're kinda hot, so conduct away." He leaned over her and sniffed; she smelled like flowers, which was pretty much what he expected.

"Okay, sir." She flipped a page on the clipboard and clicked her pen. "Are you here on business or for pleasure?"

"This time it's business but if you know anyone's offering pleasure—"

"And are you traveling alone, with a tour group, or with family or friends?"

"Well, I came by myself but my brother's here somewhere, and this other guy's here, too, and I swear to Christ if I find his ass—"

Lani wrote something on her form. "I see."

Frank scratched his nose. "You could say I need to find both of them but more important, I need to find some stuff I lost."

"Oh, well, I don't mean to pry, sir, but if there's any way we at the Bureau can help you locate—"

"No." Frank cleared his throat. "There's no way."

The girl named Lani took more notes. "And how long will you be staying?"

"Shorter the better," Frank said. "It's crazy-ass humid here."

She nodded. "And your accommodations—are you staying at a hotel, a motel, timeshare, vacation rental…?"

"A dump," Frank said. "There's these stupid green lizards all over the walls. I mean, come on."

Lani said, writing on the paper, "Our geckos. Aren't they cute?"

"Tell you what, you ever see those things at the Bellagio, they'd be comping me the biggest suite they got. Unlike this shithole here, where the manager treats the things like pets."

She nodded. "And I assume you're visiting us from the mainland."

"Uh huh, the States." He grinned as he again sized her up and down. "You know how to do the hula dance?"

Lani smiled and said no, then she thanked Frank for his time. As a token of the Bureau's appreciation, she handed him a black baseball cap with "Hawai'i" embroidered in red, green and yellow Rasta colors.

"Ah, sweet," Frank donned the cap backward, the bill covering his sunburned neck. "I dig free stuff."

"I hope you enjoy your visit but I also hope you find whatever it is you're looking for, sir," Lani said.

Frank sucked in his gut. "Listen, maybe later me and you, we can hook up."

Lani showed him a gold band on her left ring finger. "Sorry."

"Figures."

Lani thanked him for his time and as she turned and walked away, Frank stared at her butt. *Hmm, built for speed, not comfort,* he thought. Then he checked his watch.

Inside her car, Noelani Lee removed her wig and the fake wedding band and stowed both items in her glove box. She called Wanda. "Do you have the monitor with you there?"

"Yep," Wanda said, "and no, I still don't see the Tom man anywhere. I think he's not here or if he was, he's gone even though I know he didn't, like, get past me or—"

Behind the oversized sunglasses, Noelani closed her eyes. "First, no more coffee," she said. "Second, turn on the monitor." She waited a moment. "Now, do you see a yellow dot?"

"Yeppers, I do."

"And is it moving?"

"Uh huh," Wanda said. "Looks like south, past the big hotel with the funny-looking roof…it's still going…still going…wait. I think it stopped."

"Where?"

* * *

Ryan Campanella's snores snapped him out of a nap. *Dammit,* he thought. *That could have been fatal.*

Ordinarily, he found staying awake for hours on end to be an unremarkable feat. He'd done it hundreds of times. This was no different. All night he toughed it out, as he waited for the person in the Ford Taurus at the other end of the lot to make a move.

But they never did.

What pissed Ryan off this time about catching a few quick Zs was doing it seated behind the wheel of his rental, in the Kona Winds Timeshare Village parking lot.

The plush seats in the Chrysler 300 were way too comfortable.

Ryan checked the clock on the car's console. He needed a shave and he was starving. He hoped he could find a free-range egg white omelet with fresh-grated goat milk parmesan somewhere on this Godforsaken rock.

After another minute passed, Ryan decided he had enough. He knew sometimes, the best way to flush someone out was to make the first move. Even if it meant he had to expose himself in the process.

He got out of the car and took the stairs to the second-story condo, Tommy Chunks's vacation retreat. With his left hand, he slipped the key into the door's lock. With his right hand, he held the Colt Python .357 Magnum—with its serial number filed off—he'd bought from Jules Matsumoto's anonymous friend.

He looked down the stairs and into the parking lot. Nobody was in sight.

He unlocked the door and crept inside. He locked the door behind him and looked at the floor, where he found a tiny slip of yellow paper, a quarter-inch square. The night before, he'd tucked the paper between the top of the door and the doorjamb.

He released the Colt's safety.

Yet the condo was dead quiet and everything was as he'd left it. A quick inspection of the living room and the kitchen showed nothing was out of place. He opened a door in the hallway. Inside a small closet were a stackable washer and dryer. He moved to the neighboring half-bath, but it, too, was unoccupied. As he backed out of the room, he didn't notice the faucet was dripping.

Stepping across the hall, he opened the door to a bedroom. Ryan checked the closet and, on his hands and knees, peered under the two single beds. But all he saw were dust bunnies.

A few feet down and to the left, Ryan raised the gun and entered the open doorway of another, larger bathroom. He flipped on the lights and threw open the shower curtain to reveal an empty tub.

He then crept across the hall to the master bedroom, furnished with a queen-sized bed, two rattan nightstands, and a matching dresser. With his gun still raised, Ryan slid the mirrored closet doors open; he saw his clothes and his shoes on the floor next to a small safe, but nothing else.

He edged toward the bedroom window and looked at the parking lot, but seeing nothing, he turned away.

As he did, a Ford Taurus drove by.

Ryan went back to the bathroom and lifted the toilet lid. He placed the Colt on the vanity next to the sink, unzipped, and took a leak. When he finished, he returned to the master bedroom and opened the safe; he slid the gun inside and locked it using his usual four-number combination: 2480—24 being the number of wins for Hall of Famer Steve Carlton, in 1980, when the Phillies won their first World Series.

He needed a shower. The grunge he'd accumulated sitting in the car all night was too much for him to bear. Smelling bad was not an option, especially in Hawaii, where he'd need at least two showers a day to compensate for humidity-induced perspiration.

Ryan stripped, folded his clothes, placed them on the bed, and then returned to the bathroom and turned on the water. When it reached the perfect temperature, he stepped into the tub.

That's when somebody gripped the back of his neck and pushed his face against the wall.

With his nose mashed into the cheap white tile, Ryan caught a whiff of mildew mixed with bleach. He felt another hand grab the back of his hair and squeeze, hard.

"Okay," a familiar voice said, "where the fuck'd you put them?"

Chapter Sixteen:
The Long View

His feet aching and his eyelids drooping, Mr. Lim transferred two lau lau bundles—taro and ti leaves wrapped around fish, chicken, and pork—from a steamer to a plate. As he did, he heard someone pounding on the rear service door.

He called out, *"Mai char siao lah,"* but his plea not to be disturbed didn't stop whoever was out there. He groaned and set the plate aside, wiped his hands on his apron, and opened the door.

Outside, he found a woman in faded jeans and big dark sunglasses, with long, ratty brown hair. She said, "Hey. Esther here?"

Mr. Lim nodded and held up a hand and stepped back into the kitchen and looked out the pass-through. He saw Esther Halekealoha, chatting up guests, loud and laughing. He waved to her but she didn't react, so he stepped into the dining room and tapped her shoulder.

Esther said, "What's up, cook?"

"Soa pa kâu." Mr. Lim grinned, knowing Esther had no idea he'd just called her a "jungle monkey," and motioned for her to follow him to the kitchen. He led her to the back door, where the woman in sunglasses paced back and forth, talking all kinds of gibberish to herself.

Esther said to the woman, "I'm not hiring no more waitresses, sistah."

She stopped, looked at Esther, and held up a white rectangular box.

Esther turned to Mr. Lim. "We got an order of kalbi ribs coming up, so get back to work." Then she stepped outside, slamming the door behind her.

Mr. Lim returned to the flattop grill, lit a cigarette, and tried to suppress a laugh. *"Tshau tsi bai,"* he said, as he prepared for his next task.

* * *

Esther studied the woman. She shook like a leaf and her head twitched toward her right shoulder. "Who the hell are you?"

"Don't matter."

"What's a tweaker like you want with da kine honest businesswoman like me?"

"A friend told me about you. He said you can help me."

"And how?"

The woman kicked at the ground. "I need some cash."

Esther noticed the woman refused to make eye contact. "Uh huh. What makes you think I got good money for you?"

The woman brushed hair from her face. She held up the white box. "My boyfriend bought these for me but we broke up. And he's an ass and I heard you—"

"I don't need to know any shit," Esther said. "You show me what's in there."

The woman handed her the box. Esther opened it. She blinked at its contents. "These're okay," she said. "Now, what's your name, sistah?"

"Lee."

"And who's this friend you said sent you to see me, Lee?"

"Some dude knows this other bruddah who wears these shorts and talks funny."

"Uh huh." Esther squinted. "I ever seen you before?"

Lee didn't answer, just kept kicking the ground.

"You look like someone I know is why I ask." Esther thought Lee's explanation was bullshit because Gerald never referred business to her. And this chick was not one of her regulars. She figured, if it mattered, she'd ask around later.

Esther read the red lettering inside the box lid. "These things being used, I can't give you full price. Understand?"

Lee nodded as Esther reached inside her bra. She sorted through a wad of cash and held out two twenty-dollar bills. "Take it or leave it."

Lee glanced at the bills, and then averted her gaze to the ground. Esther noticed she was still shaking. "I was hoping for a little more. You see I have a—"

Esther peeled off a ten and added it to the first forty dollars. Lee snatched the money and ran away. "Shoots," Esther said. "Bitch didn't even say 'thanks.'"

She went back inside the kitchen as Mr. Lim worked on an order of chicken katsu. "Hey, cook," she said, "be back bumbye.

Got me a business meeting."

Mr. Lim watched Esther amble back outside. When the door closed behind her, he looked into the dining room—where he saw his wife. She held a document in her right hand and a pen in her left hand.

From a distance, he could tell she'd already signed it, just above a blank line reserved for his signature.

* * *

Frank Campanella said, "Well, if you don't got them, who the hell does?"

Ryan Campanella sat naked and tied with belts and bungee cords to a rattan chair on the lanai of Tommy Chunks's timeshare condo. "Dipshit, it's raining out here."

Frank leaned back on a matching a chair on the opposite side of an open sliding door. "Dry in here, sis." He drank beer from a bottle and gripped his brother's Colt in his other hand. "Don't worry, it's one of them Hawaiian rains. It won't last long, unless of course you think you're gonna melt, in which case, you're in deep shit."

Ryan looked at the gray sky and mumbled something Frank couldn't decipher.

Frank pointed at him with his beer bottle. "Allow me to repeat the question which, if you answer it to my satisfaction, maybe I'll let you back in here." He leaned forward. "If you don't have the old broad's jewelry, who the hell does?"

"Why would I tell you even if I did have them? Come on, Frank, I'm not stupid. You must think I'm a total retard."

Frank swilled beer and wiped his mouth with the back of his left hand. "Let's try this again. You come to the Aloha State because you figured out Tommy's coming here to dump the shit with Jules. Maybe you and him are working together, you got him by the balls since you know he came here instead of going to Bermuda."

"Barbados."

"Huh. You two make some kind of deal, you both make up this story about the rocks being lost, and Jules buys it like a five-dollar blowjob."

"Oh please."

"Then you let Tommy have some of the rocks; he takes them to someone else and you get the rest, thus screwing Jules *and* me. I bet you're about to fly off to give the dough to your French flamer buddy in the Bahamas."

"Barbados and no, I am not."

The brothers heard a sliding door open at the condo next door. A middle-aged woman wearing a mu'umu'u stepped onto her lanai, but as she made eye contact with the naked Ryan, she scurried back inside.

Ryan said, "I haven't seen the stones since I gave them to Tommy the other day. As far as I know, he still has them because Jules told me Tommy told him he lost them." He stopped himself and tried to backtrack but nothing came out except "Wait, ah, what I, uh—"

Frank sat up, a toothy smile splayed across his mug. "Hey now, the truth may have just set your ass free. Well, not quite. But you met Jules already. And so did Tommy, fancy that. See, funny thing, I did, too, just this morning."

Ryan slumped in his chair and closed his eyes.

"Yeah, at this weird-ass diner's got fish and eggs for breakfast," Frank said. "Jesus, who ever heard of such shit? Well, back to the topic at hand—Jules told me the same story about Tommy supposedly losing the rocks. If it's true you and Tommy aren't partners in crime, then where's that leave us? Huh?"

From another condo in a neighboring building, they heard a child say, "Mommy, that man doesn't have any clothes on."

Ryan said, "Happy now?"

Frank rose, picked up a towel, and dropped it in Ryan's lap. He untied him from the chair and pressed the Colt against his kidney. "Be advised, little bro, you'd better not do anything too stupid."

Ryan held the towel to his crotch as he examined the bruises on his chest. His stomach hurt from the flurry of punches Frank administered in the shower. He stepped into the living room and plopped on a sofa.

Frank adjusted his chair to face him and drank more beer. He kept the gun trained on his brother. "How'd you figure out he was coming to Hawaii?"

"You think I'm going to tell you?"

"What's it matter—we're all here now, like one big happy family. As for me, I figured it out when I was in Vegas the other day. The same day you and Tommy had your meet at that Texaco station."

Ryan blinked at him.

"I kinda dropped by his place unannounced, just to see what he's up to these days," Frank said. "I figure as he's on the payroll, I'd check in on our star employee. I let myself in—the front door was unlocked. Caught the chick he lives with, Yolanda, doing something on her computer. By the way, what's with her tits? One's bigger'n the other. And those lips—I swear to Christ, she could suck the black off LeBron James."

Ryan said, "Getting back to your story."

"I waltz in like I own the place and this Yolanda chick tells me Tommy's gone. Says he went out for a drive or some such bullshit. I says it's okay, he had something I let him borrow up in his room and I needed it back. She says 'okay,' and parks her tush in front of the computer and starts typing like she's on speed."

Frank drank some beer. "I go to Tommy's room and lo and be-fucking-hold, there's the key to this condo. Right out there in the open, on his desk. I knew something was up, him only being here like a few months ago. Too soon for another vacation and I got no deliveries planned for no connections in Hawaii and neither do you. At least if what you told me was true."

Ryan said, "You're boring me."

"That's when I figured out about you and the old lady in Needles, and this place you and Tommy meet. Like you figured I didn't know about it." Frank adjusted his butt in the chair. "I drive down there and wouldn't you know it? There you two fuckers are, both screwing me out of the old broad's jewels."

"Frank," Ryan said, "you screwed yourself out of them. Besides, did you think I was going to let this opportunity get away because you screwed around Vegas all weekend?" He shook his head. "You should've seen the old lady, laying there damn near dead. One more day—hell, one more *hour*—and I would've been too late."

"Yeah, I should've seen her because me and you, we were gonna be a team on that gig. I remember what you told me."

"You turned it down, dumb ass."

"As I was saying," Frank said, "I left the key where it was, knowing you'd come looking for it because Tommy, he's too damn smart to stay in his own condo. Besides, you should've seen it coming."

Ryan said, "What's that mean?"

"What do you think I was doing in Vegas?" Frank said. "Okay, there was non-stop partying and gambling and hot chicks crawling out of the woodwork, but give me a break, there's no other reason why the town even exists."

"Get to the point."

"The point is, little bro, you should spend more time getting the straight shit on the people we employ, instead of taking them at face value." Frank had another swig of beer. "You know the Swede does the skim for us from the liquor distributor?"

Ryan shrugged. "What about him?"

"Seems the Swede and Tommy, they go back years, did some time together in county, the whole nine yards," Frank said. "The Swede tells me Tommy's been talking shit about us. They watch football or basketball, whatever, and Tommy tells the Swede he's done with us, he's looking for the first chance he can to screw us, or the first one of us he can. Turns out, you drew the short straw."

"And you didn't do anything to stop him."

"Me, I got no reason," Frank said. "I figure, he's doing it to you, or thinks he is, it's not my problem."

Ryan said, "You're a paragon of virtue."

"The Swede tells me this and I figure, because you prefer keep your dainty hands off Vegas in favor of the Ariz and Cali operations, I'd get him to watch Tommy for some scratch under the table."

"It better be out of your own money, not ours."

"A percentage above the usual but don't worry, the Swede's not breaking us." Frank belched. "I could've left it alone if it was one of your solo jobs. But it became my problem when I found out you were taking the old broad's jewelry on your own and Tommy split with it for himself."

"I did all the work," Ryan said, "and besides, you turned down—"

"I told you about her to start with. Remember? I recall me

saying, 'There's some stuff we, me and you, us, brothers, business associates, we need to get our hands on,' so shut the hell up. Bottom line is, all I gotta do is find the rocks and I get a bonus."

"Which is?"

Frank said, "I screw you and Tommy at the same time."

Ryan waited a beat. "All right, you're here, I'm here, and Tommy's here, and the old lady's gems are somewhere on this island and neither Tommy nor Jules claim they have them."

Frank scratched his forehead with the gun's barrel. "Uh huh."

"Where does that leave us and what do you plan on doing about it?"

Frank finished the beer. He tossed the empty bottle to the floor.

Ryan cringed. A trashcan was maybe five feet away.

Frank leaned forward and said, "Me and you, we're gonna be a team. And this time, it's gonna be for real—no dicking with me."

* * *

As he drove his rented Ford Taurus toward downtown Kailua-Kona, Tommy Chunks now knew *both* morons were on the island.

Oh, happy day.

* * *

Against her better judgment, considering she wasn't hungry and had work to do, Noelani Lee nonetheless took Wanda Tess Fong to the Loco Moco Mama for lunch.

The cousins found a table near the jammed restaurant's entrance. A young waitress, her form-fitting logo tee shirt displaying a bare midriff, brought glasses of water and took their orders. Wanda chose the special, a Spam-and-ham-and-hamburger burger with extra cheese, and rice and macaroni salad on the side. Noelani ordered a grilled mahi mahi sandwich minus the bread and mayo.

When the waitress left, Noelani took a pen and a notepad

attached to a clipboard from her canvas tote bag.

She flipped her paper placemat, embellished with the restaurant's logo and the words, "As seen on Food Network—Great Luau Food Without the Big Time Luau Prices," to its blank back side. Then she went to work.

Wanda watched her cousin draw circles and write things on the placemat. "Noe, what are you doing?"

"Putting what I know or what I think I know on paper," Noelani said, as she consulted her notes on the clipboard. After a minute or two of writing and diagramming, she showed her flow chart to Wanda.

Noelani pointed to a circle in the middle of the paper, in which she'd written *missing jewels*. "Now *these*"—she moved her finger along a line linking the first circle to another labeled *Jules Matsumoto*—"are why *he* hired me." She pointed to another circle with the name *Benjie Zamora—courier?*, which she connected to the *missing jewels* with a dotted line.

"You think he's the jewelry dude's courier boy," Wanda said.

"I'm not sure yet." Noelani pointed to a fourth circle, labeled *Dean Pahukoa—employee*, and said, "This guy works for Jules. As for these gentlemen"—she pointed, in order, to more circles with *hip-hop dude*, *brother*, and *this other guy* written inside—"I'm not sure yet. Except for one thing." She then drew a solid line from Jules to *hip-hop dude*.

Wanda raised her eyebrows. "Those guys're buddies?"

"They seem to know each other." Noelani drew a circle around the word *Esther* and connected it to Jules and, below *Esther*, wrote *bastard son* in another circle.

Wanda whispered, "Noe, you're telling me the sistah's involved in all this, too?"

Noelani motioned toward Esther, who stood cross-armed beside the cash register, and told Wanda about the big woman's informal meeting with Jules and the fact Jules wrote something on her hand. "Like his asking price for the missing jewelry," she said.

"Did you see how much it was?"

"I was too far away. But I think he gave the hip-hop guy an offer, too. So…"

Wanda nodded. "He's seeing who can get the jewelry to him first."

"Exactly. And I bet he doesn't care who it is."

Wanda said, "But what happens if you get them before anyone else can?"

"He gets a discount," Noelani said. "He knows all I'd charge is my fee above the retainer he's already paid me."

"Ah, pretty smart. Unless you…" Wanda stopped herself and smiled. "Would you do that, Noe? I mean, get in some bidding war thing."

"Well, professional ethics and the law tell me I shouldn't."

"Uh huh. And what's telling you you should?"

"Nothing. Yet." Noelani winked at her cousin as the waitress delivered their food.

When she left, Wanda pointed to a circle on Noelani's diagram. "Who's this 'bastard son' on here?"

Noelani said she had no idea. She said she also didn't know why the foul-mouthed hip-hop dude, now wearing a Rasta ball cap with a GPS device hidden in the button on top, went to a timeshare complex called Kona Winds.

"From what I've been told," she said, cutting a piece of fish with a fork, "the place is *not* a gecko-infested dump."

But Wanda said nothing in reply. Noelani saw her cousin's expression morph into something resembling mild shock. "You okay? Wanda?"

"Daddy." She pointed out the restaurant's plate-glass window.

Noelani turned and looked outside but saw nothing out of the ordinary. "What is it, sweetie?"

"Noe, this dude in ugly-ass shorts, he's got on my custom-made necklace and pendant." Wanda pushed herself from the table and trotted outside. Noelani tossed some cash on the table, grabbed her canvas tote and her notepad and pen, and chased after her cousin.

"It's him," Wanda said when Noelani caught up to her. She pointed ahead to a man in plaid shorts. "He's the one who's got it."

Wanda overcame the limitations of her body's apple shape and plump legs and set a blistering pace for the taller and leaner Noelani.

Although amazed at her cousin's rapid transformation from a jovial cherub to a vengeful bowling ball, Noelani had seen it happen before and feared what might happen if Wanda got hold of the guy. She flashed on an incident from their adolescence when some brat walked off with Wanda's favorite Bananarama cassette. Wanda caught him and beat the living snot out of him before she force-fed the kid mud and dead flowers.

"Wanda, ease up. If you take off after him, we'll lose him."

"But Noe, he's got something important belongs to me."

"I understand, but this is not how you do it," Noelani said. "Come on, just slow down and let me help get it back for you."

They maintained a safe but shrinking distance behind the young man as he turned north on Ali'i Drive. The cousins blended with tourists and kept the dude in sight, which worked until he slipped across to the *makai*, or ocean-side of the street.

"You stay over here," Noelani said. "I'll cut across and follow him."

"Yeah, well, you better hurry, cousin," Wanda said, panting, "because I'm about to run over there and pull his hair out."

Noelani looked both ways and crossed the street and followed her quarry to the corner of Ali'i Drive and Hualalai Road. There, she watched as he lifted a man's wallet as he waited for cars to pass before he re-crossed the street.

As she followed him, Noelani looked to the opposite corner where she saw Wanda waiting, her hands balled into fists. Noelani knew her cousin was about to go off in a big way. "Wanda, don't—"

The moment the guy hit the curb, Wanda jumped on his back. She wrapped her left arm around his throat and pounded the back of his head with her right fist. Noelani raced to the corner as the guy in the plaid shorts, his knees buckling, carried Wanda into an adjacent parking lot. Wanda held on and continued whacking his head, even as he slammed her against the side of a minivan.

Noelani tried to pull Wanda off the guy but she maintained a stranglehold with one arm as she directed blows into his lower back with her other fist. She demanded her pendant while calling him, in no particular order, a "thief," a "loser," and a "dumb idiot."

Just then a tall, older man in a maroon shirt and khaki shorts rounded the front of the van. He managed to remove Wanda from the guy, who he then grabbed by the shoulder before he flung him to the ground. In the same motion, he punted the guy right in the crotch. The young man yowled in pain and rolled into a fetal position and used his hands to shield his privates from a second kick.

A handful of tourists gawked and took pictures, until the older man gave them a nasty look and snarled, "Leave. Now." They did. He stepped away from the dude and turned to face Wanda and Noelani. "Something wrong?"

"What's wrong is this fool's got my necklace my Daddy bought for me for my birthday." Wanda strained against Noelani, who held her back with both arms wrapped around her waist. "Thieving dumb idiot loser."

"Wanda, chill," Noelani said.

The older man reached down and lifted the necklace and pendant from the dude's neck and showed it to Wanda. "You mean this?"

Wanda accepted the jewelry with a toothy smile. "Sweet. Yeah, it's mine." She showed it to Noelani. "I told you, cousin, it's beautiful."

Noelani saw the pendant consisted of the letters WTF, each about an inch high and fashioned from pieces of cubic zirconium. Metal trim showed through chipped areas of gold plating.

"My initials." Wanda slipped the necklace over her head. She said to the man, "Hey, I know you from somewhere. You're staying at the King K, right?"

Noelani got a good look at the man in the maroon shirt, and the black backpack in his left hand. "Um, thank you for helping us, Mister..."

"Tommy." He held up the pack. "This is yours, too?"

Wanda snatched it and looked inside. "Oh, yeah, my book and my keys and my cell phone. Thank you, thank you, Mr. Tommy." She hugged him.

Noelani said, "Where did you find that?"

Tommy pointed to the dude in the shorts, who mustered enough strength to sit up. "Caught him trying to hide it."

"Well, we appreciate your help," Noelani said. She reached into her pocket and took out her phone.

Tommy locked eyes with her. "What are you doing?"

"I should call the cops."

Noelani was about to dial when Tommy covered the phone with one of his big hands. "No need."

"Well, but the cops should know about—"

Tommy grabbed the phone and turned it off, and then returned it to her. "I said, no need." His voice was a growl. Noelani knew it wasn't a suggestion.

Tommy lifted the young man from the ground. "I'll take care of him."

Noelani drew a breath and said, "But the cops…"

This time, Tommy leaned in close, giving Noelani a sense of his true, imposing size—he was a good six or seven inches taller and twice as wide, with not a trace of fat in sight. He dropped his voice even lower. "Not your problem now. We're all happy." He looked at Wanda. "You're happy?"

"Sure am."

"She's happy." Tommy motioned toward the necklace. "And it's okay?"

"Just like new," Wanda said.

Tommy stared at Noelani. "Have a good day." He dragged the younger man away, through the parking lot and toward Hualalai Road.

Wanda hugged Noelani. "Dang, cousin, now I got all my stuff back. Who knew?"

As she watched the two men wander away, Noelani said, "Yeah. Who knew?"

* * *

After the women—one short and plump, the other tall and lean—jumped from their table and raced from the restaurant, Esther Halekealoha thought, *Huh. And they didn't even eat nothing yet.*

She rolled around the cash register to the window, but the women were long gone. She waddled to their table, where she found names and circles and lines written on the back of a placemat.

One name jumped out at her.

Esther folded the placemat and stuffed it in her bra and ordered the skinny-girl waitress to bus the table.

* * *

"Dude," Gerald Kapono MacTavish said, "come on, it hurts. Straight up on that."

Tommy Chunks tossed him into his rented Taurus, parked behind the funky, old, half-doughnut shaped Uncle Billy's Kona Bay Hotel, just across the street from the parking lot where they had encountered the two women.

Tommy slid behind the wheel, glowered at Gerald, and started the car.

They drove to the King Kamehameha Hotel, where Tommy parked in a distant space on the resort's far west side.

He killed the engine and said, "You screwed up big back there."

Gerald slumped in his seat. "Better bend than break." His brogue lacked its usual vitality.

Tommy rolled down his window, took a pack of cigarettes from a cup holder, and lit one. He looked out the window and blew smoke into the humid air.

He let several moments pass. "Don't do it again."

"No way, I won't. Word."

Tommy said, "You don't understand. From now on, you steal only the stuff I want."

"But Esther, she'll be all like—"

"I don't care. You find what I am looking for. I don't want to catch you with so much as someone else's used chewing gum."

When Gerald didn't respond, Tommy said, "You understand."

Gerald sat up and puffed his chest and thrust his chin forward. The brogue came back, with gusto. "Clap a carle on the culs, and he will shit in your louf."

Tommy blew more smoke out the car window.

"Tide and time, bides na man."

Tommy let a few moments pass, before he reached into the glove box and took out a cell phone. He handed it to Gerald. "Use this. Updates every hour."

Gerald turned his nose up at the phone. "It's a piece of garbage. I got better ones; I can get on the Internet with them."

"It's disposable. Yours belong to other people."

"Still."

"Updates every hour," Tommy said. "You won't want to forget."

Gerald took the phone. "No problem, boss."

"Don't call me 'boss.' If you find them, call me right away. And I mean, right away." Tommy pointed at the passenger door. "Get out. Now."

Chapter Seventeen:
The Pas de Deux

Dean Pahukoa sat in the passenger seat of his silver Infiniti and pointed to the house at the end of the block. "It's that one."

Behind the wheel, Veronica Keawe sipped Evian. "You're positive?"

"No, I mean, I am, baby. I saw the kid ride his bike from there, yeah."

They said nothing for several minutes as they watched the house. But there'd been no activity there since they arrived on Olua Place a half-hour earlier, and except for a rooster's occasional crow, the cul-de-sac was quiet.

Veronica screwed the cap back on her water bottle. "All right, you know what you have to do."

"You sure about this?"

She leaned over and kissed him. At the same time, she grabbed his crotch. "You're tense. Want me to help you with that before you do this for me—er, us?"

Dean felt his cheeks get warm. "Roni, here?"

Ignoring his feeble protest, she unzipped his pants, reached in, and pulled his limp schlong from his Scooby-Doo boxers. Then she removed the Cook Islands fertility god from her purse and pressed it against Dean's penis.

She bent over and whispered to the statuette, "Work your magic, fella."

* * *

After their encounter with the dude in the plaid shorts and the man named Tommy, Noelani Lee and Wanda Tess Fong regrouped under a palm tree across the street in grassy, little Hale Halawai Park.

As a light rain fell, Wanda stretched out on the lawn and closed her eyes. Noelani meanwhile realized she left the placemat with her diagram back at the Loco Moco Mama, so she tore a blank page from Wanda's Big Island guidebook and re-created her flow chart.

"What just happened to us wasn't random," Noelani said. "I swear, there's something weird going on between this Tom

Lohmiller and the other guy." She drew a circle and wrote *Tom* in it, and another next to it, in which she wrote, *Dude in shorts.* She used solid lines to connect *Tom, missing jewels,* and *Jules Matsumoto.*

Noelani said, "Do you remember, when we checked in at the hotel, this Tom Lohmiller person was ahead of us?"

Wanda, eyes shut, said, "Yeah, the good-looking old guy."

"And he had a backpack that looked just like yours. Well, today, he just happened to have *your* pack when you jumped the weirdo. But not his own. And as you recall, he didn't have it when he bumped into you in the lobby." Noelani turned to face her cousin. "Now, how would he know it was your backpack?"

Wanda looked at her with one open eye. "Lucky guess?"

Noelani linked the *Tom* circle and *Dude in shorts* with a solid line and crossed out *this other guy.*

Wanda said, "So you think maybe this Lohmiller is the diamond delivery dude."

"Yes, Jules Matsumoto's courier."

"Not the college boy, the one with the stuffed koala bear."

"You saw how he stopped me from calling the cops. I get the feeling he's working an angle with the *hapa haole* you beat up."

"Well, to heck with that loser. I got my bling again. Life's good." Wanda held up the WTF pendant and kissed it. "Noe, I still think you and the Tom dude, you'd make a nice couple."

"Please."

"If you didn't hate men, I mean."

"I never said I hate men. All I said was, you can't trust them under any circumstances whatsoever." Noelani turned her attention back to the diagram. "What I don't get is..." She erased one of the circles.

Wanda rolled onto her stomach and looked up at her. "'Sup, Noe?"

Noelani leaned back against the palm tree and studied the diagram. The intermittent raindrops falling on her skin felt divine. "My most favorite cousin, Wanda," she said. "Can I ask you something?"

"Sure, anything."

"When you were a kid, I remember you used to drive adults absolutely crazy."

"Daddy always said I was a 'character.' Why?"

Noelani said, "What I need to know is, are you still good at it?"

* * *

Wearing a red-and-white striped terrycloth bathrobe, a beautiful, dark-skinned girl with long black hair emerged from a tunnel and approached Benjie Zamora, who sat on a stack of boxes. A plate of eggs and bacon and diamond rings sat on a table in front of him.

Sweat dripped from the girl's nose. She bent over and batted her eyelashes. "Are you still hungry?"

Benjie lifted a camera and took her picture. "It must have been a glass of juice."

The girl took a step back and removed the bathrobe, tossing it aside to reveal baggy black jeans and a white baseball jersey. Gemstones of various colors formed the "Dodgers" script lettering across her chest. She lifted her arms in the air and began gyrating like a dervish as she sang the "I like to move it, move it" song.

Partway through the tune, she glared at Benjie and said, in a man's voice, "What the fuck're you looking at?"

Benjie felt like he was floating. The girl continued her song and dance even as Benjie's head slammed against something hard.

"Hey, brah," a man's voice said. "Dude, come on. Wake up."

Benjie opened his eyes. No longer alone in a cave with a beautiful dancing girl, he instead found himself staring at the ripped dude from Jules Matsumoto's shop, who had him jacked up against the wall in his room, a hand under each armpit.

Benjie looked at his empty bed, and then back at the big guy. "Dude, my mom and dad stash money in the freezer—"

The ripped dude slammed him against the wall and held him there. "Sorry about your nap, but your back door was unlocked, yeah. And don't worry, I'm not going to hurt you."

"Brah, take what you want, all right?" Benjie knew his parents would understand, what with him being home alone and left to defend himself against this monstrous burglar.

The ripped dude looked around the room. "What I want ain't here." He lowered Benjie to the floor but kept a firm grip on him. "You gotta come with me."

Benjie's bladder was about to explode. "You're gonna kill

me."

"No, huh? Brah, no way." The ripped dude looked over his shoulder, out Benjie's bedroom door, to the hallway. "No one's gonna hurt you, I swear. But just so you know? All this is my wife's idea."

* * *

Ryan Campanella felt the Colt's barrel poke his ribs and said, "For Christ's sake, put that thing away."

Frank Campanella stuffed the pistol in his waistband. "Yeah, I guess even *you* aren't completely stupid."

The brothers, Ryan leading the way, went downstairs from Tommy Chunks's condo to Ryan's rented Chrysler. Ryan took the keys from his pocket and prepared to unlock the driver's side door, but Frank twisted his arm and pushed him face-down on the hood.

"Right, like I'm gonna let that happen," Frank said, wresting the keys from him. "Allow me to drive, Miss Daisy."

Ryan rubbed his shoulder and examined the front of his purple-striped, short-sleeved shirt. It had fresh wet spots from raindrops that had collected on the Chrysler's hood. "Look what you did, ass munch."

Frank unzipped his hoodie. "Just get in. I'll let you have shotgun."

Inside the car, Ryan looked at his brother's head and rolled his eyes.

"Yeah, what?" Frank said.

"Nice cap."

* * *

A Kona Winds housekeeper watched the Chrysler drive away, and then looked at Unit 202 in Building 6. She took out her walkie-talkie and called Sabina Zamora at the front desk.

Sabina met the housekeeper at the unit and knocked, but when nobody answered, she opened the door with a master key. Inside, she found a beer bottle on the living room floor and a towel on the sofa. The sliding door to the lanai was open. She entered the master bathroom and saw someone had torn the shower curtain from its hooks. She stepped through small puddles on the floor to examine a red smear on the tile.

"Oh, my." She crossed herself.

Standing in the master bedroom doorway, the housekeeper said, "Sabina, look in here."

Sabina shuddered—both bedside lamps were smashed, and their shades torn; the linens were rumpled and pillow feathers covered the bed like snowflakes; and several vertical blinds sat twisted on the floor under the window. The safe in the closet stood open and empty; men's shirts and pants hung above it. Sabina noticed sharp creases on each article of clothing.

Sabina told the housekeeper to stay put. She went to the office and looked up Thomas Lohmiller's primary contact number.

In Las Vegas, Yolanda ignored the telephone as she updated her Facebook page for the twelfth time that day. In this installment, she described how she sold a massive house to the owner of the West Coast's largest office-supply retail chain. Then she detailed how she celebrated her hard-earned success with a discreet lunchtime appletini.

Because the answering machine's volume was on mute, she didn't hear a woman named Sabina Zamora leave a message for Thomas Lohmiller to call her immediately.

When she hung up, Sabina called Thomas Lohmiller's secondary contact number.

The cell phone on the passenger seat next to Tommy Chunks buzzed. He looked at the incoming number. It was local, in Hawaii.

He ignored it and instead stayed two-car lengths behind a pearlescent white Chrysler 300.

Chapter Eighteen:
The Chameleon

Because it was critical to the success of her investigations, only a handful of Noelani Lee's closest friends and relatives knew about her hyperadrenalism and its occasional effects on her voice.

Even fewer knew about the process she called "getting my man on."

* * *

Noelani took the preparatory method when she assumed an undercover male identity.

She kept her hair cut in a mop-top similar to Ringo Starr circa 1964 minus the sideburns and could gel or mousse it into different styles depending on need and circumstance. She also kept a collection of wigs in various lengths and colors and considered her flat chest a professional blessing.

Through time she became proficient with make-up, so good she developed—and patented—a foolproof method of creating a five o'clock shadow. She sometimes let the hair on her legs grow out which, thanks to her hyperadrenalism, didn't take long. When she added appropriate selections from her wardrobe of men's clothing, Noelani transformed herself from an attractive woman to just one of the guys. The ruse worked so well, she couldn't remember the last time anyone figured it out.

She displayed her handiwork to Wanda Tess Fong, emerging from their hotel bathroom in faded jeans, a plain blue tee shirt, black Chuck Taylor sneakers, and a mesh ball cap silk-screened with the name of a South Dakota truck stop.

"You look just like this kid I knew in high school," Wanda said. "He listened to Willie Nelson a lot and tried flying off his house once using a trash bag for wings."

"I notice you said he tried it 'once.'"

"What voice are you gonna use?"

Noelani responded with a dead-on Mike Myers-as-Wayne Campbell from *Wayne's World*. When Wanda laughed her approval, Noelani opened the closet and retrieved one of two black backpacks. She double-checked its contents: a tube of SPF

30 sunblock, a cheesy romance novel, and an inexpensive, paper-thin beach towel purchased from the ABC Store in the lobby.

She handed it to her cousin and picked up the other pack. Its contents included a plain, white, rectangular box and items Noelani purchased cheap at a local thrift shop—beat-up binoculars and an old-school portable CD player with a C+C Music Factory disc inside.

She said, "Do you have your cell?"

Wanda held it up. "All charged up, too."

"Okay, set it on vibrate. And remember, if you see him before I do, call me but please, be careful about it."

"Come on, Noe, you know I wouldn't do it no other way."

"Just saying." Noelani inspected the battery level on her own phone. "I'll always have you in sight and I won't be far behind you, until it's time." She checked her watch, an old digital with fresh scratches across the crystal. "All right, let's go."

* * *

Two floors below, Ryan Campanella slid a key card into a door lock. "You knew he was staying here—why didn't you just do this yourself?"

Frank Campanella said, "Because this way you do all the work, and *I* get to hold *your* gun."

The lock's red light turned green. Ryan opened the door. "Seriously, you did not have to scare the living shit out of that poor woman."

In exchange for a couple hundred dollars—and at gunpoint—Frank obtained a key card from a housekeeper named Pearl. She in turn promised not to tell anyone what Frank and Ryan were doing. Just to be sure, the elder Campanella bound and gagged Pearl in a utility closet. He said he'd return the key card and let her go when they finished with it.

As Ryan opened the door, Frank pushed him into the room. "Little bro, you think some minimum-wage hag is gonna keep her pie hole shut, even after I give her some Cs? You believe such shit and you're a bigger dummy than I gave you credit for." He closed the door and again aimed the Colt at Ryan. "Now, be a good boy and find the stones."

"Please, dipshit."

"What?"

"He's not going to hide them in his own room," Ryan said, "even if he still has them."

"Start with the closet."

In it, Ryan found some shirts and pants—low-budget stuff, from Sears or JC Penney—and an ironing board and iron on a rack attached to the wall, and a suitcase on the floor.

Continuing his search in a dresser, Ryan rifled through underwear and socks. In the nightstand, he found a phone book and evidence the Gideons were still in business. He found nothing in the bathroom, except a toothbrush, cheap cologne, and a can of shaving cream.

After a half-hour search under Frank's constant watch, Ryan failed to find the toiletry kit he gave Tommy back in Arizona.

"What did I tell you?" Ryan wandered toward the open closet.

Frank lowered the Colt to his side. "Well, then, if the rocks aren't here, I can only deduce you lied to me. Which is to say, you hid them somewhere."

"For once and for all, what are you talking about?"

"I'll ask again, Miss Manners, this time more politely. Could you pretty please with sugar on top tell me where the fuck you hid the goddamn diamonds?"

"Listen, you pinhead," Ryan said, "I told you, I haven't seen the things since I handed them to Tommy." He took a step closer to the open closet. "And for your information, I haven't laid eyes on the thieving son of a bitch since I've been here. Because if I did, I would've killed him by now."

Frank snorted. "You forget about the CPA in Phoenix. I'm the one who told Tommy to take care of him while you were saying not to."

"What's that got to do with anything?"

"Bro, you couldn't tell Tommy to kill him and you expect me to believe you'd kill *Tommy*?" Frank snorted again. "Admit it; he scares your candy ass."

"Getting back to why we're here," Ryan said, "he's got to have them stashed somewhere. He lied to Jules and he still has them; maybe he found some other schmuck—"

"Yadda-yadda-yadda."

"—who paid him more for them. Or else he's trying to

extort more cash out of Jules. Did such a consideration ever pass through the bowl of pudding you call a brain?"

"Well then," Frank said, "to see if this theory of yours has anything going for it, it looks like me and you get to camp out till our pal Tommy comes back. When he does, we can ask him where the rocks are ourselves."

"Speaking of theories," Ryan said, "how is it you've managed to avoid evolution all these years?"

Frank said, "Little bro, get a firm grip on your ears and pull your head out of your ass, because if we don't welcome the back-stabbing son of a bitch to the island personally, those rocks'll be lost forever."

Ryan shook his head and again checked out the contents of the closet. From the corner of his eye, he watched as Frank turned his back to him and adjusted his Rasta ball cap as he surveyed the room. Three walls were painted chartreuse green, the fourth, white. A flat-screen TV sat atop the dresser and sliding glass doors led to a small lanai with an ocean view.

Frank whistled. "Shit, Tommy's got some taste. This ain't bad. Better'n that dump I'm at. Place got those green lizards running up and down the walls."

"They're called geckos," Ryan said.

"I've been told." Frank turned to face his brother. "Okay, what—"

The last thing Frank saw, before his world went black, was the bottom of the hotel's complimentary iron as it approached his forehead.

Ryan watched Frank flop backwards and his eyes roll up into his head.

He bent over, the iron poised to strike again if necessary. He checked to see whether his brother was breathing and if he had a pulse. Blood trickled down his face, but he was alive—just out cold.

Ryan lifted the Colt from his brother's hand and slid it into his own belt. He wiped the iron clean and returned it to its perch in the closet.

He looked at Frank again, and then at a chair on the other side of the room. Then he removed Frank's belt from his saggy jeans.

After he left the room, Ryan walked down the hall to the utility closet. He untied the towels and duct tape that bound Pearl, the housekeeper, to a metal shelf.

Pearl kept her eyes on the gun in Ryan's waistband.

"Sorry about my brother doing this to you," Ryan said. "He has serious issues with women. Our mother hated him." With great care, he removed the tape from her mouth. She winced but didn't make a sound. "The guy can't help it. It's just sometimes, he can be a total dick."

From his wallet, Ryan took a pair of hundred-dollar bills. He handed them to Pearl, along with the master key card. "This is a little extra for the trouble. Should be enough to keep your boss off your ass."

Pearl gathered herself. She tried to flatten the wrinkles in her uniform. "Can I get back to work now? I'm way behind schedule."

"Of course. And listen, if you need an excuse, just tell your boss the fumes from the crap you use to clean rooms with made you faint, or something."

Pearl reached for the doorknob. Ryan grabbed her hand. "But just so we're clear on this and so I get my money's worth," he said, "you never saw me or my asshole brother and nothing bad happened to you today. Got that?"

Pearl nodded.

Ryan opened the door and looked down the hallway, and then winked at her. As she stepped from the closet, he said, "Hey, when you get the chance, the room down there, the one you just finished cleaning before my sorry-ass brother fucked up your day?"

Shaking, Pearl stopped and said, "Yes?"

"You might want to replace the iron. The one in there's busted." He smiled as he nabbed a couple of rolls of duct tape from a shelf. "*Mahalo nui loa.*"

* * *

As they drove, Benjie Zamora could feel Dean Pahukoa's

eyes drilling holes in the back of his head. But it didn't stop him from sizing up Veronica Keawe for most of the trip.

Damn, this chick's hot.

"What?" she said.

"I just think I've seen you somewhere before," Benjie said.

"She's famous," Dean said. "My wife's the big-time foot model, yeah."

Benjie looked at the hiking boots and white socks on Veronica's feet. "Cool. So, are you, um, a Dodgers fan?"

"Am I what?" Veronica gave him a funny look. "Kid, you're weirding me out."

Minutes later, Dean instructed Veronica to pull over. Benjie felt sweat form on his palms as Dean got out and opened the passenger door. He reached in, grabbed Benjie and pulled him from the car.

Veronica came around to join them. "Now you remember our deal?"

Benjie nodded.

"We get seventy-five percent and you get a quarter, which, considering my plans for a luxurious new master bath with a spa-like feel and a big family room, I think is fair."

Benjie figured it was okay, too. He'd get rid of Thomas Lohmiller's jewels and still get the comforts of home he needed to make his post-college life tolerable.

"Yeah," Dean said, "and maybe then I can play for a team like the Yankees. You always wanted to shop at the one big Macy's store in Manhattan, right, Roni?"

Veronica rolled her eyes. "I don't know what that has to do with anything, but, fine, whatever. Let's go."

With a firm grip on Benjie's arm, Dean led the way, with Veronica trailing behind. The trio ended their hike at the opening to the lava tube.

"This is it," Dean said.

Veronica looked at the hole in the ground, and then at her husband. "You fit those big, broad shoulders through this itty-bitty hole?"

"Wasn't easy but yeah, I got in okay."

Benjie watched Veronica press her body against Dean. When she began rubbing his upper arms, Benjie said, "I think I need to pee."

She let go of Dean and glared at him. "Do it in there." She pointed to the hole. "Both of you, go in and get the jewels, and then we can find someone to buy them, the sooner, the better."

Dean hesitated. "Baby, it's okay he goes in by himself, yeah?"

"Why?"

He wiped sweat from his forehead. "See, like I told you, the animal down there's really ugly and loud."

Benjie danced from one foot to the other. "Seriously, I need to go bad."

Veronica said to Dean, "I never figured you to be chicken, baby."

"It was real, yeah."

"Well, he can find the bag on his own." She handed Benjie a flashlight. "Go for it, kid."

The first thing Benjie did inside the tube was relieve himself. Then, he turned on the flashlight and searched for the backpack containing Thomas Lohmiller's jewels.

But he couldn't find it. In fact, some of the items he'd seen on his last visit to the cave—cameras and MP3 players—were gone. The only thing he'd taken was a fancy Canon digital SLR, now hidden in his closet at home.

He heard Veronica, outside the cave: "Did you find it yet?"

"Nun-uh," Benjie said, "I don't see it."

"Then keep looking and don't come out till you have it."

Moments later, with help from Dean, an empty-handed Benjie emerged into the sunlight. "It's not in there."

"You're kidding." Veronica bent over and peered into the tube's darkness. "Are you sure? Didn't you say you put it in there?"

"Yeah, but it's gone now."

"You're not lying to me."

Benjie shook his head. "Nope. Sorry."

Just then Veronica grabbed Benjie hard by the ears; he felt her manicured nails dig into the cartilage. She said, "I don't believe you. Where did you put the jewels, you freak? You're holding out on me, you spaz."

Benjie grimaced as he tried to unlock her fingers from his ears. "No way. Honest, I left them in there and now they're gone." The sudden excitement spurred a renewed urge to urinate.

Dean pulled his wife off Benjie. "Roni, baby, chill, I believe the kid." He looked at Benjie. "Be honest, brah. You didn't steal them, did you?"

Benjie looked at his fingers and felt relief at seeing no blood. "Like I told you, I left them here but now they're gone."

Veronica stared at the sky. "I can't believe it. Somebody stole my—our jewelry." She paced in a circle and checked her watch. "Great. Now I'm running late for Pilates. Dean, baby, you need to find the diamonds. Get the kid here to help you."

Benjie excused himself and ran behind a tree.

"Kid's weak," Veronica said. "Not like you, my big, strong masculine husband. You'll do this for me, please? It means a lot to me, baby."

"Yeah, I know."

Veronica grabbed his crotch. "There's my slugger."

* * *

Frank Campanella, his head throbbing, came to after he'd been out for, well, he didn't know how long.

When he opened his eyes, the first thing he saw was the wide, blue Pacific. He was outside. The sun's hot rays and the Hawaiian humidity smothered him.

He looked down. He was stark-ass naked, his pale skin baked to a bright red, and bound to a chair with duct tape around his chest and ankles. His hands were tied behind him, and he tasted leather in his mouth. *My belt. Son of a bitch.*

A breeze filled his nostrils with the aroma of flowers. Frank didn't know what kind because, to him, they were all alike. When the airstream shifted, he swore he smelled burgers on a grill. His mouth began watering.

Behind him, he heard a sound; someone was taking a shower. Moments later, he heard whoever was in there shut off the water. He heard the shower door slide open, followed by sounds he couldn't figure out.

Goddamn Ryan. Little bro's ass is grass.

He heard a drawer open, and then close, and then the sounds of someone moving hangers and, moments later, the faint rustle of clothes.

Next thing he knew, someone dragged his chair, backwards, from the lanai into the room. It became a green-and-white blur as the chair spun around. When it stopped, he saw Tommy Chunks standing over him.

"Hello."

Through the belt, Frank said, "Uck oo."

Tommy walked across the room. He closed and locked the lanai doors and pulled the drapes shut. He turned on the television. It defaulted to the hotel's internal channel, continuous looping information with hours for the hotel's shops and restaurants and its luau, accompanied with generic and, to Frank, mind-numbing hula music.

Tommy took a piece of paper from the dresser and held it in front of Frank.

Frank read it and grimaced.

Tommy folded the paper and put it in his pocket. He spun Frank's chair to face the TV and turned his attention to the three toes on Frank's left foot. The second and third toes were missing, the result of an episode from his childhood in suburban Philly involving Ryan, a dare, and a hatchet.

Frank screamed through the gag as Tommy mashed his right heel into the fourth and pinky toes.

Through eyes squinting from the torture, he watched as Tommy picked up a car key from the dresser. "Don't go anywhere." Then he left the room.

Frank, pain arcing from his foot to his brain, stared at the television. The incessant whine of cheesy steel guitars joined the musical mishmash in his skull.

Above the cacophony, Frank heard a voice, coming from deep inside himself.

Man, you are fucked.

* * *

On a bench across from the Loco Moco Mama, Ryan Campanella leafed through *This Week on the Big Island*. The magazine brimmed with coupons for helicopter excursions to the Kilauea volcano, snorkeling adventures, and discounted rounds of golf. All pleasant diversions, Ryan assumed. But until he took care of business, there was no time for any of them.

Ryan looked up as a couple entered the restaurant. He knew nothing about Hawaiian food except it was loaded with carbs and gluten and other indigestible shit. And, if consumed in ridiculous quantities, could lead to diabetes or death. Neither of which appealed to him.

The only thing about the diner which interested him was the chance he may run into the skilled thief Jules mentioned. Well, along with the hot waitress he saw through the window, the young one with the nice rack and bare belly. He'd have to remember her for later.

For now, he'd wait.

* * *

Pearl the housekeeper called her husband, Maxwell. "Guess what?"

"What?"

She sat in the King Kamehameha Hotel's employee break room, cell phone in one hand, Pepsi in the other. "I made four hundred easy dollars today."

"Oh, no joke? Tips?"

Pearl stared at a quartet of C-notes, stacked on the table in front of her. "How fast can you get up here?"

Chapter Nineteen:
The Bait

Wanda Tess Fong, a black backpack over her left shoulder, viewed Kailua-Kona through her digital camera's LCD screen.

Atop the seawall, three boys cast fishing lines into the deep blue waters of Kailua Bay. Behind them, the spire of Mokuai Church, the oldest house of worship in Hawaii, shone bright white in the sunshine. Beyond, the green bulk of Mauna Loa emerged from a fringe of gray clouds.

The place was pretty much the same as it was when she was just a kid. As for herself, well, over time there were changes—not all of them good.

Wanda took the picture.

Her cell buzzed. On the other end, Noelani said, "Wanda, can you move along a little faster?"

"Noe, where are you?" Wanda scanned the street and nearby buildings.

"You can't see me?"

"Nope."

"Good. Keep moving, sweetie."

* * *

Gerald Kapono MacTavish filched a bag of taro chips from the pantry as Mr. Lim busied himself with an order of teriyaki beef.

"You know," he said, as he tore the bag open, "Esther, she's all up in my business again."

Mr. Lim looked at him for a moment, his face blank. Then he went back to his work.

"She's messing with me. She wants all the stuff I take. I should go on strike." Gerald munched on a chip.

Gerald often blew off steam by talking to Mr. Lim, as the chef's nonexistent comprehension of English made him an ideal sounding board. Gerald could vent to his heart's content and because he knew Mr. Lim had no idea what he was saying, none of it would get back to his mother.

"It's all good, though." Gerald popped a whole chip into his mouth. As he crunched it, he said, "She don't know about the stash place in the tube. Big-time secret. And when I find Mr. Tom's loot, she'll never know that, too."

He watched Mr. Lim scoop rice onto a plate.

"I mean I told her about it, but no way I'm telling her if I find it. I hide it from her and Tom, get my independence." Gerald slipped into his brogue: "A child may have too much of his mother's tit."

Esther Halekealoha entered the kitchen just as Gerald bit into another chip. "Boy, what I tell you about eating the profits?"

"Enough is as good as a feast."

"Knock off the Scottish." She grabbed the chips and tossed them to Mr. Lim. "Put them on the side with the grinds—now we gotta use them."

Mr. Lim muttered something indecipherable and resumed cooking.

Gerald followed his mother out of the kitchen, through the service entrance. She said, "I dunno how your brain cells work, boy, I swear."

"A man is a lion in his own cause."

Esther slapped him upside his noggin. "Look, you done good with the one video camera. I got big money for it, maybe enough for me to get me a new Blu-Ray player."

Gerald winced as he rubbed the fresh sore spot on his head. "You're welcome."

"But sometimes, I wanna squish you like a little bug, cuz I know you lie at me, like now." Again, Esther assumed her pose of authority—arms folded across her chest, staring at her son.

Gerald squinted at her. "What do you mean?"

"Where's them lost jewelries you told me about?"

He shrugged. "Not found them yet. But I will, I promise."

"Your promises, they're all empty, like your head." She poked a fat finger in Gerald's sternum. "Why is it you don't have them yet?"

"I've been busy." He rubbed his chest. "And we live on a big rock."

"Eh, well, I got no worries," Esther said, "cuz I know you'll find them and bring them right to me, with no delays. And you know why?"

Gerald said, "Uh, because we have a special mother-son

bond?"

"Because you know what's good for you, *hapa* boy. If you find them and you don't bring them to me, and if I find out you did and didn't and you lie at me about it, then this time, there's gonna be no accident."

As Gerald tried to sort out what she said, he remembered Esther's stories about the accidental fates of his illegitimate father and Uncle Herman.

Esther took the folded placemat from her brassiere and opened it. "You read this."

Which Gerald did. *Not good*, he thought.

"One sistah wrote all this and left it on the table, about the time her friend got all nutty and ran out of the place."

"What did they look like?"

"One skinny, one fat. Why you ask?"

"Think I might've met them."

Esther said, "Whatevahs. I find this and I wonder, what's this one sistah know about missing jewels? I ask myself, and then I think, the bitch is looking for them, too. Seems like there's lots of people looking for them." She bent at the waist, leaning over Gerald. "Who all you told about da kine jewelries, besides me?"

"Nobody. Honest."

"All right, who's this Benjie she got wrote here?"

Gerald shrugged. He was relieved not to see Tom Lohmiller's name on the paper.

Esther blinked. "You be honest now."

"Nope. Truth."

"Jules tell you? This one 'hip-hop dude'? He tell you?"

Gerald shook his head.

"My boy Dean didn't say nothing, did he?"

"No. I swear."

Esther stood upright. "Don't matter. You find them before anyone else. Forget all those electronics—I need you all focused on jewelry." She pointed toward Ali'i Drive. "Get back to work, and don't go walking out through the restaurant. You know I don't want my customers seeing you ever."

* * *

Wanda Tess Fong's cell vibrated as she stopped in the

middle of the Kona Inn Shopping Village to read a page in her Big Island guidebook.

"Noe," she said, "it says here the Inter-Island Steam Navigation Company built the Kona Inn in 1928 to bring wealthy tourists to the island."

"Uh huh, interesting, Wanda."

"Yep, and it says before then there was no nice place for them to stay, until they built the inn. It says the inn helped develop tourism on the Kona Coast. But the hotel closed—"

"Sweetie, have you forgotten I am watching every move you make?"

Wanda looked at other people in the shopping center. Old, young, families, couples, but not one of them was her cousin.

"You bought some postcards," Noelani said. "One was really cute, with a cartoon dolphin wearing a lei, and the other one had a picture of a sea turtle. I'm not sure which of your nieces is getting which card, but I'm sure you have it figured out."

"Dang, you're good."

"You also bought a ball cap for Uncle Arthur, because I know you don't wear them because you hate 'hat hair.' It's red and it has 'Hawai'i No Ka Oi' on it."

"Geez, Noe."

"You also bought a poster for Aunty Mimi."

Wanda looked at the white cardboard tube in her hand. "How'd you know it's for Mom?"

"It's a *Blue Hawaii* poster," Noelani said. "Aunty Mimi's still a big Elvis fan, yeah?"

Wanda said, "You're freaking me out big time since I can't see you."

"Let's keep it that way. Now keep moving. Our friend is probably coming out to play and we don't want to miss him."

* * *

The moment Gerald hit the sidewalk, he lifted a wallet from an old man's unzipped fanny bag.

He took a couple hundred bucks from the billfold and stuffed it in his pocket and left the remaining sixty or so dollars in the wallet, a token he'd give Esther when his shift ended.

He hung a right and made his way toward the Kona Inn Shopping Village. There, he nabbed another wallet, and the contents of an ice cream vendor's tip jar.

His pockets bulging, a problem made worse by the cheap cell phone Tom Lohmiller forced on him, Gerald looked for something to carry his latest haul.

About then, he spotted a familiar sight, sitting on a bench beside a yellow hibiscus plant.

* * *

Wanda felt her phone vibrate. "Hiya, Noe."

"I see him."

"Where?"

"Don't look—he'll figure out you're on to him."

"What is it you want me to do?"

"Just act natural, like we talked about."

* * *

Gerald slipped past souvenir and tee shirt shops and groups of tourists, his attention on a black backpack parked on a bench. He paid no mind to the woman seated beside it. She was irrelevant.

What was important was he found a black backpack.

This is it. I'll snag it, hide it from Esther and Tom the haole, *and sell the stuff to Jules myself. Then, and only then, will I be a free man.*

The bench sat in the middle of the shopping center's boardwalk, which meant he'd have to act with even greater quickness than usual to lift the pack. But he had confidence in his skills. They had served him well to this point, and he knew they would again.

Gerald looked at the woman on the bench. From behind, she was short and round with thick, dark hair. She was talking on a cell phone.

He hummed "O'er The Muir."

Ten feet between him and the backpack was all that separated him and—

Some dude dressed all in blue came out of nowhere. At first, Gerald didn't see the backpack under the other guy's arm, but he caught a glimpse of it when the dude exchanged it for its look-alike. The move was so nimble, so lightning-quick, the woman on the cell was oblivious of what happened. It seemed to Gerald the only people who saw anything were himself and the dude in blue.

The dude, a ball cap on his head, gave Gerald a dirty look. Then he continued southward through the shopping center.

An odd notion crossed Gerald's mind: *For a guy, he's got pretty eyes.*

Gerald watched the fat woman stand and grab the other backpack and wander in the opposite direction.

This was unacceptable. Gerald was, after all, the greatest thief in the history of the Kona Coast. He had the stockpile to prove it, in the lava tube. Not counting the good stuff Esther kept or sold over the years.

Nobody stepped on his turf and got away with it. *Never happened before; never will again*, he thought.

He wanted to yell at the dude in blue. Instead, though, his brogue was a hiss: "He has licked the butter aff my bread."

* * *

Benjie Zamora's anxiety percolated as he wondered what Dean Pahukoa and Veronica Keawe had in store for him next.

They returned to the Pahukoa home from the lava tube in time for Veronica to change into her Pilates attire. Benjie sat on the leather sofa in the living room. On a recliner, barefoot Dean flipped through channels on his massive television mounted above the fireplace. He paused at a telecast of a world's strongest man competition.

"Come on, brah," Dean said. "Anyone can pull a freight train with *both* hands."

Benjie said, "When can I go home?"

Dean clicked through more channels. He stopped at a Chicago Cubs baseball game on WGN. "Dude, Wrigley Field. I could hit lots of homers there, yeah. No need for the wind to blow out either."

"See, my 'rents might come home early and I kinda need to be there so they don't get worried about me."

Dean watched one of the Cubs hit a routine ground ball to the Houston Astros' shortstop for the third out of the inning. "Sinkerball. Hate that." As the broadcast went to commercial, he lowered the volume. "Roni wants us to find da kine diamonds and gold the Tom man was bringing to Jules. The stuff you found and then got lost. All I can say is, sooner we find the stuff, sooner you can go home."

"No," Benjie said. "I mean, no disrespect, but I need to get home. Mom'll be making dinner in a few hours and if I'm not there, I could get into big trouble."

"You'll be in bigger trouble if you and my husband don't find those jewels." Veronica emerged from the bedroom in tight brown cotton yoga pants and a form-fitting, cream-colored tank top. An embroidered lotus flower embellished the shirt, right between her breasts. Benjie's eyes widened as he stared at the flower. What he didn't see was the TV remote Dean threw at him, until it thumped his chest.

Veronica pulled her hair into a ponytail and secured it with a rubber band. "Kid, because you had them and lost them, it's up to you to find them again because I have plans for the money."

Dean rose from the recliner. "Roni, I'm kinda worried about how this is gonna turn out."

"What do you mean?"

"See, the Tom man, he seems all nice but I dunno, there's something about that *haole* gives me chicken skin. Then there was this other guy, the one in black." Dean looked at Benjie and nodded.

Benjie held the remote in one hand and rubbed his chest with the other. "Yeah, the dude's scary. I got a bad feeling off him."

"I leave the room for fifteen minutes and you two are already knee-deep in conspiracy theories."

Veronica slung a gym bag over her shoulder. She went to the kitchen, took a bottle of water from the fridge, and returned to the living room.

"I'm not asking you to do anything impossible," she said. "All I want is for you to put your pointy heads together and find my jewels. Considering my birthday earrings have disappeared, I need you to make up for them."

On her tiptoes, she gave Dean a long kiss. She fondled his butt with her left hand. "You'll do it for me, right, baby?"

"Yeah," Dean said, "for you, for sure."

"And for our little wooden friend."

Benjie diverted his attention to a beer commercial on TV.

Veronica picked up her keys from an end table. "This Pilates class costs a ton, so I can't be late. You boys do what you have to do." She left.

Benjie watched the Cubs take the field on defense. Dean grabbed the remote from him, flopped back on the recliner, and turned up the volume.

Benjie said, "I need to get home before my 'rents do."

Dean pushed the recliner as far back as it could go. "What do you think about the one *haole* in the black, the fat guy? What's he doing here?"

"Well, he said he wanted to see your boss. Maybe about the diamonds."

"Uh huh, like Tom did. Jules went and left the shop early yesterday, too, said he was gonna meet someone else come to town." Dean sniffed. "Jules got lots of friends in town all of a sudden."

One of the Astros hit a pop-up to the Cubs' third baseman. Benjie said, "How big's that thing?"

"Sixty inches, full HD, 1080p, got da kine speakers came with it but we went and got the full-on surround sound, yeah."

"Awe, sweet."

"You should watch pro-wrestling on it," Dean said. "Feels just like those bruddah's are gonna jump out of the screen and throw a metal chair at you, it's so lifelike."

Benjie made a mental note to research prices for sixty-inch hi-def TVs, once he had his share of the jewel money.

He said, "Your wife seriously wants us to find the stuff."

"Once Roni gets an idea in her head, there ain't no turning back."

"But how are we going to do it?" Benjie said. "I mean, you count all those *haoles*, there's a lot of people looking for them, not just us."

Dean grinned. "Chill, little brah. I already got that figured out."

"You do?"

Dean reached into his pocket. "Found this in your room." He held up a business card. "All we got to do is hire this private detective chick."

Benjie remembered hiding the card under his alarm clock. "You read the stuff she wrote on the back, right? I think Tom Lohmiller hired her."

"No, he didn't. I know it for a fact."

"He didn't?" Benjie gave him a puzzled look. "Well, who did?"

"There's beer in the fridge," Dean said. "You get us a couple and we can talk about it while we're watching the game, yeah."

* * *

Gerald sized up the dude in blue: five eight and one-twenty or -thirty. He figured he could take him down easy if he had to.

Then Gerald remembered an encounter from his youth, with a Tongan kid. Same situation—the Tongan lifted a lady's bag before Gerald could reach it. Gerald caught the kid and planned to tell him by all rights, he had dibs on the bag because he saw it first. But before he could say a word, the Tongan—fat but quick—launched into wicked jiu-jitsu. He knocked Gerald out in the parking lot behind a Thai restaurant on Kuakini Highway.

It happened when Gerald was new to his craft. Still, the memory of waking up next to trashcans filled with rotting fish heads in peanut sauce convinced him to maintain a cautious distance behind this new scoundrel.

The dude in blue exited the Kona Inn Shopping Village and crossed the street at Hualalai Road. Gerald thought about crossing, too. Then he remembered, it was the same place where the fat chick jumped him. So, he stayed on the *makai* side but kept the dude in sight as they both continued south.

A little farther on, the dude slipped through an opening in a lava rock wall and wandered into the Kona Farmers Market. Under his breath, Gerald said in his deepest brogue, "What's before you will not go by you." He cut across the street.

Chapter Twenty:
The Hook

Tommy Chunks looked at his watch as he sat on a sofa in the lobby of the King Kamehameha Hotel.

The idiot in the plaid shorts was late calling in.

He turned his attention to the local newspaper. Doing something as mundane as reading a paper often gave him an opportunity to clear his mind and ponder solutions to pressing problems. Like Frank Campanella, tied naked to a chair in his room, tacky canned hula music no doubt pushing his nerves to the breaking point. He wished he could've hung around to watch it happen.

He could return him to Ryan. Better yet, he could call an old friend who owed Tommy a favor, a man who ran a deep-sea charter fishing boat out of a marina up the coast.

Just then, a now-familiar woman's voice knocked him back to reality.

* * *

The dude in blue strolled through the farmers market with no apparent interest in stealing anything. So it seemed to Gerald Kapono MacTavish, who tempered his frustration with the interloper so he wouldn't pummel the guy right there amid the organic produce, cut flowers, and genuine handmade Hawaiian souvenirs from China.

He watched the dude check out suitcases made from aloha-style fabric before he moved to a vendor who sold herbal teas and Bob Marley Rasta flags.

The dude stopped at another booth and sniffed handmade soaps. Gerald spied him as he admired a row of cheap ukuleles in an array of colors. He strummed a pink one, chords from a Clash song Gerald had on one of his many iPods. Gerald watched the dude set the uke down and moved to the next booth, where he dawdled over carved koa wood sea turtles.

Gerald noted the dude's loopy grin and sleepy eyes. He got close enough to hear him make small talk with vendors, saying "excellent" and "all right" and "party on" a lot. This guy had nowhere to go, nothing to do, and all day to do it. And, as far as Gerald could tell, he didn't have a lot upstairs, either.

For a moment, Gerald withdrew Tommy's cheap cell phone from his pocket. The old man wanted him to check in every stinking hour. He was worse than Esther. Gerald hated the phone. It was a leash.

Screw it. He slid the phone back in his pocket as the dude in blue moved to a fruit stand, where he bought an Asian pear and a banana. He dropped the pear in the backpack, peeled the banana and took a bite.

A minute later, the dude exited the farmers market the same way he entered. Gerald followed, swiping a mango on his way out.

* * *

Wanda Tess Fong held the WTF pendant up for Tommy to see. "You know, what you did for me, you know, catching the loser dude who stole my necklace?"

"Yes."

"Well, it was just completely awesome of you, what with us being total strangers."

They sat at the Billfish Bar at the King Kamehameha Hotel. Outside, little kids did cannonballs in the hotel's pool. Inside, Tommy wished he could join them. Anything to get away from the chatty Wanda, who cornered him in the lobby and insisted she buy him a drink in gratitude for his chivalry in subduing the pendant thief.

Tommy said, "It's nothing."

"I mean, this has been an interesting trip so far. Did I tell you I used to live here? See, I'm visiting my cousin. I haven't seen her in, like, years. She's single, you know, and gorgeous."

Tommy nodded but said nothing.

"You met her when you caught that dude," Wanda said. She pointed at Tommy's drink. "You like their mai tais? Get enough in you and you'll forget most of your vacation. You're on vacation, right?"

"No."

"When you grabbed the loser thief bruddah in the parking lot, what'd you do with him?" She whispered, "You didn't like, you know… I mean he's still alive. Isn't he?"

"Sadly." Tommy sipped his drink.

Wanda polished hers off and ordered another round for them both. "They make them good here. I live in Las Vegas but you can't get good fruity tropical drinks this good there. Most people there drink martinis. Me, not so much—I wind up puking after a few. But these? They're smooth. Where'd you say you're from?"

"I didn't."

Wanda stopped for a moment, and then laughed. Loud. "Eh, well, no worries. Maybe we all can talk story if you join me and my cousin for dinner. You'd like to do that?"

"Where is she now?" Tommy said.

"Up in the room—she's got a headache real bad. I told her just to relax and take a nap. I got her some aspirins so I think she'll be all good to go by the time we gotta eat."

Tommy looked at his cell phone. Still no call.

Wanda said, "I know some cool places we can go." She hoisted her backpack from the floor to her lap. "I got a guidebook in here; it rates restaurants with forks, like from one to five. Five being the best. You been to the Loco Moco Mama yet?"

"No."

"Huh. I could've sworn I seen you in there yesterday. Oh well, probably some other handsome man." She winked and gave Tommy a playful punch to the arm.

"Look," Tommy said, "I don't mean to be—"

"Let's check out my guidebook." Wanda opened the backpack. As she did, her eyes popped wide and her mouth dropped open.

Tommy waited a moment. "Something wrong?"

"I don't believe this. I mean can you believe this?" From the backpack, she took a beach towel, a tube of sunblock and a Harlequin Romance. "This isn't mine. This ain't my stuff at all."

Wanda placed the pack's contents on the bar. "I bet it must've been the loser thief bruddah again, da kine stupid one in the ugly shorts. He got me again. He took my pack and swapped this one for it." She slapped a palm on the bar. "Dang it."

Tommy studied the items. "You sure?"

"Positive." Wanda buried her face in her hands. "Why's this

always happen to me? It's like he's out to get me."

Tommy returned the items to the backpack. He zipped it shut and placed it on the floor at his feet. "I'll handle this."

She looked at him. "You will, I mean, you can help?"

Tommy nodded.

"Oh. How're you gonna do that?"

"I have ways."

Wanda giggled. "You must think I'm *lolo* or something, Mr. Lohmiller. Oh, that word *lolo* means 'crazy.'"

He waited a beat before he said, "Dinner sounds nice."

"Listen, I don't—um, what'd you say?"

"Dinner. You and your cousin."

"Cool. I'll let her know."

"Please do."

They made small talk for several minutes. Tommy watched as the woman knocked back two more mai tais and followed them up with his untouched drink. She rose from the stool and wobbled.

Tommy said, "Are you okay?"

"Uh, yeah, I'll be fine if I just snooze or something." She hiccupped.

He tossed a couple of twenties on the bar. "Drinks're on me, Miss…"

"I'm Wanda Fong."

"And your cousin's name?"

"Noelani Lee. Our mothers were twins. Sisters, I mean." Wanda held a hand over her mouth to suppress a belch.

"Get some rest," Tommy said. "I'll meet you and your cousin in the lobby at seven."

Wanda gave him a hug and a sloppy kiss on the cheek, said good-bye, and staggered from the bar.

When she was gone, Tommy wiped his face with a napkin and looked at the backpack on the floor.

He thought, *How does she know my last name?*

* * *

With no sign of the weirdo in plaid shorts and the humidity what it was, Ryan Campanella decided to go back to Tommy's condo and change into fresh clothes. He was getting hungry, too, and wished there was a decent vegetarian place around there *somewhere*.

He rose from the bench outside the Loco Moco Mama and tossed the tourist magazine in a trashcan. As he did, two nubile, tanned hardbodies walked by, clad in matching pink bikini tops and white cotton shorts that hugged their delectable asses. They smiled at Ryan.

He took a deep breath and followed them.

Fresh clothes could wait.

* * *

Gerald drew closer to the dude just as he hung a left into the Ali'i Sunset Plaza, a moment after two hot blondes and a guy in a purple-striped shirt went south on the sidewalk.

As he closed in, Gerald primed himself to unleash his fury on the miscreant.

Then, the dude stopped and turned to face him. Gerald hit the brakes.

"Sh'yeah, right," the dude said. "What, are you mental? This following thing of yours is so totally not excellent." He bolted away.

Gerald gave chase, past the Loco Moco Mama and Jules's King of Diamonds through an exit between two buildings at the rear of the center, and into the parking lot.

The dude turned to taunt Gerald, thumb on his nose, fingers waggling. As he did, he didn't see the car parked in front of him. It happened to be Gerald's Saturn. The dude ran headlong into it, slid up its hood, and rolled over its passenger side. He landed on his back and dropped the backpack. It landed at his feet.

Gerald amped up his brogue as he stood over the guy: "Fancy a doin'?"

"No need for violence." The dude covered his face with both arms. "I've always found that giving in to one's inner vengeful beast is bogus."

Gerald ignored him. He grabbed the pack and held it aloft. In his throatiest brogue, he said, "Be happy while you're living, for you're a long time dead."

The dude sat up. "Uh, are you gonna kill me?"

"Nope. Word."

"Well, if you are, I wouldn't mind maybe having some time to first get my considerable personal affairs in order."

Gerald unzipped the backpack and pulled out a portable CD player. He slipped the earphones on and hit Play, and then removed binoculars from the pack. His head bopped to C+C Music Factory's "Things That Make You Go Hmmm..." as he scanned random objects through the binoculars.

The dude said, "Please allow me to take my stuff and depart this most bogus scene of the crime."

"Yo, who are you?"

"They call me Bruce."

"You look kinda girlie," Gerald said.

"I'm all man, man. Would you like physical proof of my awesome masculinity?"

"I've never seen you. You're not from here. You're an unwelcome stranger."

"True, I am a visitor to your fair shores from the distant metropolis of Hilo. Over there, I am kind of a big deal."

Gerald held up the backpack. "You had no right to steal this. Only I had the right to steal it."

"What, the fruit?"

Gerald took the Asian pear from the backpack and tossed it to Bruce. "The rest is mine."

"I'm confused, oh wait, maybe I'm not," Bruce said. "Maybe that's because I can't hear you over the sound of how epic I am." He bit into the pear.

Gerald felt his blood heat up. "Awa an bile yer heid."

"Um, exsqueeze me? *En Ingles*, party favor."

"You need to leave Kona. This is my land. Be gone. Steal no more black backpacks."

"Oh, I get it. You're upset because I pilfered said bag before you could. Hey, the awesome meter never lies."

"Laddie, you're the one sittin' on his bahookie." Gerald's brogue thickened. "A word to the wise—here, you're as welcome as water in a holed ship."

Bruce adjusted his ball cap and took another bite from the pear. "I will say this—you are unique, just like everyone else. Okay, I'll take my leave of your humble 'burg, but only if you tell me what's up with the backpacks."

Gerald waited a beat. "If you promise to leave when I finish my tale."

Bruce responded with a Boy Scout salute. "And hope to die, though considering the circumstances, such a result may be a bit extreme."

Gerald looked to his right, and then his left. He leaned over and said, "Just this—a gray-haired *haole*, he wants one of them bad. No one else gets it. If I don't, there's trouble, because of what's inside."

"What's that?"

"I'm not telling you. But the man'll rip my face off. So will Esther."

"And Esther is…?"

"My illegitimate mother. She's a hogbeast. Which is why when I find it, neither of them will ever know."

Bruce held up a hand and Gerald helped him to his feet. *Guy's got soft skin.*

Bruce pointed at something behind Gerald. "Uh, who or what is *that?*"

Gerald looked over his shoulder. Esther Halekealoha, arms folded across her massive bosom, gave him stink eye. "She's Esther."

"You are correct," Bruce said. "She is definitely not mega babe-a-licious."

Gerald turned to Bruce. "Now is when you leave Kona and don't come back."

Bruce nodded, his eyes locked on Esther. "Good call. Have a pheasant plucking day." He took another bite from the pear and wandered through the parking lot.

As he did, Esther—temples throbbing, nostrils flaring— marched toward her son.

* * *

Not only were the hardbody blondes gifted attackers, they also were skilled at deep-setting and penetration.

Amber and Ashlee—"with two *e*'s"—friends vacationing from Santa Barbara, asked Ryan Campanella to join them in a threesome. Together, they challenged a trio of local kids to beach volleyball on a sand court next to Ali'i Drive.

"You're kinda cute," Amber said to Ryan.

"Yeah," Ashlee said, "you're hot in an old-guy kinda way."

"I'll take that as a compliment." Ryan removed and folded his shirt and placed it at the edge of the court. He hid the pistol inside the shirt, removed his shoes and socks, and adjusted his sunglasses. In a matter of minutes, his hairless chest sheened with perspiration, as did his abs, which were more pronounced thanks to his manscaping regimen and his ability to suck in his stomach without being obvious. Using those lures and his undeniable charm, Ryan convinced himself Amber and Ashlee would join him for a post-game shower and serious multi-orgasmic group sex in Tommy Chunks's condo.

Then he'd dump them somewhere and get back to work.

Except for a handful of well-placed overhand serves and a few decent blocks on defense, Ryan sucked. Although volleyball wasn't his game, he made up for his shortcomings with solid trash talk aimed at the other team. The smack earned flirty smiles from his teammates. The girls told him they had played beach volleyball for all their natural-blonde California lives. Their skills overcame Ryan's liabilities, and they beat the boys by five points.

Yielding their half of the court to a new team, Ryan and the girls sat on the grass. For their benefit, he let the sun reflect on his glistening muscles. In turn, he admired the beads of perspiration on each girl's modest bosom.

"So," he said, "you girls play in school?"

"Yeah, Santa Barbara," Ashlee said.

"Ah, yeah, UC Santa Barbara. They're called the Gauchos, right?"

Amber giggled. "No, we like go to Santa Barbara High School."

"Yeah, we're totally, like, juniors," Ashlee said. "Silly."

Oh, fuck me to tears, Ryan thought.

The girls told Ryan they had to meet their parents at their hotel and left him to roast in the sun. With both his spirit and libido deflated, he waited a few minutes and picked up his shirt. As he did, his heart fell out of his chest.

The Colt was gone.

He threw on the shirt without buttoning it and scanned the ground for the gun. It was nowhere in sight. He mentally replayed the game, recalling as best he could every move he made, and tried to remember whether anyone approached the shirt while he and the girls played. But he came up empty.

Making matters worse, his shoes and socks also were missing, but he didn't give a shit about that. Barefoot, Ryan scrutinized everyone he encountered, looking for telltale bumps in waistbands and in pockets. He peeked into shopping bags and baby strollers, and retraced his steps and again reconnoitered the volleyball court two, three more times.

Nothing.

Now his palms were wet and his stomach was in knots. This wasn't good.

Hoping to collect his thoughts and jog his memory, Ryan crossed the street. He sat on the black lava rock seawall overlooking Kailua Bay.

The water was an incredible shade of blue.

"Kind of young for you," said the voice of Tommy Chunks.

"Not if you combined them." Ryan turned and looked into Tommy's deadpan mug. "It's true, I see. Your pilot got lost on the way to the Caribbean."

"Funny."

"I'm expecting a refund for your ticket."

Tommy said, "Walk."

Ryan pointed at his bare feet. "Be nice to have my shoes."

He felt the gun burrow into his back.

Tommy said, "Walk."

Chapter Twenty-One:
The Castaways

As she entered the King Kamehameha Hotel, Noelani Lee—still wearing her Bruce disguise—saw Tom Lohmiller walking through the lobby.

With him was another man, barefoot and in jeans, a purple-striped short-sleeved shirt, and sunglasses. The second man's expression told Noelani he was unhappy with the situation.

Convinced neither of them saw her, Noelani followed them to the elevators.

Tommy Chunks waited for a couple to exit the elevator before he shoved Ryan Campanella inside. "After you."

"Kiss my ass."

"Maybe later."

Tommy reached behind Ryan and pressed the fourth-floor button. At the same time, a young man in a blue tee shirt and a mesh ball cap ran to the elevator.

"Dude, thanks for waiting," the young man said. "Missing this elevator would have been most totally bogus."

"Do not call me 'dude.'" Tommy pegged the guy to be in his mid to late thirties. "Which floor?"

Seeing a circle of light around the number four, the guy said, "Why, it just so happens to be the same as you fine gentlemen."

The doors closed and the elevator began its ascent. The younger man said, "How are you fellows enjoying your visit to the island?"

Tommy said, "Shut the fuck up."

"Ah, okay then." The young man did as told.

The elevator doors opened at the fourth floor. The young man stepped out and walked to the far end of the hallway. Tommy watched him fumble with his wallet and drop his key card.

Tommy took his own room key from his pocket, opened the door, looked again at the young man in blue, and pushed Ryan inside.

* * *

In her sixth-floor room, Noelani Lee found Wanda Tess Fong lounging in bed and singing along to the theme from *Gilligan's Island*.

"Wanda, what is going on here?"

"Hey, Noe, wassup?" The tipsy Wanda tried to sit up but remained prostrate when she could not manage. "You're just in time for Giglian…Gilgian…Galagian…Uhhhh…"

Noelani removed the South Dakota truck stop cap, closed her eyes, and hung her head. "Great, you're drunk."

"Naw, just feeling good is all. Like more of like a serious buzz."

This is why I work alone, Noelani thought.

"You glike illigan, don't you?" Wanda grinned. "Back in the day, if I was around then, I'd let the professor do all kinds'a experimenting on me, you know what I mean?"

Noelani sat on the foot of the bed. "Wanda, listen to me. How did it go with Tom, if you can remember?"

"Who?"

"I asked you to—"

"The handsome, hunky, older Tom dude hero man," Wanda said. "He don't talk much but it's okay because he's nice, and because he bought me good drinks. I mean *damn* good and he said he's going to dinner with us."

"He did?"

"Yeppers," Wanda said. "Mr. Lohmiller, he said he'll meet us in the lobby."

Noelani put a hand on Wanda's forearm. "What did you just call him?"

"Who him, Mr. Lohmiller him?"

Noelani closed her eyes and rubbed her temples. "Please tell me you didn't call him that to his face."

"Yeah, I did, Noe. I mean, that's his name." Wanda hiccupped. "Isn't it?"

Noelani took a deep breath. "Sweetie, you shouldn't have done that. He doesn't know we know his last name." Noelani figured Wanda's mistake meant she'd have to revert to Plan B. First, however, she would need to develop a Plan B.

Afraid she'd say something she'd later regret, Noelani sat on her bed and took a miniature laptop from her nightstand. She powered it on. A GPS monitor, it displayed a map of Kailua-Kona, with the streets labeled and represented as white lines. A couple of seconds later, a green dot appeared on the screen.

The green dot was an electronic signal from a GPS tracking device Noelani attached inside the portable CD player, now in the hands of Gerald Kapono MacTavish. Noelani watched as the green dot followed a straight line along a street labeled Keolani Drive. A moment later, it followed a zigzag path off the road. A couple of minutes later, the dot stopped moving. Noelani waited for it to continue whatever course it was going to take. But it stayed put.

She toggled the monitor's view to a satellite image. It showed an undeveloped swath of land studded with trees and brush.

Noelani pressed a button, which changed the view on the monitor. A red dot appeared. Based on what she saw, Noelani realized the second tracking device, hidden in a tube of sunblock, sat motionless two floors below her. Beside it, a signal in the form of a yellow dot beamed from a black Rasta ball cap.

Noelani took her diagram from her pocket and wrote, "*sunglasses man*," in a circle. She connected it with solid lines to both "*Tom*" and a new circle labeled "*other man*," and "*hip-hop dude*." She also crossed out "*bastard son*," and drew a line from "*dude in shorts*" to "*Esther*."

She reviewed the diagram and it hit her. "They're the same person. Both of them."

"Who is, Noe?"

She turned to Wanda. "Do you remember anything about the conversation with Tom? I mean, before you got wasted."

"He took the backpack like you said I should let him to do."

"What did he say he'd do with it?"

"I think he still had it when I left the bar," Wanda said. "Then he says he'll, like, go to dinner with us. Real nice of him, huh?"

Noelani felt her cell buzz. She didn't recognize the number but answered. "Hello?"

A male voice responded. "Yeah, um, hi, is this N. B. Lee?"

"Yes, it is."

"The private detective? From Hilo?" He sounded young.

"Yes, how can I be of help to you, Mister…?"

"I was wondering if maybe, like, you could help me find

something we—I lost."

Noelani picked up the hotel-issue pen and pad of paper from her nightstand. "How about you give me a little information first?"

"Like what?"

"Your name is a good start."

"I'm Benjie Zamora." Noelani heard a muffled voice in the background. Benjie whispered, "Hey, do you think we can keep my parents out of this?"

* * *

"Hope you enjoyed the music." Tommy Chunks lowered the volume on the TV.

He looked at Ryan Campanella, lashed to a chair opposite his brother with the same duct tape he stole from the utility closet down the hall.

Ryan nodded at Frank's swollen toes. They were a hideous mix of green and purple. "Hey dipshit, want me to get an axe and cut those off for you?"

Frank said, "Uck oo."

Tommy said, "Not like you have room to talk." He reached into a pocket and removed the handwritten note he found when he discovered Frank in his room. "This was clever." He held it up for Ryan to read.

He's all yours.
I'm getting my rocks back.
Fuck you very much. -- RC

"You have to admit, finding his fat ass tied to a chair in the great outdoors?" Ryan grinned. "Funny stuff if I say so myself."

"Hilarious." Tommy wadded the note and tossed it in a wastepaper basket.

"Listen, Tommy," Ryan said, as he eyeballed the Colt in Tommy's waistband, "you're going about this all wrong."

"No, I am not."

"There's ways we can salvage this situation and make us all happy. Well, except for limp dick here."

"Uck oo."

"Okay. Explain."

"I look at it this way: those jewels were mine in the first place, which counts for something," Ryan said. "Even if you decided you wanted them for yourself. At first, I didn't understand. It's not like you needed the coin, considering all the legal tender you have stashed overseas."

Tommy produced two pieces of paper. One was a napkin and the other, a scrap. On each were numbers in the same handwriting. He showed them to Ryan.

Ryan scrunched his brows. "The son of a bitch."

Frank looked at his brother, and then at Tommy. "Uh?"

Tommy put the papers in his wallet. "Same amount he said he'd pay me."

"He told me you two didn't have a number," Ryan said.

"Uht tuh uck?"

"It's going to change," Tommy said, "now that you two are out of the way."

"Look," Ryan said, "I know you were trying to screw me with all this, sort of a parting shot as you ride off into some tropical sunset. Personally, I don't know what I did to earn it, unlike red pepper-pecker here."

Frank gazed at his sunburnt penis. "Ucking hing urts."

"Given half a chance, I'd pull the same shit," Ryan said. "But now we know where Jules is coming from, I'm thinking we can work out a deal."

Tommy said, "You're tied to a chair."

"I also know you don't kill people on a regular basis. It's been, what, seven years since the CPA in Phoenix?"

"You still owe me for him."

"No way, Tommy, that particular call came from the three-toed sloth here."

"Uck oth, athole."

"I also doubt you'll cap my ass with a stolen gun I bought from a friend of a friend of Jules," Ryan said.

"What does it matter, once I wipe the prints?"

"You wanna hear me out, or should I save my breath?"

Tommy looked at his watch. "Be quick."

Ryan said, "First, because you have a head start on this already, I suggest we ditch dumb ass here. Get him out of the way and that's one less aggravation for us both."

"Tempting," Tommy said.

"Uck mah ock."

"Then," Ryan said, "you lose the idiot in the fugly shorts."

The statement piqued Tommy's attention. "You know him."

"Not personally but Jules may have mentioned him in passing," Ryan said. "Weird dude, thinks he's a Scotsman. I dropped by the restaurant; I didn't see him but got two eyes full of his mother. She's one grotesque broad. Didn't stick around, what with me being on a low-cholesterol diet."

"Tick tock," Tommy said.

"But you, you've always looked for locals to do the heavy lifting when you're outside of the Southwest. I'm not entirely shocked you might have asked him to lend a helping hand. That's what you did, huh?"

"Five seconds."

"Like I was saying," Ryan said, "after we dispose of Frankie Fuckwad here, we figure out who was on the plane with you. Who might've grabbed my property when your flight bought it here on the wrong side of the globe? There are ways we can do that without attracting what you could call 'undue attention.' Ways I can help you and you can help me."

Tommy said nothing.

Ryan continued: "You let me handle that end because, no offense, I'm better at it than you. 'Brains of the outfit,' you know. All I ask is a third share. It should be enough for me to get my associate in Barbados off my back for the time being, and still leave you with enough to eke out a decent retirement."

"Go on."

Ryan leaned forward. "First, we need to find someone cooperative we can dump the stones on. Someone who is not Jules, who doesn't have a vested interest."

"Uh huh," Tommy said.

Ryan nodded toward the nightstand. "Yellow Pages're in there."

Vague as it was, the scenario Ryan presented gave Tommy pause. He also thought about Wanda Fong, the chubby Hawaiian gal from Vegas. In turn, he pondered what role Wanda Fong's cousin had in all of this.

"I can't trust you," Tommy said.

"Well then, we have something in common," Ryan said. "Listen, you and me both want this over so we can get our hands on some currency. Am I right or am I right?"

Tommy stared at Ryan for several seconds before he opened a drawer in the dresser. He took out a pair of socks and made a ball out of them. He approached Ryan and said, "Open wide."

"Hey, goddammit, I—"

Tommy rammed the socks as far into Ryan's mouth as he could without choking him. "It's okay. I've only worn them once since I last washed them."

Through his belt-gag, Frank snorted.

Tommy walked across the room and opened the closet. He picked up a black backpack from the floor and closed the door. He returned and showed it to the brothers.

A wide-eyed Ryan looked at Frank, who again snorted through his gag.

Tommy slung the backpack on his shoulder and picked up his car keys. He looked at the TV, grabbed the remote, and changed channels. He settled on a SpongeBob Squarepants marathon on the Cartoon Network.

"Enjoy," Tommy said, as he slid the "Do Not Disturb" sign in the key card slot and left.

Using his tongue, Ryan tried to extricate the rolled-up socks from his mouth. He fought against the tape that bound his ankles and wrists to the chair. He took a deep breath and looked at Frank—who laughed and snorted though his belt.

Chapter Twenty-Two:
The Squeeze

Noelani Lee's phone conversation with Benjie Zamora drove her patience to its limit, even though she knew it provided a break she needed.

She suggested they arrange a meeting, even though he made excuses about his parents and studying. As they spoke, Noelani was sure she heard another man talking to him in the background.

"Look, Benjie," she said, "you called me, not the other way around. I can only help you if we discuss the situation face to face. Either we meet or not; it's up to you. Otherwise, I have plenty of other things to do."

The scolding had an effect. "Hold on." She heard Benjie say something to the other man, who responded in a raised voice. Although she couldn't make out what Benjie's friend said, she could tell by his tone it wasn't pleasant.

The argument almost drowned out Wanda Tess Fong's snores. Noelani noticed a thin line of drool rolling from the corner of her cousin's mouth and onto her pillow.

Benjie came back on the line. "Okay, well maybe we can meet like real quick in a couple of hours. I don't have much time, see, because like my mom is making—"

"Do you have a car?"

"I don't but my friend does."

"Who's your friend?"

"He's just… He's a cool guy," Benjie said.

Noelani looked at the clock radio on her nightstand. "You know the Walmart on the Queen K Highway?"

"Yeah, sure."

She said, "Meet me in the far south end of the parking lot in two hours. Look for the white Nissan Sentra. I'll be in an orange blouse and white Capri pants."

"White what?"

"What are you—what is your friend driving?"

"It's a …" She heard Benjie's muffled voice say something to his friend. "A silver Infiniti. Sick ride."

"Okay, I'll try to make this quick so you can get home in plenty of time."

Benjie, and his unseen pal in the background, agreed to Noelani's terms.

When she hung up, she did a reverse trace on the call. It came from a phone number listed to a Pahukoa, Dean.

She flipped open the small monitor for her GPS tracker.

The yellow dot two floors below remained still. The red dot, on the other hand, was on the move.

Noelani raced to the elevator and reached the hotel's ground floor at the same time as the red dot on her monitor left the building. She dashed across the lobby in time to see Tom Lohmiller walk through the doors, alone, fifteen feet ahead of her.

In the parking lot, Noelani ducked behind an SUV. She peered around the vehicle and watched him get into a Ford Taurus. She looked to her left at her Sentra, a few spaces away. She heard a car start and again peeked around the SUV as the Taurus backed out of its space and turned toward the exit.

Noelani ran to her car and followed Tom from the lot.

The Taurus hung a right on Ali'i Drive and continued to Hualalai Road, where it turned left and drove uphill. Waiting at the light at Kuakini Highway, from her vantage point a couple of car lengths behind, Noelani saw Tom Lohmiller pick up his cell phone.

* * *

"You didn't call me." Tommy hoped his tone would emphasize his displeasure.

Gerald Kapono MacTavish said, "Sorry about that."

"You were supposed to check in."

"I stopped by the crib for food. Real."

"You there now?"

"Yeah," Gerald said. "Why?"

Noelani watched Tom Lohmiller drive straight on Hualalai. A car between him and Noelani turned right on Kuakini. Noelani slowed a bit to avoid detection and followed the Taurus on Hualalai.

At Queen Kaahumanu Highway, Tom turned right. Noelani

followed suit, letting a rusted pick-up slide between them. Less than a half-mile south on Queen K, Tom turned left—back on Hualalai, where the road continued uphill and eastward beyond the main highway.

With her GPS monitor open on the passenger seat, Noelani allowed Tom to open a hundred-yard lead. At a T-intersection, the Taurus turned left. Noelani turned right and pulled into a side street, where she stopped the car.

On the monitor, the red dot indicated Tom was driving north. He went about a half-mile to a street called Wehilani Drive, and then turned left for another third of a mile. He then turned in to a cul-de-sac, where the dot stopped moving.

Meanwhile, the yellow dot remained motionless back at the hotel.

Noelani zoomed the monitor out. Both the green and red dots blinked on the screen. She figured they were about a mile apart, as the crow flies.

The red dot in Tom's car moved. Noelani switched the monitor's view from "map" to "satellite." She watched the red dot advance toward a small building behind a big house.

Tommy pushed the backpack with the beach gear in Gerald's face, interrupting Gerald's game of tennis on the Wii. "What the hell is this?"

"Looks like a backpack to me." Gerald served an ace against his animated opponents.

"Not what I mean," Tommy said. "You stole another one from the fat chick."

Gerald watched the replay of his impressive serve. "Now *that's* mad skills, brah. Way good. McEnroe-esque."

Tommy found a ten-pound dumbbell on the floor and threw it at the television. A crack formed a spider web across the flat screen as the free-weight knocked the TV to the floor.

Gerald's jaw dropped. "Dude, my—why'd you destroy the teev?"

"I tell you to do something, you do it." Tommy's stare punctured Gerald's swagger. He tossed the backpack on Gerald's cot. "I tell you not to do something, you don't do it. But you did it anyway."

"No way. For real, innocent here."

Tommy grabbed Gerald by the collar and slammed him against the shed's plywood wall, next to the yellow-and-red flag. "I told you not to fuck up."

"Aye."

Tommy took the Colt from his pants and pressed its side against Gerald's face. "Guess what happens next."

Noelani called Wanda at the hotel.

"Hiya cousin."

"Wanda, how are you feeling now?"

"Oh, great, Noe. Nap felt good but I'm still buzzed."

"All right, what I need to know is if you can function like a normal human being."

"Well, yeah, sure. It's not like I was *completely* stinko. What's up?"

Noelani said, "I'm in a situation here and it may take some time, plus I have to do a few things after this, whatever it is. I need a favor. And sweetie, please, do not mess it up this time."

"Anything for you, Noe."

Gerald felt Tommy tighten the grip on his shirt, so tight he thought he might stop breathing.

"Brah, I got nothing to do with this bag," Gerald said. "I've tried to find yours but no luck. Haven't seen it. That's true."

Tommy pressed the gun's muzzle into Gerald's forehead. "Not good enough."

Gerald stammered. He panted. The words didn't come, until he said, "I'm not worth killing, you know."

Tommy tilted his head to one side.

Gerald felt sweat roll down his face. "So, do I live?"

Tommy stared at him for several moments. He didn't blink. "I'm thinking."

Noelani turned left on Wehilani Drive and continued toward the location of the red dot on her monitor. She found Tommy's Taurus in front of a two-story house. She parked on the street, adjusted her mesh ball cap, and then got out of the Sentra. She walked toward the house.

About then she heard a loud engine. She looked over her shoulder as a Ford pick-up with a camper shell came to a screeching halt in the driveway.

Esther Halekealoha hopped from the cab and glowered at Noelani. "Who the hell are you on my property?"

As Bruce, Noelani said, "Uh, I think I'm lost. Might this be the Bergdorff residence?"

Esther spat on the ground. "Babooze, do I look like a Bergdorff? Get outta here." She stormed into the house.

"Done thinking," Tommy said.

"Okay, good," Gerald said. "And what say ye?"

A loud voice bellowed across the backyard: "Boy, where you at? You playing with yourself and not doing what I need you to do?"

Tommy released Gerald and edged toward the shed door. He looked outside and saw a massive woman walking in his direction. "What the hell is *that?*"

"Esther," Gerald said. "She calls herself my mother."

Esther's voice again boomed: "Dammit, boy, I find you in there playing the game thing, you gonna be walking funny with a controller thingy shoved way up your ass."

Tommy stepped away from the door.

The big woman bowled her way into the shed. "Boy," she said, "why ain't you—" She stopped. In order, she looked at Tommy, the gun, Gerald, and the television's mortal remains. She jerked a thumb toward Tommy and said to Gerald, "Who's the asshole?"

"Esther," Gerald said, "this is Tom."

She looked at Tommy. "Oh, you're the *haole* wants my boy to find those missing jewelries." Esther arched her eyebrows. "Say, you look kinda okay, for an old dude."

Tommy waved the gun at Gerald. "He told you."

"Damn straight he did."

"Then I guess I have to kill you both."

"Yeah, right, like no one never pointed a gun at my big fat ass before." In a swift, almost athletic motion that belied her heft, Esther grabbed the gun from Tommy. She pulled out the magazine and dropped the pistol in her cleavage, hoisted her dress, reached down and over her huge belly, and slid the clip inside her circus tent-sized panties. "Okay, handsome," she said, pointing at her crotch, "go get it."

Stunned, Tommy looked at Gerald, who shrugged and said, "She's had practice."

Esther held her palms up. "Looks like I got your attention."

Tommy saw something written on her hand: a number, the same as the ones he'd found on Ryan and Frank. "You negotiated with Jules."

"Not officially but we will once *hapa* boy here finds the gems." Esther cocked her head and held up her right index finger. She whispered, "Shhhh…You hear that?"

Tommy looked at Gerald, who gazed at his demolished television.

Esther shook her head. "Must be my imagination."

"Imagine giving me my gun," Tommy said.

Esther smirked. She reached inside her bra and removed a piece of paper. Tommy snatched it from her and studied it for several seconds.

"Now you ain't no 'hip-hop dude' far as I can tell, and I know my boy Dean, and you sure as hell ain't no Benjie Zamora, whoever the hell he is," Esther said. "And unless you got a 'brother' here on this island, then you gotta be the *haole* man the boy told me about."

Tommy said, "Screw you."

Esther pointed at her chest. "Reach in for the gun and we can call it foreplay. Better yet, go for the clip and you can say you got to third base."

Tommy rubbed his eyes. "What do you want?"

"Leave my bastard son, the island's best thief, to me to do this shit."

Gerald beamed. "Mom, I didn't know—"

"Quiet, dummy." Esther said to Tommy, "I taught him all he knows. Back on Oahu, there's nothing I can't steal and sell for profit. Same here, except now the boy helps. Plus, the restaurant takes up a lot of my time."

Esther lowered herself onto Gerald's cot. It bowed to within an inch of the floor. She picked up the pack beside her and looked inside. She glared at Gerald. "You dummy, what you doing stealing beach towels and this book?"

Gerald pointed at Tommy. "Wasn't me. He brought it."

She turned to Tommy. "You ain't much of a thief." She tossed the pack to him, and then patted the white plastic arm of a lawn chair, ignoring a pair of binoculars in the seat. "Sit down, handsome, we'll talk story."

Tommy slipped the pack on his shoulder. "I'll pass."

"'Kay den, I'll do the talking." Esther took a deep breath, and then said, "My cousin Herman, he got me to move here after the boy was born and I got in trouble back in Pearl City. Some bitch says she's gonna kill me, told me I was doing her man, which technically was true. When my apartment gets all shot up, I tell Herman, 'On my way.'"

Esther said, "I come here and cook for Herman at home. He says my grinds're way *ono*. One day the cops bust his cook, stupid bruddah has all these Laughing Buddha plants growing in his backyard. Well, Herman can't cook to save his life, so he makes me his chef. Then when he gets killed picking opihi, I take over the place."

Tommy said, "Opihi?"

"Kinda like barnacles, except you eat them," Esther said. "They live on sea cliffs and such. Anyway, we ran out one day, so I told Herman. He says he'll go get some. But this one big wave come up and washed his ass in the ocean."

Tommy said nothing.

"Him dying was kinda my fault," Esther said. "Sort of like the boy's Scottish daddy."

"'Tis a sad tale," Gerald said.

Esther said, "I take over the place and change the name to the Loco Moco Mama. Got it from Dean, my boy works at the jewelry store. You know Dean, I bet, 'cause you know Jules, too."

Tommy nodded.

"Dean comes in one day and he says to me, 'Mama, your loco moco, it's da kine.' Laters, I hire Mr. Lim, and taught him all the recipes," Esther said. "Rest is history. Speaking of Dean—one good kid, don't make no trouble. You think he knows about the diamonds?"

Tommy assumed Jules said something to the muscular ballplayer. Hell, he'd already spilled it to the Campanellas, why not get his own employee involved? "No idea."

Esther read the writing on her palm. "You think this is a good deal?"

"If you find them."

"And they're in some backpack, yeah?"

Tommy glared at Gerald.

"Brah," Gerald said, "look at her. Try lying to her when she's in a *bad* mood."

Esther laughed. "So, you make Scottish boy here help you find the gold and diamonds so you'd sell them to Jules. The boy, he'd get nothing from it. Maybe you'd kill his ass."

"What makes you think I would?"

"I'd do the same thing, I was you."

Gerald said, "Hey, wait a minute…"

Tommy held up the placemat. "Where'd you get it?"

"Two girls," Esther said, "they left it at the restaurant. You want I should describe them for you?"

"It's not necessary."

"Yeah," Gerald said. He reached back and rubbed his kidneys. "The fat one's mean. Truth."

Esther was about to say something when she again cocked her head and held up a hand. "You hear that?" She waited a beat. "Sounds like a car starting up."

Tommy said, "I don't have all day."

"Yeah, fine, okay. All right, who's the Benjie Zamora whose name's on the drawing? Someone else you tried to get to find your stuff? Maybe *he* got it all."

"No idea," Tommy said. But he decided he'd better find out.

"Well, since it looks like you ain't gonna kill me or my bastard son," Esther said, "maybe we can make us a deal."

"A deal."

"Uh huh."

"You and me."

"Is that so bad?"

In measured tones, Tommy said, "To hell with you, lady. To hell with you, to hell with your weirdo son, and to hell with Jules Matsumoto."

Esther said, "Wouldn't hurt you to expand your vocabulary."

He pointed at Gerald. "I should've known better. You were my biggest mistake."

"No worries," Gerald said. "Esther tells me the same thing all the time."

"And twice on Sundays, 'cause that's the day he was conceived," Esther said. "This means you're gonna try to find the jewelries on your own?"

Tommy nodded.

"You know," Esther said, "something goes wrong, you might be the third man I killed by accident."

"I'm not worried."

"Just be careful is all I'm saying. Besides, it looks like me and you, we're in a race." Esther stood, reached into her bosom, and removed the gun. She handed it to Tommy. "Take the damn thing. I got lots more."

Tommy slid the pistol in his waistband. "The clip?"

Esther raised her dress, exposing her gargantuan thighs and size six-XL underwear. "Dive in, baby, the water's fine."

"Perhaps another time."

Esther said, "How about before you split, we make a bet on the side? High stakes, just for fun."

"Fine."

"First one to get the jewels and gets most for them wins my restaurant."

"It'll never happen," Tommy said. "I'll be gone."

* * *

In a dripping wet mint green bathing suit, a white towel wrapped around her waist and Big Island guidebook in hand, Wanda Tess Fong crossed the King Kamehameha Hotel lobby to the front desk. "Howzit."

The desk clerk, a young woman, said, "Yes, ma'am, how can I help you?"

"Well, you see I was at the pool—it's an awesome pool."

"Thank you."

"Okay, this is the funniest thing," Wanda said. "I was having a good time and was getting ready to leave, and when I got out of the water and went to the lounge chair I was using, I couldn't find my room key card thingy."

"Oh, too bad."

"Yep," Wanda said. "I think maybe I forgot to take it with me plus I didn't have no place to keep it safe there by the pool, anyway, and I don't have my ID on me, either."

"I can help you," the desk clerk said. "What's your room number?"

"Um…" *What was it Noelani said?* "Yeah, it's 419."

Wanda watched the girl type something into her computer. She looked at the monitor, and then at Wanda. "You must be Mrs. Lohmiller."

"Yep, I am. My handsome hubby got into town like a day before me. I had to take care of some stuff back home in Vegas and just got here earlier today. He's off fishing or something, so I figured I can wait for him to get back, or get a new key, know what I mean?"

As Wanda rambled, the girl encoded a new key card. She handed it to Wanda. "There you are, Mrs. Lohmiller. Is there anything else I can do for you today?"

Wanda smiled at the key card. "Nope, I'm good."

"Have a great evening."

"Yeah, you too. *Mahalo.*" Wanda scurried across the lobby toward the elevators.

She got off on the fourth floor and tiptoed toward room 419, a zillion crazy ideas washing through her still-buzzing mind. Like, what if someone is dead in there, maybe the man in the striped shirt Noe saw with the Tom man earlier. Or maybe he was alive and waiting to kill Tom, or whoever walks through the door. He might have a gun.

Wanda felt her throat go dry.

Seeing the "Do Not Disturb" placard in the key card slot, she looked up and down the hallway. No other guests were in sight.

"Noe, I don't know how you do all this detective stuff," she said to herself. Then she removed the card, slid the key in the slot, and entered the room.

* * *

Hearing a loud noise in the shed, Noelani Lee drew her Ruger and ducked behind a trash can, just as Esther Halekealoha barreled across the yard, yelling at her son.

After Esther went inside the shed, Noelani sneaked across the yard until she was next to the outbuilding. She pressed her ear against the thin wall and listened to Tommy and Esther and Gerald discuss the missing gems—and her own diagram. But when Noelani smacked her arm in a failed attempt to swat an annoying fly, and heard Esther's resulting shush, she backpedaled to her Sentra. She double-checked the GPS monitor as she turned over the ignition. The green and red lights blinked but were not moving.

She drove toward the green signal, to an undeveloped area about a mile from Esther's house. The light glowed brighter and blinked with greater frequency as Noelani crossed scrubland and approached a hole in the ground.

Noelani lowered herself into the hole. She fell and landed on her butt, stood, dusted herself off, and checked out her surroundings. Even in the darkness, she made out bags and boxes scattered about the cave. Without a flashlight or a cigarette lighter, Noelani improvised and used her smartphone to provide illumination.

She sucked in a breath and said, "You have got to be kidding me."

She found two backpacks nestled against a box filled with small electronic gadgets. Noelani snatched the packs and prepared to exit the tube when the light from her phone reflected off something shiny, buried under rocks a few feet to her left.

It was a zipper. Noelani knelt and uncovered a third black backpack. She opened it; inside, she found a toiletry bag and an airline ticket.

Fiji, she thought. *I should go there one day.*

She opened the toiletry bag and looked inside. "Hmm."

As she prepared to leave, she made a last scan inside the cave. The light from her phone illuminated another object. *Don't see that every day. This could make things fun.*

She tossed the backpacks through the hole, picked up the other object—handling it with care as she'd never held one of those things before—and pulled herself out of the lava tube.

A moment later, as she collected the objects, her cell rang. "Hey there."

"Noe," Wanda Tess Fong said, "you need to get back, like soon."

"What's going on, Wanda?"

"You wouldn't believe me even if I told you."

Chapter Twenty-Three:
The Negotiations

Noelani Lee took it all in.

Two men, lashed to chairs. A fat one, naked—except for a black Rasta ball cap he wore backwards, and a bath towel covering his privates. He was cherry red and hairy all over and smelled like a mix of sweat and Old Spice.

The other one was slimmer, well-groomed, and wore sunglasses. He had frosted hair and bore an aromatic hint of Calvin Klein's Obsession. His unbuttoned, purple-striped shirt revealed a baby-smooth chest.

Neither one could talk. But they both wanted to, after Noelani told them Jules Matsumoto hired her to locate a backpack full of missing precious stones and jewelry.

SpongeBob Squarepants played in the background. Noelani turned off the TV.

"Ank oo," the one in the striped shirt said behind whatever was stuffed halfway down his throat.

Noelani said, "You found them this way?"

"Yep," Wanda said. "Like you told me to, I didn't touch nothing, except for throwing the towel on the naked dude. His, little *thing*, was nasty looking."

Through his belt-gag, the naked one said, "Iddle?"

Noelani bent over to get a good look at their faces. The fat red one was the same man she'd seen spying on Tom Lohmiller and the guy in the plaid shorts, and who also had breakfast with Jules Matsumoto. His eyes were belligerent. The other one was the same man Tom escorted into the hotel earlier in the afternoon. She removed his sunglasses and saw unbridled cockiness in his eyes.

Wanda said, "So who are they, cousin?"

"Friends of a friend or two." Noelani set the sunglasses aside. "We know them as 'hip-hop dude' and 'brother.'"

The one in the striped shirt: "Uht tuh uck?"

The other one squinted at Noelani. When it dawned on him, he closed his eyes and slumped in his chair. "Oh thit."

Noelani turned to face her cousin. "Wanda, do you remember the old game show called *Let's Make a Deal?*"

"Uh uh, people dress up funny and try to win cash or fabulous prizes."

"I'm sure you fellows are familiar with it, too."

Both men nodded.

"Good. Well, here's how we play the Hawaiian version," Noelani said. "I'll start by making an offer to you both. The first one who accepts gets a free pass, but only if he tells me everything he knows about Tom Lohmiller, Jules Matsumoto, and a backpack full of missing heirloom jewelry."

The men looked at each other with poker faces.

"The loser," she said, "will spend the night with one of my favorite Big Island police detectives. I should warn you, he has severe anger management issues and lives in the middle of nowhere." She clapped her hands. "Okay, who's ready to play?"

The men pleaded through their gags and, despite the binds around their ankles, tried to kick each other. As they got louder, Noelani turned the TV back on. SpongeBob Squarepants and his friends in Bikini Bottom again filled the room with their boisterous foibles. The two men compensated by increasing the volume of their mumbles.

"Looks like we don't have a winner," Wanda said.

Noelani watched in mild amusement as the sunburnt one continued his unintelligible protests. She also noticed as the clothed one calmed down and evened out his breathing. He looked her in the eye as the naked one continued his muffled bitching.

Noelani muted the TV and pulled wadded-up socks from the man's mouth. She tossed them to the floor and wiped his saliva on his shirt.

"Hey, ease up," he said. "Thing's custom-tailored."

Noelani said, "Get to the point and fast."

The naked one whined and slumped in his chair.

Noelani said, "And your name is…?"

"Ryan, and the first thing I want to say is, considering I've had those nasty socks crammed in my mouth, you think I can have something to drink?"

Wanda went to the bathroom and returned with a plastic cup filled with water.

"Are you serious?" he said. "Tap?"

Wanda blinked once before she poured the water over his

head. The sunburned one snorted.

"Before we continue," Noelani said, "I'm going to go out on a limb and say you're this one's brother."

"No matter how many times I flush, he never goes away," Ryan said. Water dripped down his face. "But yeah, Frank here's my brother, which in essence makes me an only child. How'd you know?"

Noelani looked at Frank. "Nice hat."

Frank mumbled through his gag.

Noelani asked Ryan to tell her his story. He cleared his throat and claimed he obtained the gems from a wholesaler in Arizona with the intent of brokering them to an overseas retailer.

"Iar," Frank said.

Ryan ignored him. "I handed them to Tommy Chunks to—"

"Excuse me?"

"What?"

"Who?"

"Tommy Chunks," Ryan said.

"Who's he," Noelani said, "Tom Lohmiller?'

"Yeah, if you wanna be formal about it."

"What kind of name is 'Chunks'?"

"A term of endearment."

Noelani shook her head. "Go on."

Ryan said he gave Tommy the gems for delivery to a good friend in the Caribbean, as a gift. But instead, Tommy jetted off to Hawaii. Ryan detailed his conversation with Jules after his arrival on the island, including the explanation of how Tommy lost the backpack during the crash landing of Island Skipper Flight 2.

"Jules told me Tommy's planning on using the money so he can retire in Japan," Ryan said.

"Ount Uji," Frank said.

"Whatever."

Noelani took it all in. "Then Tommy Ch—Tom Lohmiller's the anonymous courier Jules claimed lost the gems at a restaurant."

"He told you that?" Ryan laughed.

"So then, it wasn't the kid," Wanda said.

Ryan said, "What kid?"

"Don't worry your pretty little head," Noelani said. Frank laughed behind his gag. "You said Jules hooked you up with a gun."

"And now our mutual friend Tommy's got it."

"Um ath," Frank said.

Noelani turned her attention to Frank. "You have a lot to say."

"Uh huh."

"Then let's hear it."

"Big mistake," Ryan said.

"Uck oo, oo aggot."

Noelani removed Frank's belt-gag.

Frank looked Noelani up and down. "Shit, girl, you're kinda hot for a semi-Asian Hawaiian chick."

"For the record," Noelani said, "I'm part Chinese and Korean but also part native Hawaiian and Portuguese. With lots of other stuff thrown in."

"What-the-fuck-ever," Frank said. "I hope you don't believe all the garbage my heterosexually-challenged brother here just laid on you."

Before Ryan could respond, Noelani said, "Right now I'm not sure who or what to believe, but I've got an open mind. Go ahead, and hurry, please."

Frank told Noelani he lined up the jewels from a wholesaler in California and planned to re-sell them to the same overseas colleague Ryan mentioned.

"And there's the bullshit," Ryan said.

However, Frank continued, the California wholesaler told him Ryan swooped in on them first, which Frank said was a Grade-A violation of the family business code. He then told Noelani about his meeting with Jules, which included the same explanation of how Tommy lost the gems.

"As you can see, little bro here screwed me over," Frank said. "The weasel's got balls on him, but no family loyalty at all."

"Wow, Noe," Wanda said. "I'm no expert but I'm thinking after hearing these guys talk story, they're both liars. Don't you think?"

"Up to a point," Noelani said. "Look, fellas, I don't care where those diamonds and gold rings came from. It doesn't matter to me, and it's a good thing you keep it to yourselves. But what I understand based on what you two…gentlemen…just said, is my client, Jules Matsumoto, lied to me."

"Yeah." Frank grinned. "Ain't that a pip?"

"Now you know what's going on," Ryan said, "what are you going to do next, besides letting me go and leaving him here?"

"Not so fast." Noelani nodded at Frank. "Where are your clothes?"

"Ask numbnuts here."

Ryan said, "I thought it was a nice touch, leaving him here for Tommy to find like this."

"You're a true artist," Noelani said. "Speaking of which, I have something to show you." She went into the bathroom and emerged a moment later with a black backpack.

Frank and Ryan's eyes widened. "Oh, fuck me," Frank said.

Ryan flashed on the pack Tommy displayed before he left the room. "Uh, wait, what the hell?"

Noelani unzipped the pack and removed a brown toiletry bag. Its contents made a tinkling sound when she shook it.

Ryan said, "Okay, we can work something out, right?"

"Screw you," Frank said, "those're just as much mine as yours."

"For the last time, dipshit," Ryan said, "you fucked up, so I—"

"Screwed me, yeah, I know." Frank said to Noelani, "Give 'em to me. All he'll do is give them to a douchebag French poker shark in Bimini."

"Barbados, dammit."

"Both of you," Noelani said, "be quiet."

Ryan glared at her. "Lady, those're mine, all right?"

Noelani dropped the toiletry bag in the pack. "I'm not sure I follow."

"Yeah, me, too," Wanda said.

Noelani looked at Frank. "What's all of this about Barbados?"

"Here's the truth as God is my witness," Frank said. "Baby bro here stole them from some old broad behind my back and him and Tommy worked together to screw me out of my cut."

"Frank, just shut your mouth for once." Ryan turned to face Noelani. "The truth is, Tommy stole them from *me*—"

"After you stole them from the dead woman," Frank said.

"Give them to me and let me go. What you do with my useless brother is your problem, not mine."

Noelani said nothing for several long moments.

Wanda scrunched her eyebrows. "Noe, what are you thinking?"

Frank said, "She thinking she's gonna give me the gems, right, sweetheart?" He leaned over and whispered, "I'll cut you in for a quarter of what Jules gives me."

"Frank, I'm sitting right here," Ryan said.

Noelani told Frank to whisper to her how much Jules offered him for the gems. When he did, she stood upright and stared past them, out the lanai toward the ocean. Frank smirked at Ryan.

"What'd he say, Noe?" Wanda said. "How much?"

"Same as what Jules was going to pay me," Ryan said. "Come on, lady, you're not serious about this. Are you?"

Noelani said, "I'm thinking, I'm thinking." She scratched the side of her nose. "I'm also thinking we need to get you both out of here before Tom Lohmiller comes back. Tell me, where are his clothes?"

"Dumpster out back," Ryan said. "Where they belong."

"Jesus H. Christ," Frank said, "you know how much those garmz cost me?"

Noelani looked at Wanda. "Let's get them to our room as best we can, without anyone noticing. Especially the red one."

"Shit's already itchy," Frank said. "One guess where it itches the most, babe."

"You're one gross buggah," Wanda said. "Okay, cousin, so after we do that, what happens next?"

Noelani said, "I'm not sure yet."

"Just a warning," Frank said, "you cannot trust my little bro at all."

Ryan said, "Yeah, and you're a regular Boy Scout."

"Knock it off before I change my mind." Noelani leaned over. "Once we get you upstairs, I have other business to attend to. In the meantime, be good and treat my favorite cousin with the respect she's due. Because if you don't, Tom Lohmiller will be the least of your worries."

She said to Wanda, "There's a luggage cart in the hall—can you get it for me please?"

Then, over the brothers' strident and foul objections, she stuffed the socks back in Ryan's mouth and tightened the belt around Frank's yammering trap.

* * *

After Pilates, Veronica Keawe met a pair of girlfriends for shopping at a high-end resort on the rugged Kohala Coast, north of Kailua-Kona.

One friend, married to the CEO of a commercial real estate development company, splurged on a Tahitian black-pearl necklace for herself and matching cufflinks for her husband.

Her other friend, the wife of Hawaii's leading restaurant food wholesaler, couldn't resist the temptation of a bottle of Clive Christian No. 1 perfume.

As the trio meandered through the shops, an empty-handed Veronica excused herself and went to a nearby restroom. Inside a locked stall, she called her husband. "Hi, baby, so what are you up to today?"

"All kinds of good stuff," Dean Pahukoa said.

"Has the…Jules person called you in?"

"Nope, I left him a message to say I'm sick, so he's not bothering me, yeah."

"Any progress with your other chore?"

Dean said, "Me and the kid here been talking and we got a real good plan."

"Does this mean you're about to get my—the diamonds for me—us?" Veronica's heart leaped as she recalled a red leather crocodile-print Dooney & Bourke bag, retailing for almost six hundred dollars, she had seen in one of the shops.

"Oh yeah," Dean said. "All me and the kid gotta do is—"

"Good. Love ya." She hung up and dashed from the restroom, credit card in hand.

Chapter Twenty-Four:
The Ones that Got Away

Noelani Lee said to Wanda Tess Fong, "You'll be okay. Just don't untie them."

Using a baggage cart, the cousins hauled Ryan and Frank Campanella to their room two floors up. There, they placed the brothers facing each other in their darkened closet.

Wanda said, "I swear the hairy one keeps checking out my butt."

Noelani removed an orange blouse and white Capri pants from a drawer and laid them on her bed. "I won't be late. This meeting shouldn't take long."

Wanda lowered her voice to a whisper. "It's with the Benjie kid?"

"Him and a 'friend.' I have a couple of stops after, but I'll make it quick."

"What kind of stops?"

"I need to do some shopping."

Wanda pouted. "And I can't go along?"

"It's not that kind of shopping," Noelani said. "It's for work."

"Well, be careful. Anything happens to you and I'm stuck with these buggahs, I don't know what I'll do." Wanda looked at the closet. "What *are* we gonna do with them?"

"Depends on what happens next," Noelani said.

"Which is…?"

Noelani put an index finger over her lips. She took Wanda by the hand and led her to the other side of the room. She whispered, "What I should have done all along."

"What's that, Noe?"

"I'm going to give the people what they want."

* * *

Jules Matsumoto assured the prematurely gray fifty-something woman from Missouri that the sea turtle pendant in her hand was of the finest quality, a design unlike any other in all of Hawaii.

"It's from my latest line of Island Creations," he said. "It also is the last turtle in stock from this particular collection, which makes it particularly unique."

"Well, I don't know," the woman said. "Tell me again how much."

"I have it listed at seven-hundred fifty." He flashed a condescending smile. "Look, considering this is your last day on the island, I'm willing to make a deal."

The woman blinked at him.

"Out the door, with tax, six hundred."

She hesitated. "I should talk to my husband first."

"Ma'am, I understand. But think of how this piece will remind you of what surely must be a wonderful Hawaiian holiday." Jules noticed the sunburn on her neck. "Is this your first time here?"

She said, "My husband saved up and surprised me with this trip for our twenty-seventh wedding anniversary."

"Ah, well, congratulations. Tell me, what does your husband do for a living?"

"He's director of marketing for the *Jump, Jive, and Jesus! Show* at the Down Home Countrypolitan Theater in Branson."

Jules studied the plain, chunky cross hanging on a chain around her neck. Twenty-four karat plated, and in need of a good cleaning. "I've heard of it. People tell me it's a terrific, spiritually uplifting show."

"Some people think mixing jazz and the Gospels is blasphemous," the woman said. "But we believe the Lord spoke to his flock as much through Louis Prima as he did through his many blessed miracles."

"Amen, sister," Jules said. "Well, to keep earthly and heavenly peace in your household, you tell me—what price is fair to me as a businessman, but also agreeable to your pragmatic husband?"

Before the woman could respond, the shop door flew open and Tommy Chunks stormed in with a black backpack. His expression told Jules this was not a social call.

Tommy ignored the woman holding the sea turtle pendant as approached the counter. "Your office. Now."

Jules felt his heart sink. "Well, sir, how about you wait for me for a few seconds while I take care of this lovely young lady?"

The woman blushed.

"Five minutes," Tommy said. "One second longer, and you're a dead man."

The woman blanched.

Tommy went into the office and sat behind Jules's desk.

"Goodness." The woman clutched the cross hanging from her neck. "Did he just say he's going to kill you?"

Jules reassumed his sales demeanor. "He's a friend from way back. He jokes." He looked at Tommy through the window between the office and the sales floor, and then at a handgun and the backpack sitting on the desk in front of Tommy. "Ma'am, I'm in the process of clearing out inventory because I have a new collection which will be ready soon. What would your husband say to two hundred, total, with tax?"

"Do you take American Express?"

Jules completed the transaction and, when the woman left, flipped the "Open" sign to "Closed" and locked the door.

He went to the office and took the unfamiliar seat on the wrong side of his desk. He looked first at the gun, and then into Tommy's furious green eyes.

"I wasn't expecting you today," Jules said. "I see you found the goods."

Tommy sat back, hands folded in his lap. He nodded toward the pack. "This isn't them. This is nothing."

Jules weighed the foolhardiness of lunging for the gun and shooting Tommy. He could tell the cops the man at his desk was a robber and it was self-defense. Maybe the religious lady would back his story, considering she witnessed his threat and because he gave her a generous discount.

Tommy said, "When were you planning to tell me the Moron Brothers were here?"

"What—I have no idea what you mean."

Tommy pointed to the Colt. "Recognize the piece?"

Jules knew there was no escaping the truth, so he opted to tell a variation thereof. "Tommy, they dropped in, unexpected. I had no idea those idiots would figure out you came to Hawaii. And believe me, I didn't tell them you were here."

"Uh huh."

"Come on, we're talking about two lamebrains who can't spell 'dog' if you spotted them the *d* and the—"

"What did you promise them?"

"Nothing," Jules said. "They demanded I keep my mouth shut about them being here. I would've called you but those guys? I just figured you and Gerald, working together, you'd find the gems before either of them would."

"He's a waste of perfectly good sperm," Tommy said. "And his mother is not human." He picked up the Colt. "Nice piece you got Ryan."

"He didn't give me much choice."

Tommy tucked the Colt in his waistband. "Surprised you didn't hook Frank up with one, too."

Jules glanced at the baseball bat leaning against the wall, next to his desk.

Tommy shook his head. "Don't even think about it." He took two pieces of paper, one of them a napkin, from his wallet, and slid them across the desk. "Look familiar?"

Jules worked up saliva in his arid mouth. "They pressured me; they made me do it against my will. I had to come up with something."

"Just like the big, ugly woman did when you wrote the same exact number on her big, fat hand. The same exact number you quoted me over the phone. Right, Jules?"

Silence enveloped the office as Jules waited for Tommy to say something, knowing whatever defense he offered would be pointless.

Unable to take it any longer, Jules said, "What did you do with them?"

Tommy leaned across the desk. "Tell me about the woman."

"Which woman?" Jules said.

From another pocket, Tommy produced the diagram Esther Halekealoha gave him. He relayed her story about how two women left it behind at the Loco Moco Mama.

"You don't know a flat-chested Hawaiian girl or her short, fat, talkative cousin?" Tommy said, "This is her pack. You never met either one?"

Jules shook his head. "No, Tommy."

"The tall one knows a lot. This drawing is her work. And, look, she put you right in the middle of this thing."

"Tommy, you think Esther's not going to lie to you?"

Tommy motioned toward the placemat. "Benjie Zamora?"

"Honest to God," Jules said, "I have no idea."

"Your man, Dean." Tommy placed a blue box with the name and logo of N. Romanov & Sons on the desk. "I know he's looking for this."

Jules opened the box. "Wow." *White gold*, he thought. *Not my forte but I could make it work.*

"Yeah, 'wow.' He's trying to find them. But why do I get the feeling he's also looking for my stuff?" Tommy nabbed the box from Jules. "If you want this to work, you need to double your offer."

Jules said, "Tommy, there's no way. You'll break me."

"Your inventory's low. Esther knows this, too, so she's looking now. By the way, how much does she and her son bring in for you a year?"

When Jules stammered, Tommy said, "It's what the market will bear. And I'll be a silent partner in this business of yours. At least until we're squared away."

Tommy stood and picked up the pack. Jules remained seated. "Stop dicking with me, Jules. Knock off the games. We're partners now. No local chicks, no jerk-offs in plaid shorts, no moron brothers, no buff ballplayers, and no big, fat, mean women. I'll find the stuff on my own, and you will buy it only from me, exclusively. If anyone else brings it to you, you let me know and I'll take care of them. *Comprende?*"

Jules had never heard Tommy string together so many words at one time, which unnerved him even more as Tommy's rant underscored his frustration. "I understand how upset you are right now, and sincerely, I don't blame you one bit."

"When I find the goods," Tommy said, "and I will, you will have one hour to make up your mind. You'll either hold up your end of the bargain, or you'll go swimming in lava."

"One hour," Jules said. "Okay."

"And after you go for a nice, hot dip, I'll take my business elsewhere. Understood?"

Jules nodded.

"I have things to do, long term," Tommy said. "But you've got customers to keep happy in the short run. Orders to fill. Lucrative ones, I'm assuming."

Juice to buy, too. "Tommy, I feel bad about how this all played out, so anything I can do to make amends, I will."

"Live up to your end, and you'll live."

Jules said, "You have my word on it."

Tommy slapped Jules on the shoulder. "Later, partner." He let himself out.

And at that moment, Jules threw up.

* * *

"Uck oo, aggot."

"Ith ma ath, thit foah bains."

The closet door flew open. Wanda Tess Fong said, "You dummies, shut up already. I'm trying to watch Dr. Phil."

The brothers looked at each other, and then at the floor.

Wanda slid the door shut. "Forget it. I'm out of here."

* * *

Tommy Chunks caught the attention of a young woman working at the King Kamehameha Hotel's front desk.

"Aloha," she said, "how may I help you?"

"Tom Lohmiller. Room 419. Any messages?"

She typed something on her computer. "No, Mr. Lohmiller, no messages."

He nodded and turned to walk away.

"Sir?"

"Yes?"

"How was your fishing trip?"

Tommy blinked. "Fishing."

"Yes," she said. "Your wife picked up a new key earlier today and said you were deep-sea fishing. Did you catch anything?"

"Not yet." Tommy blinked. "My wife."

"She said she lost hers or forgot it or something when she was at the pool. I hope it was okay—I made a new one for her."

"Of course," Tommy said. "Thank you."

The girl whispered, "Sir, it's none of my business, but I think I smelled alcohol on her breath."

"She likes the occasional drink."

Tommy thanked her and walked to the pool, where he saw Wanda Tess Fong reclining on a lounge, reading her Big Island guidebook. Then he continued to the elevators.

Exiting on the sixth floor, Tommy scanned the hallway before he went to his room. The "Do Not Disturb" card was still in place.

Once inside, his heart sank. There was no hula music on the TV, no sound of any kind. Not only was the television turned off, but the two chairs and their bound-and-gagged occupants were gone.

In their place, on the dresser beside the television, he found a note written on hotel stationery:

> *Hi, Tom!*
> *Your friends were bored so we took them for a*
> *ride.*
> *Meet us in the lobby at 7 p.m.*
> *The Girls*

Tommy crumpled the note and tossed it aside. He leaned against the dresser and rubbed his eyes. Then he undressed and prepared to take a shower.

Chapter Twenty-Five:
The Diversionary Tactics

Just as Jules Matsumoto finished cleaning vomit from his office carpet, he heard a knock on his door.

He opened it and felt his shoulders sag. "Oh, great."

"Awful nice to see you, too," Esther Halekealoha said. "You try the pork like I suggested?"

"Esther, what can I do for you?"

She shoved him aside and leaned over a display case filled with tiny gold-plated figurines. "Hey, ain't that the one dude, who is he? Da kine original *Hawaii Five-O* cop."

"Steve McGarrett."

"The one next to him looks like Magnum. You make Hawaiian TV cops into jewelry, huh." Esther grinned at him. "I think they call it 'irony,' yeah."

Jules said, "Those are just two of six limited-edition pieces from our discontinued *Aloha Law* collection. They're marked down for quick sale, if you're interested. Now, what the heck do you *want*, Esther?"

"Ain't what I want matters. Well, maybe a little." She pointed toward the office. "Let's go talk story."

Jules sat behind the desk as Esther squeezed her substantial frame into the guest chair. She scrunched her nose. "Damn, brah," she said, "your office smelling rank."

Jules reached for his baseball bat, but Esther leaned across the desk, her belly pushing aside everything in its path, and slapped a beefy mitt on his shoulder. "Leave it where it is, this ain't da kine social call."

He relented and placed his hands on the desk, fingers laced together. "What do you want?"

Esther sat back. "Let's start with this." She lobbed a white, rectangular box toward him.

Jules opened it. He recognized the container—several years old, yes, but one of his nonetheless—but its contents were unfamiliar.

Esther said, "How much you give me for them?"

Jules lifted an earring from the box. He took a loupe from his desk drawer and examined the piece. "Where did you get this?"

"You never ask me before. I didn't think you cared."

"I don't. It's just this is awfully cheap crap."

"How cheap you talking?"

Jules placed the earring back in the box. "Whatever you paid was too much. I've seen this same set for twenty bucks at Kmart."

Esther slapped her forehead. "No wonder the bitch ran off fast as she did."

"Next time one of your tweaker pals sells you something," Jules said, "make sure you ask for a receipt."

Esther laughed. "Yeah, you're a funny man, Jules. Well, now we got that out the way, tell me something—where's the nice Dean boy works for you? I missed him at breakfast this morning."

"Dean called in sick."

"You think?" Esther said. "My boy Dean *never* misses breakfast."

Jules tossed it around in his head. Dean rarely took days off, and never two in a row. "What are you getting at?"

"Mmmm, maybe he's trying to find them jewels you was waiting for the Tom man to bring you."

"Excuse me?"

Esther picked up the placemat diagram from Jules's desk. Jules forgot Tommy Chunks had left it there. "It's all on this paper here, brah. Looks like your buddy Tom came by to see you, too, huh? Plus what I know from talking story with the man myself."

Jules reached for the paper. "Give me that."

Esther held the diagram out of his reach. "I don't know who the sistah is who drew this, but I think she's involved someways. I get the feeling she's looking for the stuff, too. You think?"

Jules didn't respond.

"And look, there's Dean's name. Now I ain't no expert, but I see Dean on here and I think, he's gotta be hunting, too, and he's not telling you he is."

"Dean would never go behind my back."

"Eh, well, no matters, me and *hapa* Scottish boy're gonna find the jewelries," Esther said. "And when we do and if you still want them, and I know you will 'cause I know *you*, you're gonna pay, big time. I mean more'n this." She held up her hand.

Jules read his own handwriting on her wide palm. "Esther, it's the best I can do."

"Man, you're like a broken record. All I ever hear from you is 'this is all it's worth' and 'cash is kinda tight' and 'what the market will bear.'" Esther stood and dropped the placemat on the desk. "We got what they call the 'new normal' now, Jules. So how about me and you talk again bumbye when I got the shit for you?"

Jules looked up at her but avoided direct eye contact. He couldn't speak.

"'Kay den," she said. "I gotta get back to the grinds. Hey, by the way—I know this one woman, she clean this place up good. No more stink."

* * *

Noelani Lee spotted Benjie Zamora in the Walmart parking lot. He stood next to a silver Infiniti, talking with a muscular Hawaiian man.

She recognized him as the same kid she'd seen walking down Ali'i Drive with a black backpack. The muscle-bound guy was Benjie's invisible friend on the phone, Dean Pahukoa—the baseball player with the greasy hair and bad breath who worked for Jules Matsumoto.

Noelani watched as Dean said something to Benjie. Through Benjie's body language, she gathered his responses bordered on apathetic—his wandering eyes and slumped shoulders did his talking for him.

Dean said, "You got our story straight, yeah?"
Benjie nodded. "But I don't think she's gonna go for it."
"C'mon, she will."
"Not if this Mr. Lohmiller already hired her."
"Dude, she never did say that." Dean leaned over Benjie and lowered his voice. "Just like we talked about—you tell her she finds the jewels, she gets a big cut." He waited a beat, and then said, "Well, not too big, but whatever she charges to find stuff."
Benjie said, "Yeah, whatever."
"And don't forget, you don't mention me 'cause she knows

who I am."

"Okay."

"It's all your idea, as far as she knows, yeah." Dean slapped Benjie's upper arm. "All right, brah, she'll be here soon. Do your thing and pretty soon, we'll be rolling in the dough."

Noelani watched as Benjie rubbed his arm and Dean jogged to a small white building, which housed a kiosk for refilling large water bottles. She waited a couple of seconds for Dean to hide behind the structure before she made a loop through the lot and parked beside Benjie and the Infiniti. She got out of her car and approached him. "Are you Benjie Zamora?"

He nodded.

"I'm Noelani Lee." She stood facing him, with her back toward the water kiosk.

Benjie gave her a thin smile. "Thanks for meeting us—me."

Noelani said, "What are you, nineteen, twenty?"

"Twenty."

"What's a guy your age need with a licensed private investigator?"

Benjie looked around the parking lot. Noelani watched his eyes settle on a spot behind her.

"Let me guess," she said, "you think your girlfriend is cheating on you."

"No, I don't have a girlfriend. I mean, not right now."

"It's one of my specialties. Keep me in mind for the future." She winked. "Well, then why else would a college kid like you want to hire me?"

"Well, I…hey, how do you know I'm in college?"

"I saw how much U-H charged you for that botany textbook," Noelani said. "Can we say 'rip off'?"

Benjie took a deep breath. "Do you have my textbook?"

"Not any more. And I don't have the koala either."

Benjie bowed his head. "You mean Ozzie. I've had him since I was a little kid."

"And you kept him."

"He, uh, comforts me."

"So I discovered," Noelani said.

Benjie looked at her and blushed.

Noelani motioned with her head toward the water kiosk. "I know Dean's watching so don't do anything to make him think you're about to blow this. What was his plan, anyway?"

Benjie, feeling for the first time since the plane crash like someone lifted a ton of crap off his shoulders, let out a deep sigh. He told Noelani it was Dean's idea for her find a missing backpack, with the added explanation it contained valuable stuff he'd been hired to deliver from Oahu to Jules Matsumoto.

"Wow," Noelani said. "Dean thought that would work."

Benjie shrugged. "His idea was, if me and you found it, we'd take it to Dean and he'd sell the gold and diamonds to Jules, and we'd pay you part of whatever Jules paid us."

"But Dean has no plans to give them to Jules, does he?"

Benjie shook his head. "His wife, she's a beauty queen or something, she wants to sell them and use the money to remodel their house. Something about kids and a spa."

Noelani said, "You had the pack with the jewels for a while, didn't you?"

"Uh huh. I didn't know what to do with it. I mean I was going to sell them to Jules. I was in his shop and this mean, sweaty white dude walks in, and I freaked."

She grinned. "I don't blame you."

"You know the dude?"

"Kind of."

"Well," Benjie said, "I hid them in this place I used to go to when I was a kid."

"A lava tube." When he responded with a puzzled look, she said, "Been there."

"I figured I can hide them there and get rid of them later," Benjie said. "There was an airline ticket, too, for this Thomas Lohmiller. But when I found your business card at home, I figured he hired you to find them."

"No, officially I'm working for Jules Matsumoto," Noelani said. "The reason I left you my card is because my cousin was on the same plane as you and lost her backpack during the crash landing. And in the process of trying to find it, I've gotten to know Mr. Lohmiller and some other interesting people fairly well in the past few days."

Benjie said, "Wait, so if this stuff belongs to the Lohmiller dude, why'd Jules hire you?"

"To find Mr. Lohmiller's pack. It's kind of complicated."

"Will Lohmiller kill me if he knows I had his things?"

"I sure hope not," Noelani said. "Tell me how you got involved with Dean."

Benjie described how Dean Pahukoa and Veronica Keawe somehow figured out he had the jewels and forced him to hand them over. He described their trip to the lava tube but when they got there, the jewels were gone. "Do you know where the jewels are?"

"Benjie, listen." Noelani peeked over her left shoulder, and then lowered her voice to a near-whisper. "Here's what you do—when your friend Dean asks if I said 'yes' to the job, tell him I did."

"Uh, what?" Benjie looked behind Noelani. "You'll do it?"

"Tell him I promised you I'll have the jewels for him and his wife tomorrow morning at the latest."

Benjie blinked. "Wait—you can get them?"

"But understand," Noelani said, "you'll have to settle for something, um, *different* than a share of the money they'll get for selling the stuff."

"What do you mean?"

She handed him one of her cards and a pen. "Write your cell number on here for me." He did as she asked and handed her the card. She told him to keep the pen.

Without another word, Noelani climbed in her Sentra. She waved to Benjie and drove to an empty space closer to the Walmart's entrance. There, she took a small receiver device and a pair of ear buds from her glove box. Despite some interference, she listened as a tiny microphone on the pen she'd just given Benjie picked up his conversation with Dean.

Dean said, "The sistah go for it?"

"Yeah, I think she did."

"You told her we're gonna pay her when she finds the diamonds and we get them sold—she was cool?"

Benjie nodded. He had to pee bad.

Dean grinned. "Shoots, brah, I told you, you could do it. No worries."

"What're you going to tell your wife?" Benjie said.

"Don't worry, I'll handle Roni. She'll be all jacked."

"Look, now that this is over, can you take me home?"

"C'mon brah, let's get some beer and celebrate."

"See, I can't," Benjie said. "It's lasagna night."

* * *

In the parking lot behind the Ali'i Sunset Plaza, Gerald Kapono MacTavish sat in his car, eyes closed, thinking.

Freed from Tom Lohmiller's shackles, his servitude now was exclusive to Esther. The bad part was, if he found the jewelry for her, and she sold it to the Jules dude, Gerald's cut would be a pittance—if he got anything at all.

On the other hand, if he found it and left Esther in the dark, not tell her a word about it, he could rake in the windfall and be a man of leisure. No longer would he live in a steamy, stinking shed in his mother's backyard. Gone would be the days of lifting wallets and cameras from tourists to feed her insatiable demand and that of her back-door cash customers. Instead, he could commit petty theft for sport.

if someone paid him enough for the goods, he could afford a journey to ancient Alba. It would be a glorious trek, to the highlands, the lowlands, the uplands. He'd sail the seas to the Hebrides, and the isles Shetland and Orkney.

In his brogue, he said to himself, "Give me but one hour of Scotland, let me see it ere I die."

The hairs on the back of his neck stood when he heard a horrid sound, familiar yet strange, coming from the vicinity of the Loco Moco Mama.

He got out of the car and followed the noise to the rear of the restaurant, where he found Bruce, the intruder from Hilo, with a backpack over his shoulders—and Gerald's precious bagpipes in his hands.

Bruce blew into the blowstick with such force his cheeks threatened to explode. His fingers fumbled with the chanter. The sound he produced was hideous and unbecoming an instrument as ancient and noble as the pipes.

"Stop it," Gerald said, his brogue ratcheted up commensurate with his aggravation. "Ye are unworthy of the pipes. *My* pipes."

Bruce stopped blowing. "Dude, to interrupt my musical stylings is beyond bogus. It's ultra-bogus."

Gerald gritted his teeth and felt his hands form into fists. He took a step toward Bruce, ready to do damage.

Bruce said, "Allow me to extend my apologies for my off-kilter play. Get it? Off-*kilt*er?" He laughed in a hoarse snicker.

Gerald stopped and unclenched his fists. He gazed at his pipes and worried that Bruce had forever ruined them.

"Before you commence beating me," Bruce said, "I believe I may have not just one thing you seek, but two." He pointed at the backpack with a thumb.

"Aye?"

"I overheard your conversation with the freak of nature known as your 'mother' earlier today," Bruce said. "By the way, the shed you live in—did you get an adjustable or are you fixed?"

At that moment, Mr. Lim emerged from the restaurant's back door. He stepped outside, lit a cigarette and stuffed his hands in his pockets. He turned to face Gerald and Bruce.

Bruce motioned toward the cook. "What about him?"

"Not to worry," Gerald said. "No English."

Bruce eyed Mr. Lim. "All right," he said. "I know you're looking for some most excellent diamonds and gold. Your mission, should you choose to accept it, is to figure out if they are in the pack strapped to my back. If you choose the pipes as your lovely parting gift, I get to keep whatever is in the bag. But if you select the pack, I keep the pipes."

Gerald looked at the pipes, and then the pack, and again at the pipes.

"When you make up your mind, I will do something big," Bruce said. "Something mega. Something most totally excellent."

"What's that?"

"You'll never see me in Kona again." Bruce took off the backpack and held it in his left hand. He cradled the bagpipes against his chest with his right. "I'll stay in Hilo and go about my life, soaking in our annual average rainfall of one-hundred thirty inches. Although I must admit, I find the dry air on this side of the island more agreeable to my growing roster of allergies."

Gerald stepped closer. "You mean it this time?"

As Bruce hummed the countdown tune from *Jeopardy!*,

Gerald swiped the backpack.

Bruce looked at his empty hand. "Excellent."

Gerald unzipped the pack and removed a brown toiletry bag. He opened it and looked over his shoulder at Mr. Lim. The cigarette dangling from the cook's mouth enhanced his detached demeanor. Gerald turned to Bruce and smiled.

But his happiness turned to distress when he heard Esther's voice bellow from inside the restaurant. "Hey, is the boy out there? Where's the *hapa* bastard?"

"Sounds like Mount Momsuvius is about to blow," Bruce said. "Maybe you should make a hasty exit before she gets her gigantic hands on you and leaves me to mop up hurl and lung butter."

Without pausing to close either the toiletry bag or backpack, Gerald snatched the bagpipes from Bruce and bolted to the parking lot. He disappeared around a corner as Esther Halekealoha burst through the service door.

She said to Mr. Lim, "I hear my son back here?"

The cook shrugged and muttered something in Hokkien under his breath.

"Damn, I thought I heard his Scottish…" Esther stared at Bruce. "Who the hell're you?"

"I'm nobody and prefer to stay that way."

"Good, then maybe you get out of here, yeah?" Esther looked down at Mr. Lim. "When you finish the cancer stick, get your butt back to the kitchen cuz we got the dinner rush starting soon." She turned on her hefty heel and went back into the restaurant.

A moment later, Mr. Lim dropped what remained of his cigarette and stamped it out. He erupted in laughter.

Bruce scrunched his eyebrows and said, "I'm glad you find this so humorous."

The cook pointed at Bruce, and then toward the parking lot, in the general direction of Gerald. "*Phah chhíu-chhèng,*" he said. He made a motion simulating male masturbation.

Bruce scratched his nose. "Uh, *yo no hablo los* Chinese, bro."

Mr. Lim nodded toward the parking lot. "Him *khàm lān.*" He pointed at his crotch. "Big *khàm lān.*" He laughed again, said something else Bruce did not understand, and went inside the restaurant.

As Mr. Lim opened the back door, Bruce noticed something peculiar about him. Something out of place for a humble short-order cook toiling at a small but popular Hawaiian plate-lunch restaurant.

Some shiny and sparkly things on his fingers.

* * *

With his belly full of lasagna and his parents settled in to watch *Entertainment Tonight*, Benjie Zamora stepped outside. Some old high school buddies had promised they'd pick him up for an evening of lukewarm beers and rented porn.

Instead, Benjie encountered a tall, older man on his front porch, with a big gun in his hand. The man motioned toward a car parked on the street.

"Get in."

Benjie's knees wobbled. "I think I need to pee."

The man grabbed Benjie by the arm and dragged him to the car. He shoved him inside and got in behind the wheel and started the engine.

As they pulled away, Benjie gazed back at his boyhood home, certain he would never see it again. "I need to go bad."

The man said, "You're Benjie Zamora."

Benjie felt like someone or something knocked the wind out of him. "Oh." He gulped. "You're the Thomas Lohmiller dude."

Tommy gave him a dirty look.

They drove to a secluded spot Benjie recognized was close to his lava tube hideaway. Tommy killed the engine and, his gun aimed at Benjie, said, "You own a toy koala."

Benjie seat-danced his bladder into submission. "Yeah, Ozzie. You know where I can find him?"

"Where's my stuff?"

Unable to contain himself, Benjie let it out in a gush—about how he wound up with Tommy's backpack and how he wondered what to do with it and how he thought he might sell the stuff he found inside it to Jules Matsumoto. But instead, he got scared when he ran into a white guy in black, so he hid the pack in the lava tube. And how Dean Pahukoa and his hot wife forced him to go back to the tube, but it was gone when they got there.

Tommy said, "And you never once thought about just giving it to me."

"I need to go *bad*."

"Tell me why I should believe you."

"Because I think I'm gonna piss all over your car."

"About the cave, dumb ass."

"Du… I was scared," Benjie said. "I'm sorry, I didn't mean for them to get lost."

"You're positive they're not in the cave."

"Yeah. Can I please go now? I won't run away, I promise."

Tommy motioned toward the passenger door. Benjie jumped out and whizzed for a solid minute next to the car. When he finished, he got back in and closed the door.

"Besides you and Dean and his wife," Tommy said, "who else knows about this cave?"

Somebody did, Benjie thought. *Whoever it was who dumped all those cameras and other things there, as if they were hiding it all in the tube for some reason.* "Well, um, so does the lady private detective."

Tommy squinted at him. He waited a beat, and then said, "Say again?"

Benjie trembled. "I think I shouldn't have—"

"This lady detective—you've met her." Tommy turned to face him, the gun pointed at Benjie's face. "A lady private detective."

Benjie knew he'd started something he shouldn't, but one look at the pistol and he plunged ahead. He told Tommy about the business card and how he assumed Tommy hired Noelani Lee to find the jewels. But when they met in the Walmart parking lot with Dean hiding behind a water shack, she said she was working for Jules Matsumoto, who hired her to find the same pack.

Tommy lowered the Colt. "She's working for Jules."

When Benjie nodded, Tommy demanded the woman's description. Benjie said she was taller than him but shorter than Tommy, not bad looking for someone so old, and had pretty eyes and shaggy hair and no boobs.

"It's all true, sir, everything I just told you is the truth." Benjie blinked at the gun. "Please don't kill me. Miss Lee said you wouldn't hurt me."

"It's not her say *what* I do with you." Tommy took a deep

breath, and then released a low, guttural sound in his throat as he exhaled. He slammed the back of his head against his headrest, three times. "Fine."

Benjie cowered against the passenger door, unsure of what Tommy's response meant, but hoping for the best. "Um, so everything's cool now? You can drop me off at my friend's house?"

"No. First you're going to show me this cave."

"Oh, uh—"

"*Then* I'll figure out what to do with you."

* * *

A weary Jules Matsumoto shut his shop down early and was counting the till when his cell rang.

"Mr. Matsumoto? It's Noelani Lee."

"Hello, Miss Lee."

"Wow, you sound beat, Mr. Matsumoto."

"I've had better days."

"Then maybe you'd like to hear some good news for a change."

Chapter Twenty-Six:
The Green Flash

When Noelani Lee returned to the King Kamehameha Hotel early Thursday evening, she found her cousin, Wanda Tess Fong, sitting in bed. On TV, Judge Judy chewed out the defendant in a low-stakes lawsuit. "How are our guests doing?"

"For a couple of dudes who can't talk," Wanda said, "they sure talk a lot."

Noelani opened the closet. Frank and Ryan Campanella stared up at her. "I don't know how you two can stand this. Here you are, in Hawaii, and you're stuck in this Godforsaken closet."

Frank offered up a half-hearted, "Uck oo."

Noelani looked at Ryan. "Does he always talk to women like that?"

"Eth. He'th uh ath-ole."

"Uck oo, doo."

"Too bad you boys can't join us tonight, especially since we're meeting with a couple of your closest friends," Noelani said. She bent over and whispered, "Oh, the backpack I showed you earlier? Well, it's the *real* guest of honor."

The brothers moaned and groaned in protest as Noelani closed the door. She took a fresh change of clothes from a dresser and said to Wanda, "Did you see our friend around the hotel?"

Wanda changed the channel to HGTV. A young couple was searching for their dream home in Des Moines. "He was snooping around the pool and acted like he didn't see me, but I know he did. Later, I saw him walk through the lobby to the parking lot."

"When was that?"

"Like an hour ago. I came back up and been waiting for you ever since, with those buggahs in the closet." Wanda whispered, "Noe, they creep me out."

"Don't worry. Stupidity is not contagious." Noelani went into the bathroom, where she changed into a red pullover top and white linen pants. She cleaned theatrical make-up from her face, applied fresh lipstick and blush, and returned to the room.

Wanda turned off the TV and hopped out of bed. She

grabbed her purse and said, "Are you gonna tell me what you did all day?"

"Not while we have an audience. But I'll fill you in on the way downstairs."

When the elevator doors closed behind them, a man and a woman emerged from a utility closet at the end of the hall and went straight to room 619.

* * *

A few minutes before seven, Tommy Chunks, his shirt and pants dusted with volcanic dirt from his futile trip to the lava tube with Benjie Zamora, entered the hotel's lobby. He spotted Jules Matsumoto in a chair, skimming through a magazine.

About the same time the lady detective, Noelani Lee, and her chunky cousin greeted Jules, who rose and said something to them. Noelani did all the talking in response. As she spoke, she checked her watch and scanned the lobby. *Looking for me*, Tommy thought. She had a white canvas tote bag on her right shoulder but she did not, Tommy observed, have a black backpack.

Tommy could tell Jules was getting impatient. He had that look on his face, as if he wanted what he came for so he could get the hell out of there.

Forget it, Jules. Tommy retreated outside.

"Miss Lee," Jules said, "I would like to resolve matters, the sooner, the better."

"No worries, Mr. Matsumoto," Noelani said, "but Wanda and I wanted to see if you'd like to join us for a celebratory dinner."

Jules opened his mouth to say something but didn't.

"My treat," Noelani said. "Wanda, you mentioned a nice place on the water?"

"Yep, they got seafood and—"

Jules wasn't in the mood. "Miss Lee, you know why I'm here. Can't we just take care of the business at hand?"

"Well, sure, I assumed you'd—"

"Just tell me, where are they?"

Wanda's stomach growled. "Sorry."

"In my car," Noelani said, "locked in the trunk."

Jules said, "All right. Let's go, shall we?"

Outside, Tommy watched them walk past the main entrance to a set of doors on the north end of the hotel, which in turn led to the guest parking lot.

As the trio stepped outside, he heard Noelani say something like "mine's the white Nissan," so he double-timed it in that direction.

Several feet from the car, Noelani dropped her keys. As Wanda and Jules continued on, she bent down, picked up her keychain, stood—and felt someone snag the tote from her shoulder.

Tommy, a black backpack hanging on his left shoulder, reached inside the bag, and removed Noelani's Ruger. He took it from its leather holster, which he in turn tossed under a car. "Good evening," Tommy said, pointing the gun at her.

Noelani batted her eyelashes at him. "You're late."

Tommy racked the gun's slide.

"Let me guess—Esther wouldn't return your clip. Did she hide it somewhere?"

Tommy said nothing as he tossed the tote back to her.

Noelani pointed at his clothes. "You're filthy. I assume you've been exploring some of our island's underground geological features, yeah?"

He blinked at her. "Come on." He prodded her with the gun toward the car.

Wanda turned to face them, and her eyes went wide.

Jules's jaw dropped. "Tommy, what are you doing here? What—what is this all about?"

"Oh, I invited him," Noelani said, smiling.

Jules said, "You *what?*"

"Trust me," Noelani said, "this isn't happening quite the way I planned."

Tommy tossed the backpack to Wanda. "I believe this is yours."

She caught it and looked at Noelani, who said nothing but responded with a shrug.

Tommy said, "Everyone, in the car. Miss Lee, drive. Jules, shotgun." He said to Wanda, "You, back seat, with me."

Stunned, Wanda looked at Noelani, who responded with a wink.

When everyone was buckled in, Tommy told Noelani to make two lefts from the lot, and then said he would tell her where to go from there.

Noelani looked at Tommy in the rearview mirror. Unlike her other encounters with him, this time, his expression was tighter, more determined, focused. Beside him, Wanda sat statue stiff. If she hadn't blinked a couple of times, Noelani thought, she could've passed for a pear-shaped mannequin.

Beside her in the passenger seat, Jules seethed. He gave Noelani stink eye. "What did you mean when you said you 'invited' him to join us?"

"My plan was for us to do business in a nice, public place," she said. "But it seems Mr. Lohmiller has other ideas."

Jules covered his face with his hands. "And now he has us all at gunpoint."

"Yeah, there's that." Noelani peeked at Tommy in the rearview. "See, if only he'd been a little patient, it wouldn't have had to come to this."

Jules said, "What does that mean?"

Tommy said, "Quiet," in a no-nonsense growl.

They drove past a Honda dealership, a newspaper office, Kona's aquatics center, and ball fields—one of which was home to the Kona Diamond Kings. Just before the road hit a dead end, Tommy tapped Noelani on the shoulder with the gun. "Turn left, here."

Noelani steered the Sentra into the Old Kona Airport Beach Park. Ahead, the wrecked Island Skipper Airlines DC-6 rested on its belly. Police officers and people in tee shirts and ball caps embellished with "NTSB" in big gold letters clustered around the plane. Floodlights illuminated the scene, which camera-toting tourists captured on cameras and cell phones from behind Jersey barriers. At the request of island tourism officials, federal authorities had moved the plane just enough so visitors could access the beach. Its status as a visitor attraction, albeit temporary, was a delightful bonus.

"Keep going," Tommy said, "to the end."

Noelani drove on a long stretch of pavement that, from 1948 to 1970, had been an active airport runway. In the rearview, she noticed Wanda was perspiring but remained motionless. In the passenger seat, Jules was silent. His eyes were closed and his lips moved as he talked to himself. She couldn't make out what he was saying.

At the far end of the road, a handful of cars and minivans sat parked along the beach. Their occupants stood in the sand, cameras at the ready, waiting to document a glorious Hawaiian sunset. As Noelani slowed the car, Tommy told her to go as far to her right as possible, off the paved road and onto gravel, and park facing the ocean.

When she killed the engine, Tommy told everyone to get out and gather behind the car. He nodded toward the trunk. "It's in here?"

Noelani unlocked the trunk, reached in, and removed a black backpack, which she held to her chest.

"Well, then," Jules said, "you found them."

"Yes, I guess you could say so," Noelani said.

"Great, hand them over and I'll pay you the balance of your fees."

Tommy stared at him. "You can't be serious."

"Look, Tommy, I hired Miss Lee to find the jewelry and she did, so I guess it's time to wrap this up."

Tommy shifted the gun to his left hand and pointed it at Jules. "You're forgetting something." He said to Noelani, "Prove it's the right one."

Noelani opened the pack. From it, she removed a strip of paper, which she handed to Tommy. "I believe this is yours."

He read it: one-way to Fiji.

Noelani then took a brown toiletry kit from the backpack. She unzipped it and tilted it so Tommy and Jules could better view its contents in the twilight.

Tommy said nothing.

Jules licked his lips.

Noelani closed the kit and returned it to the pack. "Okay, so now the question is, now that we have them, who do they belong to?"

Jules put his hands on his hips. "Miss Lee, come on."

Tommy squinted. "Excuse me."

"Well, from what I understand," Noelani said, "or what I've been told, the jewels were stolen from an old lady in California."

"Speaking of the morons, where are they?" Tommy said.

"I left them in the dark."

Tommy said to Wanda, "Mrs. Lohmiller. The best you could do?"

She shrugged. "I kinda think we'd make a cute couple."

"No. I snore."

"So does she," Noelani said. "May I?"

Tommy nodded.

Jules folded his arms and blinked several times.

"Your problems started when the jewelry went missing, after the accident. You saw your retirement and your chance to escape from the brothers slipping away. So, you hooked up with the guy in the plaid shorts. By the way, what do you make of the shed he lives in? I mean, if my mother did that to me, I'd have bailed years ago."

Noelani waited a moment to gauge Tommy's response. There was none.

She said, "Mr. Matsumoto, you need the valuables as bad as Mr. Lohmiller needs to sell them, what with your new collection due soon."

"Of course," Jules said, "I have many loyal customers who are counting on me."

"I understand," Noelani said, "but it's one thing to lie to me about a courier from Honolulu, no big deal. But I wonder, what percentage of your gross goes toward steroids for Dean Pahukoa?"

Jules cleared his throat. "What the devil are you talking about?"

"The little man breasts, the greasy skin and hair—he has all the physical manifestations and no doubt some I couldn't see."

Jules shook his head. "You don't know what you're talking about."

Noelani leaned forward. "I found pictures of him in high school—heck, I found some from three years ago. He didn't get ripped like that from pumping iron all day," she said. "Was it your idea or his?"

"Miss Lee—"

"Wait," Tommy said. "I want to hear this."

"Playing for a team you sponsor and making the big leagues so you can take credit for being the man who 'discovered' him," Noelani said. "In exchange for a substantial percentage of whatever contract he signs, of course."

Jules looked at her for a moment, and then stared at his feet. "He just needed a little boost. If he does well here and gets into pro ball, then perhaps he can finally afford his wife."

"Ah, the foot model. I haven't had the pleasure," Noelani said. "Well, you see, Dean wanted me to find the jewels, too. Surprised?"

Jules didn't answer.

She said, "Thing is, he didn't want to meet face to face so he got a kid to front for him."

"Benjie Zamora," Tommy said.

"Another mutual acquaintance," Noelani said.

"Kid had them," Tommy said, "at one point."

"Thing is, he didn't want to be in the middle of all this, and I can't blame him. Still, it didn't stop you from forcing him to give you a tour of the lava tube, huh?"

"Wait," Jules said, "what lava tube?"

"Where Benjie hid the jewelry," Noelani said.

Tommy motioned toward the pack. "You found them there."

"See," Noelani said, "there were a bunch of backpacks changing hands like crazy, but the one with the jewelry never seemed to turn up anywhere. First Wanda and I had one with a stuffed koala, and then we had another one full of rocks." She smiled. "Thanks to the brave Mr. Lohmiller here, my cousin got her bag back."

Wanda held up her WTF pendant. "It would've sucked if I never saw this again."

"But Wanda," Noelani said, "the only reason you have it is because Mr. Lohmiller knew who took it."

Tommy blinked at her but said nothing.

"Your big problem was, he's a royal screw-up." Noelani leaned back against the car, still clutching the pack. "You were going to kill him, but his mother interrupted your fun, which meant you might've had to shoot her, too, yeah?"

She said to Jules, "It's a good thing he didn't, considering Esther's one of your primary sources for 'raw materials.'" Noelani told him about the cheap jewelry Esther delivered to him earlier in the day. "She overpaid for it big time. Like the loser who bought me the *original* contents of your box."

Jules huffed. "Lady, I have high standards."

"Think of the bucks Esther could have made for herself if she'd gotten hold of your precious stones and fenced them elsewhere."

"She'd never get what they're worth," Jules said. "Nobody would have given her what I would've paid."

"Which is what we agreed to," Tommy said, "and what you promised to pay each of the Moron Brothers."

"It doesn't matter now," Jules said, "because Miss Lee is going to give them to me as per our agreement."

"Then you are dead," Tommy said, "as per my decision." He leveled the gun with Jules's head.

"Hang on, fellas," Noelani said. "See, this is where I can't figure out what happens next."

Tommy and Jules stared at her. Jules said, "What do you mean? It's clear to me."

Tommy lowered the gun. "Me, too."

"Yes, but the problem is," Noelani said, "I'm not quite sure who owns these valuable goodies."

Jules said, "I hired you to find them; you did; and now, you give them to me."

"Well, here's the thing—you didn't care who brought you the stuff, just so long as you got it. Not to mention, it's *your* fault things got as crazy around here as they did."

"Wait—what?" Jules shook his head. "I don't know what you're getting at."

"Quiet, Jules," Tommy said.

"It's simple." Noelani kept an eye on the gun. "Mr. Lohmiller lost the jewelry, so you suggested he get the pretend Scotsman to help him find it, even though you knew he would tell Esther. Then you add in the different stories you gave Ryan and Frank and of course, Dean, because he works for you, who told his wife, which you knew would happen, then he in turn told Benjie Zamora. Which I don't think *any* of us saw coming." She looked at Tommy. "Pretty crazy, yeah?"

Tommy nodded. "Pretty stupid."

"As for poor Benjie," Noelani said, "did you know he planned on selling them to you?"

Jules said, "He did?"

"If you'd been there when he came to your shop. But Frank was there, too, and he scared him away—with no further explanation needed."

Jules ignored her. "Give me the backpack."

Noelani pointed at the gun in Tommy's hand. "Yeah, well, not a good idea."

Jules held up his hands in mock surrender. Turning up the charm, he said, "Tommy, we can discuss this like the adult businessmen we are."

"Right."

"Let's just let her hand over the bag, we'll take the materials to my shop *right now* so I can appraise them, and then I'll cut you a check for their true worth."

"Wait, you're admitting you low-balled me."

"Remember, we're partners."

Tommy glared at Jules. "Deal's off the table." He took a step toward Noelani and pointed the Ruger at her stomach. "Hand it over."

She said to Jules, "He makes a convincing argument."

Jules fumed. "Do it and so help me God I will call the cops and your license will be in peril."

"But what will you tell them?" Noelani said. "A mainlander stole gold and gems from another guy, who stole them from an old lady in California who's dead by now, and you planned to buy them from whoever got them to you first so you could make your overpriced stuff? The cops would eat it up."

Jules stared at her.

"Not to mention the humiliation you and Dean would endure when your dirty steroid secret went public." Noelani held the pack tighter.

"Hand it over," Tommy said.

"There are lots of unique pieces in here, probably date back to the nineteen twenties or beyond." Noelani kept her eyes on the pistol. "What a shame to destroy heirlooms like those to make schlocky crap for tourists. Besides, they must be worth a small fortune if Mr. Lohmiller plans on funding his retirement with them."

Jules sniffed. "Now you're being ridiculous."

"A reminder," Tommy said. "This is not a negotiation."

"You can't just shoot anyone here," Jules said. "All those cops and people down by the plane, they'd be all over you in a heartbeat."

"I didn't say *here*," Tommy said. "It's a big island."

"Oh, it's huge, bigger than all the other ones combined," Noelani said. "But who would drive?"

"However," Tommy said, "if Miss Lee gives the pack to me, everybody lives."

Noelani smiled. "Relax, Mr. Lohmiller. Put the gun away. I planned to give them to you all along."

Jules did a double take. "Wait, I'm sorry, what did you just say?"

Tommy lowered the Ruger. "I'm listening."

"Although the jewelry's true ownership is, for lack of a better term, nebulous," Noelani said, "the truth is, Mr. Matsumoto never had them in his possession."

"Hello?" Jules said. "Again, I hired you to find them."

"But Mr. Lohmiller is the one who brought them here," she said. "Now, Ryan claims they're his, because he stole them first. So does Frank, although I'm not sure how except he hates his brother, and I'm pretty sure he doesn't hold you in very high regard, either, Mr. Lohmiller."

"Fuck him," Tommy said.

Noelani shut the trunk with her left hand while she clutched the pack with her right. "In truth, the jewels belong to the heirs of the dead woman in California, or the courts or whoever. But I can only go by who had them when the plane crashed. And that would be Mr. Lohmiller."

"Thank you," Tommy said.

"If you go through with this," Jules said, his hands balling into fists, "I demand you refund me your retainer."

"Well, see, you paid me to find the jewels, and technically, I did. By the way, you'll be getting my invoice for the balance of my fees and expenses within the week."

Tommy motioned toward the backpack with the gun. "Give me my stuff."

Noelani said, "Okay, but on a couple of conditions."

"Go."

"First, leave the island as soon as possible."

"Happy to."

"There are flights to Honolulu all night. You can be in Fiji by Saturday, or Sunday. The whole International Date Line thing confuses me."

Tommy nodded.

"Second," Noelani said, "do not pass 'go,' except to pick up your clothes and stuff, and do not collect two idiot brothers."

At that moment, Jules lunged forward and snatched the backpack from Noelani. He started running down the old runway, stumbling a few times but staying on his feet.

Tommy looked at Noelani. "Oh, please."

She shrugged. "Oops."

Tommy raced after Jules and tackled him about a dozen yards away. He pulled the pack from Jules's grasp, landed a punch to his gut, and dragged him across the blacktop to the car. He slammed him against the driver's door and shoved the Ruger in Jules's face. "You're done."

Before he could pull the trigger, Noelani jumped between them, shielding Jules. "Do you really want to kill him?"

Tommy stepped back. "Yes. I do."

"But you have your stuff now. Besides, he's toast as it is, so why not just take the pack and split?"

Wheezing, Jules said, "What do you mean, 'toast'?"

Noelani turned to him and whispered, "I'm trying to save your life, if it's okay with you."

Tommy waited a beat, and then said, "The car."

She surrendered her keychain. "She's low on gas, so can you fill her up for me?"

"It'll be at the airport. Gun and keys under the seat."

"Oh, and what about your rental?"

Tommy grinned. "Not worried. It wasn't my credit card number." He shoved Jules aside and got in behind the wheel and shut the door. He tossed the backpack on the passenger seat. "Some asshole in Vegas named Jimmy Vartoogian."

Noelani recoiled. "Jimmy..." She took a deep breath. "Wait, you know him?"

Tommy grinned. "Good-bye, Miss Lee." He drove away, down the old runway.

Jules fell to his knees. "You understand, Miss Lee, you've violated my trust as your client."

Snapping herself out of a seven-year-old haze, Noelani helped him to his feet. "Mr. Matsumoto, he wasn't going to kill you."

"Don't be so sure."

"The gun wasn't loaded."

Jules squinted at her.

"I emptied the clip before I packed it in my bag. As a precaution."

"Because you knew he would be here." He cracked a smile. "It's true. You are as smart as they—as smart as *you* say you are."

"Sometimes I get lucky, too." Noelani said, "Um, despite everything that happened here this evening, believe it or not, there is something I can do for you."

"Other than destroying my reputation and Dean's baseball career, what's left?"

"I promise to keep quiet about the steroids and your dodgy business practices, but only if you cease and desist."

"You told me it's none of your business how I do mine."

"No, not the jewelry. I mean, the distribution of anabolic steroids—it violates the state's Uniform Controlled Substances Act," Noelani said. "The last time I checked, it lists about sixty such drugs. I've got a feeling you've given Dean at least one of them on a regular basis."

Jules rubbed his stomach. "Be reasonable."

"Add the fact you're not a licensed dispenser and, well, pretty soon we're talking Class C felony."

"Dean was on the threshold of being a Major League star. He's a complete five-tool player. He could've been the next Alex Rodriguez."

"Okay, I don't know anything about sports," Noelani said, "and I have no idea what a 'five-tool player' is, but I'm pretty sure you just made a lousy analogy."

Jules stared at the darkening sky. "Everything's down the drain. My business, Dean's career." He looked at her, almost in tears. "All because you think you're better than me."

"It's not just you." Noelani took a small plastic bag from her pocket. "Look, here's something, a gesture of my concern, and to give you a fresh start."

Jules studied the bag's contents—plumeria-shaped gold-and-diamond earrings and a matching necklace. He recognized them as one of his earlier, more popular editions, but they still sparkled like new.

Noelani watched his eyes light up.

He dropped the plastic bag in his breast pocket. "Please excuse me. I have work to do." He trudged down the road, back toward town.

Noelani almost felt bad for him as she watched him stagger away. Then she realized, she'd lost track of Wanda during the encounter with Tommy and Jules.

Noelani called her name until Wanda responded. She found her cousin sitting on the beach, her knees tucked under her chin and the backpack resting in the sand at her side.

"Howzit, cuz," Wanda said.

"Wanda, what are you doing? How long have you been over here?"

"Long enough to see it."

Noelani sat beside her. "See what, Tom Lohmiller taking my car?"

Wanda smiled. "The green flash."

Noelani had heard about the fabled "green flash," a phenomenon where light and atmospheric conditions cause what many observers swear is a flare of green light above the sun as it sets over the Pacific.

"All the years I lived here and never saw it," Wanda said, "then there it was. Something you never see in Vegas, either. Too bad you missed it."

Noelani removed her sandals and dug her toes in the sand. "Did you get a picture?"

Wanda shook her head. "But it was way cool. Things like the green flash, and the palm trees and the rain and the beaches, I'm never taking for granted any more now I'm moving back home." Wanda turned to face her. "Now what happens?"

"With…"

"You let Tom leave with those expensive jewels and things."

Noelani said, "I didn't, but yes, I did."

Wanda stared at Noelani, with only the surf and a child's laughter breaking the silence. "Noe, what do you mean?"

"Sweetie," Noelani said, "the first thing we need to do is

walk back to the hotel, now that my car's gone."

"And then what?"

"Then I need to tie up some loose ends." She nodded toward the backpack. "Oh, I'll need to borrow that."

* * *

When the red light turned green, Pearl the housekeeper removed the keycard from the lock.

She and her husband, Maxwell, pulling a baggage cart behind him, entered room 619 at the King Kamehameha Hotel. All the lights were on, and the television blared tinny hula music on the house channel.

Above the tunes Pearl heard a muffled noise from inside the closet. She turned off the TV and slid one of the mirrored doors open.

Maxwell rubbed his chin as he looked at two men, bound to chairs with their mouths gagged. "These're the buggahs went and tied you up and then gave you the money." He motioned toward one of them and said, "Why's he got no clothes on?"

Pearl shrugged and said, "All I know is they're both jerks." She reached in her pocket and took out her four hundred-dollar bills, and then leaned over the two men and tore them to shreds. "You dummies didn't think I'd find out?" she said, as she tossed the greenback confetti on the men.

The naked one tried to say something through his gag. The other one said something which, to Pearl, sounded like "shit."

"Passing off fake cash like it's the real thing," Maxwell said. "You ask me, it's kind of a wrong thing to do."

"Rodney down in the business office says he's seen so much of it, he said he wasn't surprised." Pearl turned to face the two men. "Then again, it means these two baboozes owe me but big time."

Maxwell pulled the luggage cart closer to the closet. "Dear, are you sure you wanna do this?"

"Damn straight I'm sure."

"All right, then. Let's load 'em up."

Chapter Twenty-Seven:
The Loose Ends

First thing Friday morning, Gerald Kapono MacTavish took the backpack he'd nabbed from the guy named Bruce and drove straight to the lava tube.

Now he had the gold and jewels and Esther Halekealoha had no clue. He figured all he had to do was stash the bag in the cave for a couple of days before he unloaded it on Jules Matsumoto, or another jeweler. He could start a bidding war and jack up the price.

It didn't matter to him because either option would work. His dreams of moving to Scotland were about to come true. The valuable stones were the ransom he'd pay to liberate himself from Esther's oppression.

Less than a mile from the tube, he passed a small car driving the opposite direction. When the driver waved at Gerald, something on his right hand glinted in the rising sun's rays.

Gerald thought, *Huh, strange—I didn't think the cook lived anywhere near here.*

A minute later, Gerald pulled his Saturn to the side of Keolani Drive. He followed the path to the hole in the ground and dropped himself inside the tube. There in the darkness, he hid the backpack under large rocks.

I'm one step closer to freedom.

His job finished, he pulled himself out of the hole, into the morning light.

Someone told him to freeze.

Several Kona cops surrounded the hole, guns drawn. He raised his hands and met each officer's stare with his own petrified gaze.

A man in a lime-green, short-sleeved shirt and khaki pants approached Gerald. He had a badge clipped to his belt. "Good morning," he said. "Are you Gerald Kapono MacTavish, by chance?"

"Aye."

"Ah, good. What do you have in the hole, Mr. MacTavish?"

Gerald felt his knees go weak. "Nothing. Word."

"I see. Then you won't mind showing us your, uh, 'nothing,' would you?"

* * *

Despite Esther Halekealoha's best efforts to keep up with demand, impatient customers—many of whom had waited a half-hour or more to be served—began leaving the Loco Moco Mama.

Drenched in sweat in the cramped kitchen, Esther cursed Mr. Lim for picking this of all days to quit. Just like that, he called and told her, in plain as day English she always knew he didn't speak, he was done. And he wouldn't be back. Not even for a severance check, which Esther decided she'd never write anyway.

Another order came in, eggs sunny side with fried Spam and hash browns. Esther looked out the pass-through to the dining room. She remembered one of the waitresses once took cooking classes in high school. It didn't matter if the girl remembered how to boil water; Esther was desperate for a pair of helping hands.

"Girl," she called out, "you get your skinny ass in here and help me, dammit."

The young waitress with the tight-fitting logo tee shirt, the cleavage, and the exposed, newly pierced navel, ignored her. Instead, she continued flirting with a pair of local boys.

Esther gave her stink eye. "'Kay den, you're fired. Unless you get in here and make—"

She clammed up when a pair of uniformed cops, accompanied by another one in a lime-green, short-sleeved shirt and khaki pants, entered the restaurant. She watched the man in civilian clothes show his badge to the waitress. She saw the skinny girl turn and point to the kitchen. The girl sneered at her as the three cops came toward Esther.

The one in the civilian clothes said, "Mrs. Halekealoha?"

"Hey, howzit?"

"I'm sorry to interrupt but I need to ask you some questions."

"Yeah, well I'm kinda busy here," she said. "You come back later and you get one big discount for lunch. All cops eat here cheap."

"Mrs. Halekealoha, we're not here for the food. Can you

please step out into the dining room?"

* * *

An unshaven, dirty, fatigued Jules Matsumoto unlocked his shop, went inside, and stared at his empty display cabinets.

He was relieved he still had some inventory to fill them. But the fact his latest, most valuable batch of raw materials were winging their way across the Pacific with Tom Lohmiller was bound to put a long-term crimp on plans for his next series of Island Creations.

He turned off the alarm system and locked the door behind him. He then began filling the displays. As he did, he removed "marked down" stickers from numerous items.

When he finished, Jules checked his watch; it as was still an hour till opening time. He decided he'd get some office work done before Dean showed up…*if* the traitor showed up at all.

At the same instant he stepped inside his office, somebody grabbed the back of his shirt and pushed him face-first into a wall.

"Okay, where the fuck'd they go?"

* * *

Benjie Zamora watched his mother scoop a huge helping of scrambled eggs from a pan and dump them on his plate.

"There you go, my hungry college man son," Sabina said.

"Thanks, Mom."

"Have some more bacon. Unless you want me to fry up some sausage. I have time still."

"No thanks, I'm good."

"She can do that, you know." Orestes Zamora picked up the sports section. "That's one of the reasons I married your mother. She's a quick fryer-upper."

"Honey, please, Benjie doesn't want to hear stories about our courtship." Sabina put the pan in the sink. "I made some tuna salad for your lunch, unless you want some of the leftover lasagna from last night."

Orestes checked his watch. "Look at the time, Mother, we need to get going." He folded the paper and set it aside, and then drank the last of his coffee. "Big day today, son. We're introducing a new air freshener for our customers. It's called 'English Rose Garden.' We're the first car wash in all the islands to get it."

Benjie said, "Cool."

"It comes direct from Mexico. You know, when you come work with me, you'll learn all the tricks of the car wash trade."

Benjie froze. "Work? Uh, at the car wash?"

"Son, there's no reason why you can't share in the rewards and responsibilities of a thriving family business." Orestes slapped Benjie on the back. "Say, how about I swing by during lunch and take you up there, so you can meet the staff?"

"Well, I—"

"They're great people, and besides, I've talked you up plenty to them."

"Now, Orestes," Sabina said, "aren't you getting ahead of yourself? I'm sure Benjie has big plans of his own for a career when he graduates."

Orestes grinned at Benjie. He whispered, "Son, low scores are great for golf, but not for your GPA." He leaned in closer. "I'd like you to pick a major by noon. If you don't, those big fellas at the wash will be happy to teach you the finer points of hand-drying."

Benjie felt the need to pee.

Orestes sat up and said to Sabina, "Say, Mother, what's new at the resort?"

"Something strange," Sabina said. "Somebody was living in a unit belonging to one of our members, but we haven't been able to reach the owner, and nobody has seen who was there."

"Oh, my goodness."

"It belongs to a man named Mr. Lohmiller, from Las Vegas."

Benjie felt a chill.

"Seems strange," Orestes said. "He's not here in Kona?"

"He didn't reserve the unit, and he doesn't return phone calls," Sabina said. "What's even stranger is it looks like somebody had a fight in the unit. A bad one, too. Some lamps were broken and can you believe, the police found blood in the bathroom."

Benjie acted as if he was focused on eating breakfast, but his mother's narrative gave him chicken skin.

"Wow," Orestes said, "you need to be careful there on the job, Mother."

"I doubt there's anything to worry about. Except one of the housekeepers said she saw two strange men leaving the unit, but nobody's seen them since."

Benjie's stomach flipped. He set his fork aside.

"Well, as long as they're gone, we should be okay." Sabina picked up her car keys and kissed Benjie on the forehead. "You have a terrific day, son, and let your brain and your body get some rest."

"Great advice, Mother," Orestes said. He looked at Benjie. "At least until noon." Seconds later, they both were gone.

Sabina's parakeet chirped in the living room. The kitchen faucet dripped.

Benjie sat in silence, staring at his food, afraid to move even in his own house. He was paralyzed, physically and mentally, what with his mother's description of Tom Lohmiller's trashed condo and his father's sudden ultimatum—go to work or start taking school seriously.

Man, could this day get any crappier?

Hearing a car outside, he stayed put on his stool until he was sure it drove away. A couple of minutes later, he steeled himself and went to the living room. He pulled a curtain back from the window and looked down both ends of the street when something on the front porch distracted him.

It was a black backpack.

Benjie picked it up, locked the door and ran to his room. His heart pounding, he unzipped the bag and looked inside.

The first thing he saw was his botany text, a round, hot-pink sticker in the upper-right-hand corner with a $1 price written on it above the typed words "Kona Coast Charity Shop." He tossed it on a chair.

Then he saw Ozzie. Benjie lifted the stuffed koala from the backpack and hugged it. A sense of calm washed over him.

He carried the toy to the kitchen and placed it face-down on the counter. He took a pair of scissors from a drawer and snipped the stitches on the toy's back. After cutting a hole about two inches long, Benjie dug into the stuffing.

They were still there—two plastic bags, one filled with

rolling papers and another containing a couple of ounces of dank Mowie Wowie.

Leaving Ozzie on the counter, Benjie grabbed a matchbook from the drawer and took the rolling papers and the plastic bags out to the lanai.

He kicked back in an Adirondack chair and rolled a fat doob, fired it up and inhaled.

The neighborhood rooster crowed.

As Benjie exhaled the smoke, he felt all his worries drift away.

Good old Ozzie, he thought. *He always comes through when I need him most.*

* * *

Dean Pahukoa was awake for fifteen minutes when he looked at Veronica Keawe. She rolled over, her eyes closed, and purred.

On her nightstand, the Cook Islands fertility god—its wooden surface sprouting several of Dean's pubic hairs—aimed its penis at Dean.

Brah, I hate you.

Clad only in his boxers, the black ones with the logos of all thirty Major League Baseball teams, Dean climbed out of bed and went to the bathroom. He took a long, healthy piss. When he finished, he shuffled through the bedroom, past Veronica's brand-new purse, and went to the kitchen. He turned on the coffeepot, and then went out the front door to get the morning newspaper.

But what he found beside it was even better.

It was a black backpack.

Oh, man. The chick private detective and the kid came through. Totally clutch.

He grabbed the pack and brought it into the living room. Inside, he found a toiletry bag. Something inside it made a tinkling sound, like metal hitting metal. Dean opened it and looked inside.

"Holy shit." He repeated the magic words three times, the volume of his voice rising with each intonation.

"Dean?" Veronica, in a bathrobe and her thickest socks,

joined him in the living room. She yawned. "Coffee ready yet?"

"Roni, check it out." He held the open toiletry bag up for her to view its contents.

She covered her mouth with both hands. "No way. Dean? No way. Where'd they—*no way*. Oh my God, how'd you get them? No way."

"Me and the kid, we got an idea then we went and—"

Veronica reached inside Dean's boxers and gripped his privates. "Baby, do you know what this means?"

"Go easy, Roni, I think I got wood slivers down there."

"It means we're gonna be rich. Now I can get the money I need for the big family room addition and the bathroom remodel to give it a spa-like feel. And I'll even have enough left over so I can go to San Francisco every other weekend to buy shoes." She released his pecker. "Baby, you did good this time. You know how proud I am of you?"

"The same way you were proud of me when I hit that game winner the other day?"

"No, no, no, not the…baseball…crap. I mean, you've made a huge contribution to our future as a couple and as a family, when we start having kids." Veronica paced across the living room. "Okay, now we have to sell this stuff."

"Well," Dean said, "I know Jules'll want to buy it."

Veronica spun on her heel. "You can't sell it to him, Dean."

"Roni, he's my boss and he wants it, and I know he was expecting it from the Tom man for da kine Island Creations we're gonna make, yeah."

She dashed to his side and put a hand on his bicep. "Dean, listen to me. We can't sell it to him because he will not give you a fair price."

"Sure, he will."

"You *work for him*. Don't you get it? He *expects* you to just hand it over."

Dean peered inside the toiletry bag at rings and bracelets, necklaces, and earrings. "Well, maybe we can sell it to someone else."

Veronica felt a shudder of inspiration. "Who's your—who's Jules's biggest competitor?"

"This chain from Maui, they're called Lahaina Treasures. Their things're nice but not like collectibles like the Island

Creations are."

Veronica wrapped her arms around Dean's waist. She caught a whiff of his bad breath. "I have an idea, but it's going to require you to stand up to your boss for once."

"But Roni, Jules has been real good to me," Dean said, "especially helping me be a great baseball player."

"Look, once he hears what we have to say, he'll have no choice but to pay us huge for this stuff. Now, do you want to know what I have in mind?"

* * *

Wanda Tess Fong packed the last of her clothes in her suitcase as she and Noelani Lee prepared to check out of the King Kamehameha Hotel. "I don't know why we have to leave so soon. We were just starting to have fun."

Noelani Lee zipped up her overnight bag. "Wanda, you said yourself you're moving back to the island. We need to go to Hilo and get you set up with a job and a bank account, and maybe even a place to live."

"This Mrs. Hanratty, she's okay?"

"One of my best clients ever. So let's get something to eat, then we'll go to the airport and get my car, yeah?"

Wanda motioned toward the closet. "Any idea how they got away?"

Upon returning to their room the night before, Noelani and Wanda found their closet empty. Except for a black ball cap with "Hawai'i" printed on it in Rasta colors, and what looked like torn-up pieces of counterfeit money on the floor, there was no sign of the foul-mouthed brothers or the chairs they'd been strapped to.

Wanda assumed Tom Lohmiller must've broken in and done something terrible, knowing how bad he because he wanted to get rid of them. But Noelani said no, because according to the GPS device attached to a ring inside the toiletry bag, he drove straight to the airport, as he promised he would.

Noelani picked up her overnight bag. "Which reminds me, I owe you a new backpack."

* * *

Sitting behind his desk, Jules said to Frank Campanella, "How did you get in here without tripping the alarm?"

Kicked back in the guest chair, his feet propped on Jules's desk, Frank said, "Trade secret, and if I told you, then it wouldn't be a secret no more, am I right?"

Jules looked at Ryan Campanella, standing beside him, the baseball bat in his hands. "Listen, you can have anything you want but I'm telling you, I don't have—"

"Save it, Jules," Ryan said. "We already told you, the Hawaiian chick had the bag, and we know she was going to give you the rocks, so don't even bullshit us."

"If I may reiterate," Frank said, "we had us a seriously fucked up night and we don't need you piling your usual crap on it this morning."

The brothers had just finished telling Jules about being kidnapped first by Tommy Chunks, then by Noelani Lee and her cousin, and later by the hotel housekeeper and her husband, who loaded them—still tied to the chairs—in a pick-up truck and hauled them to the middle of who-knows-where.

There in the boonies, they took Ryan's clothes and his wallet and all his real cash, along with his credit cards, then cut the brothers loose and left them alone and naked in the dark.

Jules said, "How did you get those clothes?"

"These by no means qualify as 'clothes,'" Frank said, as he adjusted the waistband of a pair of purple hibiscus-print board shorts. A neon-orange tee shirt emblazoned with a picture of Gumby and Pokey strained against his belly. "I don't know who wears shit like this other than pansies like my little bro here."

Ryan flattened a wrinkle in the red-and-yellow pineapple motif aloha shirt he'd paired with denim cut-offs. "All I'm saying is, I'm glad people around here still hang their stuff out to dry overnight, and that's all I'm gonna say."

"Lucky for you, maybe," Frank said. "Me, I can't wait to get back into my phat garmz and lose these threads."

"Jesus, Frank—you're the only person I know outside of Compton who wears rags like those."

"Um," Jules said, "why isn't one of you dead by now?"

"Trust me, I was tempted," Ryan said. "But dipshit here and I came to what you might call a 'truce' of sorts."

Frank smirked at his brother. "Not that we're all pals now, it's just me and Nancy here decided to set our differences aside for the time being, until we get what we came for."

"Frank," Jules said, "I already told you—"

"And anyway," Ryan said, "I think it's your own death you should be worried about." He smacked his palm with the baseball bat.

Jules ran a hand through his hair. "I told you, she gave the bag to Tommy and he flew off—"

"To Tahiti, yeah, we know," Frank said.

"Tonga," Ryan said.

Frank rolled his eyes. "Just so you know, we already checked your safe."

"Which only proves you're smart enough not to hide the stuff here," Ryan said.

Jules felt tightness in his chest as he spun in his chair and looked at his safe. Its door yawned open from a wall behind a file cabinet. "You…you cleaned it out?"

"Just a little pocket change," Ryan said. "See, me and the Brainless Wonder here still hate each other, but we know we're not getting off this rock unless we work together."

Frank said, "Here's what I don't get, Jules: If the flat-chested Hawaiian babe gave the rocks to Tommy right in front of you last night, I mean, the bag she showed us herself, then how is it Tommy already had the *same* bag when he ditched us in his closet?"

Jules squinted at Frank. "What did you say?"

Ryan admired the bat in his hands. "What's this written on here, 'Four homer game, 8-0—Diamond Kings vs. Waimea, July 14'?" He studied an autograph on the bat's thick barrel. "Who the hell's Dean Pahukoa?"

"Guys," Jules said, "I have no idea what you mean by 'another bag.' The only one Tommy had last night was the one Miss Lee gave him."

"Oh, Jules." Ryan again smacked his palm with the bat. "Jules, Jules, Jules. What did we tell you about dicking with us?"

Frank rose and rounded the desk. Standing beside his brother, he said, "You know, somewhere between this story you're telling us and what me and sis here—"

"Shut up, dipshit."

"—experienced our own selves, there's gotta be some truth. So maybe, perhaps, possibly, per-fucking-chance, you can finally tell us what it is."

Jules held up his hands. "I swear to you, guys, I don't—"

"We think," Ryan said, "Tommy had the real bag and he sold you the stuff, like he planned on doing from the start of all this shit."

"So maybe you hid it at home or somewhere else," Frank said. "Unless you can prove us wrong. So, what'll it be, Jules?"

"Show us the stuff," Ryan said.

Frank grinned. "Or we'll take turns going all Babe Ruth on your melon."

Before Jules could respond, he heard someone unlock the door and enter the shop. Then he heard Dean Pahukoa say, "Hey, boss, you here?"

Jules looked at Ryan, who nodded. "Ah, good morning, Dean. I'm in here."

Dean stepped inside the office, with Veronica Keawe trailing him. She held a backpack under her left arm. They stopped in the doorway when they saw Frank and Ryan standing beside Jules.

"You're in early," Jules said. "At least you're in today."

"Uh, yeah, sorry about being sick this week." Dean nodded toward the brothers. "Hey, if you're busy, me and Roni can go get some breakfast, yeah."

"No, we won't." Veronica glared at the two men. "Dean, baby, are these the guys you told me about?"

"Hold on, sweet cheeks," Frank said, "what did Schwarzendoofus here tell you?"

Ryan rested the bat on his shoulder. "What's in your backpack?"

Dean squinted. "Boss, is that the stick I got the four dingers with last month?"

"Yes, it is. Remember? I told you I was going to hold onto it until—"

"Save it, Jules." Veronica ignored the strangers and plopped the pack on his desk. "We're here to talk business."

Jules blinked at the pack. "Excuse me, but what's this all about?"

Veronica elbowed Dean. "Tell him, baby."

"Yeah," Frank said, "tell us, baby."

Dean looked from Frank to Ryan to Veronica, who arched an eyebrow, then to Jules. "Boss, you know I know you were looking for the Island Creations raw materials the Tom man was supposed to bring you, but he lost them."

Jules nodded. "Uh huh."

"Well, we found them."

Jules rubbed his forehead. "You're kidding."

"On the front porch, this morning," Dean said. "I mean this is the real deal. See, we got some help and we found them and, you know, they're all in there, yeah."

Frank said, "What kind of help?"

Ryan tightened his grip on the bat. "Did this 'help' come in the form of a Hawaiian chick with no tits?"

"Well," Dean glanced at Veronica, "not that I noticed."

Veronica pushed her husband aside as she approached the desk. "Jules, here's the thing: Inside this backpack are your precious things the *haole* was supposed to sell you. I—we found them, and now I'm—we're ready to make a deal."

"Hang on," Jules said, "there's been a mistake."

"Man, it's getting deeper in here," Frank said.

"Oh, there's no mistake," Veronica said, "except the one Jules made when he underestimated Dean, thinking all he can do is score home goals."

Dean whispered, "Hit home runs, Roni."

Jules said, "I'm sorry if you misunderstood, but that's not what I meant."

"I understand, all right." Veronica gripped the pack with both hands. "We've already had an offer from Lahaina Treasures. They're seriously interested. Right, Dean?"

"Uh, yeah, they are, boss."

"Now," Veronica said, "we didn't sell to them right away. We told them we needed to think it over. But Dean's like this puppy dog with you, totally loyal, and he said you should have first crack at them."

Jules said, "And what does this mean to me?"

"Correction," Frank said, "what does it mean for *me*?"

"*Us*, asshole," Ryan said.

"I don't know about you two, whoever you are," Veronica said, "but it means if Jules gives us a decent price, then he gets all the things he needs to make his silly tourist jewelry."

Jules sighed. "For starters, that's not how Lahaina Treasures obtains its materials."

Dean tilted his head. "It isn't?"

"Hardly. They have this long supply chain throughout the United States and Canada and scores of middlemen in three continents and God only knows what else. Why do you think they charge so much for their stuff?"

"Huh." Dean pondered his boss's statement. "So, if we don't have all those middlemen things, then why do we charge so much for *ours*?"

"Besides," Jules said, "these cannot be the missing gold and gems."

"No, boss, this is them."

Veronica pulled a brown toiletry kit from the backpack, unzipped it, and dumped its contents on the desk. "See for yourself. It's all there. I didn't keep any of it."

"Well, Roni, there was the one—"

"Baby, shut up."

Jules picked up what looked like a diamond solitaire. Decades of experience handling jewelry and precious stones told him he didn't need a loupe or any other tool to determine the stone was glass. Not even CZ. With his thumbnail, he scraped a thin layer of gold paint to expose steel. "Veronica, this isn't real."

"Sure it is." She again elbowed Dean. "Tell him."

"Yeah, boss, this gotta be the stuff, for sure. Like I said, we found it."

"This is all costume jewelry, and bad costume jewelry at that." Jules scanned the baubles on his desk. "The whole collection is worth maybe, I don't know, a hundred dollars at the most."

"A hundred dollars?" Veronica glared at him. "What kind of operation do you run here, Jules?"

Dean held her shoulders and tried to calm her. "Roni, chill. Maybe Jules just needs to examine it all real close."

Frank snorted. "Looks like he fooled you, too, lady."

"Your boss is an ass, Dean," Veronica said. "He says it's worth a hundred dollars. After all we went through to find his precious…crap."

Jules said, "Dean, you're fired."

Dean stared at him. "Fired?"

"How could you pull this stunt after all I've done for you and your baseball career?"

"Wait, stunt? What do you mean, boss?"

Ryan said to Frank, "Should we beat the living hell out of him now?"

"Wait one." Frank grinned. "I wanna hear this."

"I cannot believe after the sacrifices and investments I made to ensure your baseball future, you would try to make me buy this worthless..." Jules picked up a random ring. "This is the kind of garbage you find at chain pharmacies and low-end charity thrift stores."

"No, boss," Dean said, "it's all real, guaranteed."

Ryan shook his head. "This isn't the stuff. If anyone in this room would know, it would be me."

"It should be me, too, you back-stabbing prick," Frank said.

"You two stay out of it." Veronica steamed. "This is between me and Dean and Jules."

Ryan held up his hands. "Just saying."

"Three years, Dean," Jules said. "Three years, and you claim to have my diamonds and gold, and you bring me... Do you know how much I spent on juice to make you the man you are today?"

Veronica looked at Jules, and then at Dean. "Wait. 'Juice'? What's 'juice'? What 'juice' is he talking about, baby?"

Frank snorted again. "Oh shit."

"*The* juice," Jules said. "Don't even tell me you don't know. Lady, he didn't get buff from lifting weights. How could he when he never goes to the gym?"

Veronica's breath came in short spurts. "Dean. Talk to me."

Dean backed away from the desk. "Jules here got the idea for making me the best Hawaiian baseball player of all time. He said he has this one connection who's got some good steroids. He said I take that stuff, I'll hit the ball harder and farther and there's no way scouts are gonna ignore me."

Veronica stared at the ceiling.

"Um, I hate to bust your balloon," Frank said, "but they make you pee in a cup now."

Dean looked at Frank. "They what? Who does?"

"Testing for steroids and other crap," Ryan said. "Big scandal, or didn't the news get this far west?"

"Maybe Jules here kinda skipped over those details." Frank chuckled. "Listen, Muscles, you'd be screwed before you got started. But Jules often forgets details like those on a regular basis. Right, Jules?"

"Guys," Jules said, "there are certain methods available on the black market to—"

"But," Dean said, "Jules told me I could get millions from a big league team and he'd get some of it for helping me."

"He did *what?*" Veronica glared at Jules. Then, she grabbed the baseball bat from an unsuspecting Ryan and dashed into the showroom.

Frank laughed at his brother. "Jesus, did you *let* the chick take it?"

"Didn't see it coming, but what the hell. This should be good."

Jules pushed himself from the desk and rushed past Ryan and Frank to the showroom. There, Veronica stood over a display case filled with sparkling Island Creations.

She held the bat in both hands above her head.

"Don't do it," Jules's voice cracked. "I'll give you anything you want, but for the love of God, just don't do it."

Veronica spied a pair of earrings and a matching necklace in the case; the pieces were made to look like plumeria blooms. Solitary diamonds inside each flower dazzled in the display case lighting. She whipped the bat down; the glass shattered, and an alarm screeched.

Dean reached for her as she again raised the bat and swung, almost hitting her husband's head. At the same time, Jules lunged for her, but he succeeded only in taking her backhand swing to his right elbow.

Veronica growled, dropped the bat, and wrapped her hands around Jules's throat. In retaliation, Jules slapped her across the face. As she recoiled from the blow, his many rings leaving welts on her cheek, he pried her hands from his neck and pushed her to the floor. She landed near the door and wailed in agony as her right ankle twisted beneath her.

Seeing his wife in distress, Dean grabbed Jules's throat and lifted him off the floor with one hand. "Shit ain't cool, boss."

Ryan looked at his brother. "I don't know about you, but this might be a good time to make ourselves scarce."

Frank sidestepped the howling Veronica and followed his brother outside. "Fucking 'roids. Amazing what some people'll do to get ahead."

* * *

Yellow crime scene tape covered the Loco Moco Mama's glass door. A uniformed police officer stood guard, keeping a watchful eye on bystanders.

As she and her cousin approached the restaurant, Wanda Tess Fong said, "Dang, Noe, check this out."

Noelani Lee peeked past the cop through the glass door. Inside, a man in a lime-green, short-sleeved shirt and khaki pants took notes as he talked to Esther Halekealoha and Gerald Kapono MacTavish. Both were seated and handcuffed.

Esther interrupted the man and said something to Gerald, her face contorted in anger. Gerald mouthed something back at her. Esther tried to get up from her chair, but officers pushed her back down. Other cops combed the eatery, which was empty of customers and employees.

"Well, whatever this is, it doesn't look good," Noelani said.

Wanda said to the cop, "Excuse me, so like, what happened here?"

"We just busted this mom-and-son theft ring."

Noelani said, "What on earth did they do?"

"It turns out the son was stealing stuff from tourists. You know, the usual—phones, cameras. He'd bring it here, and his mother, the *tita* in there, she sold it. They've been at it for years."

Wanda sidled up beside him. He was tall, dark, and somewhat handsome. "How'd you bust them?"

"We got an anonymous phone tip last night from someone who said he spends time exploring lava tubes."

"You did?"

"The caller said he found this one was full of stuff. We followed up, and then staked it out and caught the son there this morning."

"This caller," Wanda said, looking at Noelani sideways, "what'd he sound like?"

"Well, from what I understand, he had a thick accent of some kind," the cop said.

Wanda looked at Noelani. She shrugged.

"But you should've seen his stash," the cop said. "There was tons of expensive stuff. The weird thing was, we caught this bruddah in the act, hiding a backpack."

Noelani said, "A backpack?"

"See," the cop said, "what didn't make sense was, inside the bag was a bunch of colored glass and beads and some toy rings. All of it worthless, if you know what I mean."

Wanda opened her mouth, but Noelani cut her off. "Too bad about the restaurant. It's a shame for the employees, too."

"Now there's a weird situation, too," the cop said. "Not long after we got here, this itty-bitty lady shows up with these big diamond rings on all her fingers. I mean, they had rocks on them as big as she is. She tells the waitresses, she and her husband are gonna open a new restaurant and she wants to hire them."

"Hmm," Noelani said. "Imagine that."

"Right there on the spot. Promises she'll pay them twice what the *tita* in there did, plus bennies. Her husband was with her, too. Nice man. He talked up the girls—they seemed to like him. He had some serious bling, too."

Two doors up, a shrieking alarm interrupted their conversation. Noelani, Wanda, and the cop watched as a middle-aged man flew through a window at Jules's King of Diamonds and landed on the sidewalk amid shards of glass.

As the officer and a pair of colleagues raced toward them, a muscular young man landed on the older man and pinned him to the ground. At the same time, a woman limped out of the shop. Wincing, she demanded the cops arrest the older man for pain and suffering and hindering her ability to make a living.

"Do you all know who I am? *Do you?*" But the cops ignored her indignant cries as they wrestled the younger man off the older one.

Just then, Noelani spotted Ryan and Frank Campanella approaching from the direction of the tussle. "I think we're about to have company."

Wanda covered her mouth. "Oh dang, Noe."

Noelani smiled as she studied their attire, including their footwear—oversized rubber flip-flops. "Aloha guys. Hey, just because some big moke leaves his slippahs on his doorstep doesn't mean you can steal them."

"I think of it as 'borrowing' because in no way am I keeping these stupid things," Ryan said. "But how about we change the subject?"

"I didn't know we were having a conversation."

"Oh, we're about to," Frank said, "because we want to know where the hell's the bag you gave Tommy last night. I mean, either he's got the jewelry, or he turned around and sold it to Jules, huh?"

Noelani shrugged. "I can't say for sure."

Wanda tugged her cousin's blouse. "Noe, don't mess with these dudes."

Noelani assured her the brothers wouldn't try anything too stupid with cops all over the place.

"I can't vouch for the mental midget here," Ryan said, "but knowing Tommy's gone and Jules is"—he looked over his shoulder and watched as the cops hauled Jules and Dean back inside the jewelry store—"otherwise occupied, I figure it's time to get off this rock."

"Miss Priss here's right," Frank said. "Walking through the sticks last night got me to thinking, maybe it's time we give up on the old dead broad's jewels and get back to business."

"Which means we'll need to relocate our base of operations," Ryan said. "And in case you're wondering, no, it won't be here."

"Damn right for once," Frank said. "Anyway, I think I used up my Hawaii quota."

"So, you're giving up," Noelani said.

Frank wiped sweat from his forehead. "What is it you know that we don't know?"

"Well, I'm just amazed after all you've been through this week, you're assuming the jewelry isn't still on the island."

Quiet moments passed, interrupted only by Esther yelling at Gerald through the restaurant's plate-glass window, and Veronica screaming at Jules in the windowless jewelry shop.

Frank snorted. "Lady, what the hell're you talking about?"

"It just seems to me," Noelani said, "you boys are giving up way too easy."

"Dipshit and me aren't giving up anything," Ryan said.

Noelani shrugged. "Sorry. I believe you are. You're just assuming the jewelry is no longer on the island. How do you know it isn't?"

"Because Tommy got the stuff and his ass is outta here," Frank said. "One day we'll catch up with him, what with karma being a bitch. But for now, me and sis here need to regroup."

"Well, okay, even though I think you may be wrong," Noelani said, "it's still nice to see you two have kissed and made up."

Frank snorted. "I think I just puked a little in my mouth."

Ryan extended a hand. Noelani hesitated before she shook it. He said, "All I'm gonna say is, you're awful damn sharp, and that's all I'm gonna say."

"This means you're leaving my island? Because if it does, well, I'd offer you a ride to the airport, but my car's already there."

"Don't worry," Ryan said. "There's lots of rides around here for the choosing. See any you like?"

Noelani shook her head. "I prefer mine. Besides, I could never cheat on her."

Frank stretched the waistband of his pilfered shorts. "We got a guy somewhere around here's good at making docs, so we'll be gone before you girls can say 'kamana wanna lay-ya.'"

Wanda poked him in the chest. "Don't diss the culture."

"Ignore him." Ryan winked at her, and then said to Noelani, "*A hui hou kakou malama pono.*" Then he and Frank strolled toward Ali'i Drive.

As the brothers walked away, Noelani took Wanda by the arm. "Just in case they change their minds, I think we should get out of here, too."

Wanda said, "You know, I heard you slip out of the room last night, when I went to sleep. I mean, when you *thought* I was sleeping."

"Mmm-hmm."

"And you went shopping without me yesterday—what was that all about?"

They stopped next to the coffee shop with the red umbrellas. "Wanda, do you remember when I told you I was going to give the people what they want?"

"Yeah."

"And tie up loose ends?"

"Yeah."

"Well, that's exactly what I did." Noelani smiled. "With a few exceptions."

Wanda started to speak, stopped, and then said, "Maybe it's a good thing I don't know everything, cuz."

Noelani motioned toward an empty table under an umbrella. "Latte?"

Now for a sneak preview of the next
Noelani Lee adventure,

The Hilo Hustle

by

Tom Bradley Jr.

Chapter One:
The Floater

Before dawn on Thursday, the body of a barefoot man in a blue tee shirt and khaki cargo shorts washed ashore on a beach in Hilo, Hawaii.

Another man out for a morning jog found the body, lying face down, in the sand at Bayfront Park, a few yards from a row of outrigger canoes. The jogger took out his cell and called the police—after he tweeted a picture of the corpse to all three-hundred forty-six of his followers.

* * *

Noelani B. Lee looked up at the cloudless blue Hawaiian sky and frowned.

Four straight days of uninterrupted sunshine with no end in sight.

Noelani hoped for rain. She needed it.

Sitting on the dusty ground under a tree on Coconut Island Park, as families and kids cavorted around her, Noelani switched her attention from the deplorable weather to a couple standing a couple dozen feet away. The man wore jeans shorts and a red tee shirt with the sleeves cut off; the woman wore green painters' pants and an orange button-up blouse.

Noelani watched as they played grab-ass for the world to see, unclenching only when children ran past them. Then the man and woman sat on a bench overlooking the bay. The man lit a cigarette.

Noelani's hopes for precipitation rose on Wednesday evening when word spread about a storm moving down from the Aleutians; forecasters predicted it would drench the Big Island's windward side, perhaps nonstop, for several days.

Hearing this welcome news, Noelani selected a spot in her front yard where she could sit and meditate amid the refreshing and mind-clearing raindrops.

All this aridity was out of place in Hilo, where rainfalls exceed well more than one-hundred inches in a normal a year. *I might as well be back in Vegas*, she thought.

But to her chagrin, the sun rose bright on Thursday

morning. The huge Alaskan storm, she learned, changed course and was bearing down on Northern California.

Noelani looked through the viewfinder of her Canon with the telephoto lens and squeezed off several shots of the man and woman talking. Then the man tossed the cigarette aside and rubbed his hand on the woman's right thigh; she leaned in close to him and, from what Noelani could tell, began nibbling his earlobe. Noelani prepared for the money shots.

"Come on," she whispered. "Give her a smooch. Pretty please?"

The man and woman pressed their foreheads together.

"With lots of tongue."

As if on cue, the pair locked lips. Noelani fired off dozens of exposures as the woman began pulling off his red muscle shirt and the man unbuttoned her orange blouse. Noelani kept the shutter pressed down until she caught a glimpse of braless boobs, at which point she lowered the camera, closed her eyes, and shook her head.

Hoping to avoid further retinal damage and figuring she had all the evidence she needed, Noelani slipped the camera in her canvas tote bag and made her way across the park to the footbridge connecting the little island with a parking lot on Kelipio Place.

Upon reaching the bridge, she took out her cell phone. "Hello, Mrs. Medeiros? Noelani Lee… Yes, it sure is a beautiful day… I was wondering, do you have time to meet today?... Well I have something—"

A quarter of the way across the span, a uniformed police officer and a plainclothes detective, wearing a lime green, short-sleeved shirt, and a badge clipped to the his belt, blocked her path.

"Um, Mrs. Medeiros, I need to call you back." She disconnected the call.

"Miss Lee," said the plainclothes cop.

"You're Detective Ahuna," she said. "I remember, you used to work over in Kona."

"Yes, but I transferred to South Hilo a few months back. Figured I'd retire here, be closer to the grandkids."

Noelani glanced at the uniformed cop, who stared at her but said nothing. "Well I'm sure you must be looking forward to it."

"Miss Lee," Detective Ahuna said, "I'm wondering what you can tell me about a gentleman named Milton Nihoa. He's a licensed private investigator, like you, correct?"

Noelani laughed. "In name only, and he's not a gentleman. If you want the truth, Milt gives all of us P.I.s a bad name."

"How so?"

"Because he a client-poaching, lazy, lying, slimy, cowardly weasel."

Detective Ahuna grinned. "Hmm."

Noelani held up her hands. "I know, you cops think we're all of those things and worse. Trust me, I've heard it all."

"I'm not one to judge, Miss Lee."

"But Milt's the worst of the worst. Ask anyone."

"We will."

"So what did he do this time?"

"Miss Lee, I understand, at a conference last month on Maui, you and Mr. Nihoa butted heads."

Noelani chuckled. "That's putting it mildly."

"I heard from various sources," Detective Ahuna said, "during this confrontation, you threatened to rip out his lungs."

"If it would guarantee he'd stop breathing, why not?"

"Uh huh."

After a moment, Noelani said, "So, is Milt in trouble again? Did he get in a fight with a client? Because if we're done talking about the jerk, I'm on my way to meet a client."

The uniformed cop stepped forward and positioned himself next to Noelani. She then realized how big he really was, towering a full foot taller than her five feet, eight inches.

"Miss Lee," Detective Ahuna said, "you need to come with us."

Chapter Two:
The Person of Interest

In an interrogation room at the police station on Kapiolani Street, Noelani Lee watched Detective Ahuna remove a photograph from a folder and slide it across the table toward her.

She studied the picture: In it, Milt Nihoa's shoeless body lay prone on a beach, just as Detective Ahuna told her he'd been found. He wore tan shorts and a blue tee shirt with a numeral "7" on the back.

The detective produced another photo from the folder, which showed Milt on his back. Noelani saw no signs of trauma—no apparent bullet wounds, nothing obvious to indicate he'd been stabbed or strangled. There was no blood on him or his clothing, though she figured if he'd been in the water for a while, any traces might have washed away.

She read white script lettering on his shirt: Wally's Dive Inn. "What happened to him?"

"The few friends of his we could find told us Mr. Nihoa couldn't swim," Detective Ahuna said. He picked up a pen from the table and clicked it several times.

Noelani ignored the detective's fidgeting. "Oh, so he drowned."

"We haven't officially determined cause of death," he said. "But I wonder if you can help us figure out why a man who can't swim would be in Hilo Bay in the middle of the night, fully clothed, and without shoes."

"You asked me the same question five minutes ago," she said. "And like I said, I don't know, unless he was drunk and fell in or something."

"Uh huh." Detective Ahuna sniffed. "Earlier, you said the last time you saw Mr. Nihoa alive was, what, last week?"

"Yes," Noelani said. "I ran into him when I was grocery shopping."

"At the KTA store on Holomua Street."

"Yes."

"Do you always shop there?"

"I was driving by and remembered I need to pick up a few things. Cat food, and lettuce."

"Did Mr. Nihoa shop there on a regular basis?"

"I wouldn't know. I only saw him there the one time."

Detective Ahuna clicked the pen once, twice, three times. "When you saw Mr. Nihoa at the KTA store, what did you say to him?"

"Nothing," Noelani said, staring at the pen. "I saw him coming toward me, so I turned around and went down the next aisle."

"Why?"

"Hopefully, to prevent him from making another embarrassing scene in public."

"You mentioned," Detective Ahuna said, "Mr. Nihoa had a drinking problem."

"Milt could put it away, yes," she said. "He didn't like me anyway, but when he was loaded, he was especially nasty."

"When you saw him at the KTA market, could you tell if he'd been drinking?"

"I didn't get close enough to find out."

"And you haven't run into him since, by accident or otherwise."

"Look, Detective, I did all I could to avoid Milt," Noelani said. "I didn't want anything to do with him, and"—she pointed at the photos—"I definitely didn't have anything to do with this."

Detective Ahuna waited a beat. "Where were you last night?"

"I was working."

"In the middle of the night?"

Noelani explained: When she's working cases, she doesn't take time to sleep. And since Mrs. Medeiros hired her to follow her cheating husband, she'd probably slept four hours all week.

"Help me out here, since I don't know how these things work," Detective Ahuna said. "How long does it usually take to prove a husband's messing around?"

"It depends," she said. "With Mr. Medeiros, it was several days and nights." She explained Mrs. Medeiros suspected her husband was seeing his mistress on his way home from work as a graveyard shift security guard; Mrs. Medeiros figured it was his only opportunity to fool around, since she was home three days a week and he slept until late in the afternoon on those days. So, Noelani said, she started following him home—

"Wait a minute," Detective Ahuna said, "you told me earlier you stay up all night doing computer searches and stuff."

"It depends on the situation," Noelani said. "During my investigation I observed Mr. Medeiros never visited another woman's house. I started to think Mrs. Medeiros was imagining things—hang-up calls at odd hours, him exceeding his wireless plan's text limit. But last night—well, seven this morning—after he got off work, he stopped at a house over by the municipal golf course and left a note on the door."

"He didn't knock or try to go inside?"

"No, he left a note on the door. I checked it out and saw he'd written instructions on it for the recipient to meet him today on Coconut Island. I took a picture of the note—it's still on my phone if you need proof—and sent it to Mrs. Medeiros. I knew she was working today, which meant he'd have plenty of time on his hands."

Detective Ahuna clicked the pen. "Hmm."

"Turns out he had other things in his hands."

"You're certain you went nowhere else last night."

"All I did was follow Mr. Medeiros," Noelani said, "then I went home and got my camera and prepared to catch him in the park today."

He clicked the pen four times. "You know, left unchecked, these odd nocturnal work habits of yours could be hazardous to your health."

Noelani shrugged. "I just happen to do my best thinking late at night."

"Sometimes when people are sleep deprived, they forget things they've done, or they just do things by rote, almost like they're unconscious of what they're doing." Detective Ahuna sat forward. "They might go on a long walk or go out driving and not remember it at all."

"Detective, you're confusing sleep deprivation with sleep walking," Noelani said. "The truth is, when I'm not working a case, I'm out like a light."

"And how often is that?"

"Well, ummm…" She smiled. "Not very."

"You're telling me you can swear for a fact you weren't anywhere near Milt Nihoa last night, or before dawn this morning?"

"Of course I don't have anyone who can corroborate my story except my cousin, Wanda," Noelani said. "She came over with Thai take-out around seven-thirty and stayed till ten before she went home."

"We've already spoken with Miss Fong, which still leaves plenty of time unaccounted for."

Noelani sighed and rubbed her temples.

Detective Ahuna asked her to provide details about her encounter with Milt Nihoa on Maui. She said it happened around noon on the second day of the conference when Milt, reeking of beer, accosted her and loudly berated her about a case she'd handed off to him several weeks previously.

"At the time," she said, "I had a full plate and couldn't give it—the case—all the attention it needed."

"What was the case?"

"It involved a deadbeat dad. Milt was between jobs, so I did the courteous thing and asked him if he wanted to take it. He did, but he bungled it huge and turned around and blamed me."

Detective Ahuna rubbed his chin. "Hold on—you passed a paying client along to someone with whom you had a mutual dislike?"

"Like I said, I was quite busy, and I was just trying to be nice," Noelani said. "Besides, Milt had moments when he could be human, on those rare occasions when he was sober."

"All right. So why did he blame you for messing it up?"

"He told the client it was my fault she'd never see any money the guy owed her, because he couldn't read my handwritten notes." Noelani took a deep breath. "I said I also typed them up, but he claimed they were missing from the file. I told him if he'd maybe lay off the beer for a day or two and get off his lazy butt, he could do his job in a professional manner. Then he called me a 'bitch' and a 'titless dyke.'"

Detective Ahuna glanced at her flat chest. "Are you a lesbian, Miss Lee?"

Noelani stared at him. "No, so don't get your hopes up."

He held up his hands. "Just clarifying, in case you turned down Milt's advances somewhere in the past and he took it personally."

"If he even so much as thought of it, I'd have castrated

him." She felt a lump in her throat. "What I meant—never mind."

Detective Ahuna grinned. "Tell me what happened next at the conference."

Noelani said, "We started going at it pretty loud with all kinds of name-calling. It was ugly. Next thing I knew, hotel security's breaking us up."

"And they kicked you both out."

"What upset me more than anything was it happened right before I was supposed to give my presentation on new advances in audio surveillance technology."

"Huh. You, uh, happen to have your presentation on disk?"

"I can burn you a copy."

They sat in silence for several seconds. Then Detective Ahuna asked Noelani if she knew anything about Milt's current caseload. She said no, since they never spoke, at least cordially. Then he asked if she knew if Milt had other enemies.

"Only if you count every other P.I. in the state and a bunch on the West Coast."

Detective Ahuna clicked his pen twice, and then rose from his seat. "Miss Lee, I'll have a uniform give you a ride to your car."

Noelani stood. "Let me guess—I'm not supposed to leave the island, right?"

"I also suggest," he said, "you stay away from the Nihoa investigation. We don't need you sticking your nose in it. I'm sure you understand why."

"What with me being a 'person of interest,'" Noelani said.

"But if you hear anything out there, I'm the first and only person you call." He handed her a card.

She looked at it before she tucked in it a pocket. "What else?"

"Please do the world a favor and get a decent night's sleep."

* * *

As she slid in behind the wheel of her white Nissan Sentra, Noelani noticed she had a voice mail on her cell.

Her cousin, Wanda Fong: "Noe, what's going on? The cops were here asking questions about if I was at your place last night. Are you okay? What's this about the bruddah they found on the beach? Cuz, I'm all worried big time about you. Call me."

Noelani decided she would, after her delayed meeting with Mrs. Medeiros.

She met her client at the Medeiros' modest home on Malia Street on the south end of Hilo. As she stopped her car, Noelani noticed a huge pile of men's clothing and shoes in the driveway.

"Sorry I'm late," Noelani said, as she climbed from the Sentra. "I got hung up on some other business."

"Show me the pics," Mrs. Medeiros said.

Noelani handed her the camera and explained how to view the images on the LCD screen. She watched as Mrs. Medeiros scanned the pictures without expression.

When she finished, Mrs. Medeiros returned the camera to Noelani. "You can give me the thing the pics are on, yeah?"

Noelani removed the memory card and handed it to Mrs. Medeiros. "If you want, I can help you download them."

"Not a problem. I got a twelve-year old boy who can handle it."

Noelani winced. "Oh, well, maybe he shouldn't see them."

"Please, kid's gotta learn, getting nookie on the side's a bad thing," Mrs. Medeiros said. "Send me your invoice, but understand, I don't get paid till next Friday."

Noelani nodded toward the pile of clothing. "I suppose Mr. Medeiros will be surprised when he finds all his stuff out here tonight."

"Naw, the surprise'll be when he gets home and finds all's left is a pile of ashes." Mrs. Medeiros picked up a can of gasoline and took a lighter from her pocket. "You might wanna take a step or two back."

* * *

Noelani finally arrived home after five o'clock. She entered her tiny house on Iwalani Street to find Master Po, her flame-point Himalayan, sitting on the kitchen counter, eating granola from a knocked-over cereal box.

"At least it's not bran flakes this time," she said to the cat.

"But I've had a long day and I'm hungry, too, so you get a free pass."

Noelani took a Styrofoam container of khanom chin namya, left over from Wanda's Wednesday night visit, from the fridge. She placed it in the microwave and, as the nuker heated the rice noodles, fish sauce, and veggies, she went to the living room to check her answering machine.

The first message was from Wanda, much the same as the one she'd left on Noelani's cell but sounding a bit more urgent.

The second message was from another woman: "Hello, my name is Cinnamon—spelled C-Y-N-A-M-I-N—Allgood, and I need your help." She left a number, which Noelani dialed.

"Hi, this is N.B. Lee returning your call."

"Oh hey, thanks for getting back to me so soon," Cynamin Allgood said. "Look, I need to meet with you but tonight isn't good since the natural light's getting bad."

Noelani looked out her front, west-facing window. There were still a couple of hours left until the sun would set over Mauna Kea. "The light?"

"We'd prefer nice, early morning light from the east for a good shot."

Noelani stared at the receiver for a moment. "Oh. Okay."

"So, if you can—do you know the little jetty in the bay with the park benches on it, across from Lili'uokalani Gardens?"

"I'm sure I can find it."

"Great," Cynamin said. "Meet me there at eight tomorrow morning. If it's sunny again, and what I hear it's supposed to be gorgeous, the producer said we'll have fantastic views of the bay in the background."

The microwave beeped in the kitchen. "Producer?"

"Don't you worry none, though. He may have the title but everyone knows, I run the show."

Noelani stared at the ceiling. "Miss Allgood, I'm a little confused here. What is it you're asking me to do?"

"I need your help, especially since…"

When she trailed off, Noelani said, "Are you in trouble?"

After a beat, Cynamin said, "You heard about the dead man they found on the beach this morning."

"I wish I didn't know as much as I do, but, yes. Why?"

"Miss Lee," Cynamin said, "he was working for me."

About the Author

Tom Bradley Jr. is a former print reporter and current public relations professional who is a late bloomer in the world of fiction, self-publishing the first novel in his Noelani Lee mystery series in 2013.

After serving as a Journalist in the US Navy, Tom wrote for community and daily newspapers in San Diego County and later launched a career in public relations in Las Vegas and San Antonio. He has won numerous awards for both his news and PR writing.

A native Pennsylvanian, Tom holds a BA in Communications from National University in San Diego, and an MA in Strategic Communication and Leadership from Seton Hall University in South Orange, NJ. When he's not writing, Tom can most often be found reading, watching far too many foreign crime dramas on TV, and shopping for unusual craft beers.

He resides in suburban Las Vegas with his wife, Donna; a Bengal cat named Malia; and a basset hound who sometimes answers to Lola. *The Kona Shuffle* is the first novel in his Noelani Lee mystery series.

www.ingramcontent.com/pod-product-compliance
Lightning Source LLC
Chambersburg PA
CBHW071559150726
48000CB00004B/1516